SECRET

Evonne Swingler

America Star Books
Frederick, Maryland

First printing

All characters in this book are fictitious, and any resemblance to real persons, living or dead, is coincidental.

America Star Books has allowed this work to remain exactly as the author intended, verbatim, without editorial input.

Softcover 9781611023527
PUBLISHED BY AMERICA STAR BOOKS, LLLP
www.americastarbooks.com
Frederick, Maryland

1

February 17th, 1987, is a birthday that I will NEVER forget. I had just turned eight and I had gotten everything I had asked for. I remember it like it was yesterday. My big chocolate cake, gifts on the table and decorations everywhere. Uncle Mike and Daddy were sitting in the living room blowing up balloons.

"Hey daddy!" I said, running to hug him.

"Hey baby girl!" he responded, kissing me on the forehead.

"Hey Uncle Mike." I said holding my hand out. "It's my birthday."

Daddy and Uncle Mike fell out laughing. When they were done, Uncle Mike shook my hand as if that was the reason for it being there. He let go and I kept my hand out.

"What you want now?" he asked.

"Some money for my birthday." I said in the sweetest little voice.

"Aww okay. I see what you tryna do." he said, playfully. "You tryna hustle me. Is that it?"

I just smiled.

"Nigga shut up and give my princess some money." Daddy said, winking at me, while tying up the last balloon.

"Well you lucky you my favorite niece."

He dug into his back pocket and handed me a ten dollar bill.

"Thank you Uncle Mike!" I said jumping to give him a hug.

"No problem baby doll. Happy birthday." he said, hugging me back.

As I walked away, I heard Uncle Mike tell my dad "she get all that hustling from you," and they shared another laugh.

I felt like a rich kid with ten dollars. I could do a lot with ten dollars at my age. My daddy never let me carry money because I always would lose it, so my mom would always try to sneak it to me. Even though I always lost her money, she never seemed to care.

It was still kind of early and there was really nothing to do. I played with my balloons for awhile, but that got kind of boring so I watched some cartoons.

"Has anybody seen my birthday girl?!" I heard my mom yell from the back door.

Being distracted from all of everything, I didn't even realize she was gone.

"Mommy!" I yelled, jumping into her arms.

"Hey baby! Happy birthday ma-ma." she said. "Wanna see what I got you?"

I shook my head yeah and she grabbed my hand. We headed towards my room, but before we went in there she whispered something into daddy's ear.

"Aight." he said as we walked into my room.

When we got in there, she pulled out the prettiest dress that I had ever seen. It was pink and white with little shoes to match. She reached into the bag again and pulled out a birthday tiara. I felt like a real princess. I was in a rush to put it on but mommy made me take a bath first.

"I know princess Secret don't wanna be dirty on her birthday" she said.

I got in, washed up, got out, put my clothes on and mommy did my hair. My tiara went on perfect. Now I was officially a princess. We walked into the living room and daddy was blocking the door way. I heard some noises behind him but I couldn't see.

"Daddy what's behind you?' I asked.

"Do you really wanna know?" he asked playfully

I shook my head yeah.

"Do you really really wanna know?"

"YES!" I yelled, excited and anxiously.

He jumped to the side and about ten of my friends from school and around the neighborhood jumped up. "SURPRISE!" They all yelled. I was so shocked. It was the first time I had had any friends over for my birthday. They all ran up to me complementing my dress and trying to take my tiara off. It was crazy and I didn't even care. I was just so happy to see all of them. Daddy shouted "Say cheese!" and the camera went off. Flick, flick, flick was all I heard. All I could do was pose like the little princess I was. Couldn't nobody tell me nothing.

They took us to Camp Snoopy and bought us all unlimited wrist bands. We rode on almost all the rides until we had enough. When we got done, they sang happy birthday, ate cake and ice cream and we left. Before we got to the house, we dropped all the girls off at their homes. As bad as I begged for a sleep over, mommy wasn't having it. She'd had had enough and was ready to go to bed. By the time we got done dropping them all off, I had fallen asleep in the back seat. We pulled up to the house and daddy had awakened me with his yelling.

"What the fuck is this shit?!"

I sat up, wiped my eyes and looked out the window. There were police lights flashing everywhere. My parents were going crazy.

"Baby, Mike sold us out!" Mommy replied. "What we gone do?"

"I don't know. Just keep driving." daddy said..

I was so lost I didn't know what was going on. What in the world did "sold us out" mean? I began to wonder about Uncle Mike. He was still at the house when we left. What if he went to jail or something? What if somebody robbed the house? What if something bad happened to him? My little mind was just going crazy.

"What happened daddy?" I asked.

"Nothing baby girl. Just lay back down and go to sleep." he said as I laid back down.

"Baby call Mike." Mommy said.

5

As soon as daddy got on the phone I hopped my nosy ass right back up.

"Mommy I'm scared." I said whining.

"It's okay ma-ma." she responded.

"But why the police at our house?"

"Not now Secret." she said.

Now I knew something was wrong. Whenever mommy was in a situation she couldn't explain to me, she would always say "not now Secret." Daddy didn't get in touch with Uncle Mike and I just knew something bad happened. I began to cry hysterically. I don't know why, but seeing my mom and dad on the verge of losing it was very scary.

I looked out the window and we were blocks away from our house. I guess daddy thought the coast was clear because he told mommy to pull over and park. I was still crying so daddy pulled me up to the front with him.

"I need you to calm down baby girl." he said. "You aight. I'm not gone let nothing happen to you."

"O...kay." I said between sobs.

As I laid there on my daddy's chest, I felt safe. Like nothing or no one could touch me. They began to discuss what was happening. I didn't understand none of the grown-up talk they were doing, but it sounded real serious. Moments later, my safe feeling was gone. The police came rushing around both ends of the street surrounding us.

"Mommy!" I yelled.

"Give me my baby." she said as I crawled over to her.

"Everybody put your hands where I can see them!" one of the cops yelled.

My parents did as they were told.

"Now let the child out of the car!" he yelled again.

I didn't budge. I was too scared to move anywhere. How did they even know that I was in here?

"I said, release the child from the vehicle!" the cop was persistent.

"Go head baby girl." Daddy said.

Mommy put her hands back through the window and grabbed me.

"Hell naw! They not finna take my baby." She snapped.

"Vic, they gone take her anyway. Just let her go." he said.

"No! If they want her they gone have to go through me to get her." She responded.

"Do you really think its necessary for all that?" he asked.

Just then, the cop spoke again.

"I'm going to give you one more chance to release the child into our custody or we're going to come and get her."

The look on my moms face told my dad that she wasn't changing her mind and that she was ready for whatever.

"Aight then. Lets do this." he responded.

As we sat back, we waited for their next move.

"Place your hands back where we can see them. We're coming to retrieve the child!" the cop yelled once more.

"Mommy I don't wanna go." I cried.

She didn't know what to say. She knew they were going to take me no matter how hard she fought them off. Tears began to form in her eyes.

"Get in the back and get on the floor ma-ma." she said.

Even though I was confused, I did as I was told.

"What you doing Vic?" Daddy asked.

"I can't do life Perry." mommy said. "I aint no animal. I cant live in no fuckin' cage."

"Step out of the car NOW!" the cop demanded.

"Man hell naw Victoria! I can't let you do that bae." daddy said with tears rolling down his face.

"It's the only way. They finally got us and I'm not going down without a fight. We already talked about this P!"

Daddy took a deep breath. "We really finna do this?"

"STEP...OUT...NOW!" The police shouted again.

"Secret, Mommy loves you princess. Don't ever forget that." She said crying, grabbing something out the glove compartment. "Stay down baby."

"Hands where I can see them!" they constantly yelled.

7

Daddy wiped his tears as he made some type of noise with his gun. My parents looked at each other and kissed for the last time.

"Give daddy a kiss baby girl." he said.

I hopped up and kissed both of my parents without any knowledge of what was going on. Then they told me to get back down. Right after that, they got out of the car. It was silent for about a second. Next thing I heard was gun shots coming from everywhere. As I laid on the floor in the backseat, I covered my ears and screamed through what I thought was a nightmare. That was the last time I saw my mom Victoria McKay Adams, and my dad Perry Earl Adams.

2

My first foster family wasn't so bad. I was still the only child and got whatever I wanted. The only problem was that they were old and white. I was black. It was totally obvious that I didn't fit in. It was boring and I didn't have any friends. White kids from school were kind of boring and black kids, well, there really weren't any. Miriam and Ed were so boring and they never invited people over. If they did, it was always some old hag that looked older than the both of them.

I knew I wouldn't last there. I mean, they were nice and all, but I had to get out one way or another before they tried to adopt me. I started acting up in school because I had a feeling that that would tick them off. I would bully kids for no reason at all and steal their money, start fights, curse out the teachers when they would try and tell me what to do and the number of visits to the principals office were outrageous. I knew that I wasn't doing right, but I didn't care. I didn't want to live with some old ass white people who would probably die at any moment. I had to get out.

Just as I suspected, I was right. Miriam couldn't handle all the bad phone calls from my school. Let alone the countless number of trips she had to make up there. She was a sweet little lady who never raised her voice or frowned, but you could always tell when she was unhappy. One night I had finally heard the argument that I had been waiting for.

"I can't take this anymore Ed. The girl is driving me crazy." Miriam said.

"So what do you think we should do?... Counseling?" Ed asked.

"Counseling?!... No. I think we should send her back." Miriam yelled.

"Send her back?!" Ed yelled. "No. We can't send her back. We've got years in with this girl. She ours now."

"I can't handle her anymore. She's making me sick. The doctor told me that I have been stressing too much and where do you think that its coming from Ed? Old age?...She has to go."

"Miriam calm down." Ed said. "Maybe it's just a faze. We'll get passed this."

Miriam paused for a moment. I knew she was taking in what her husband had just said to her. Then I heard the magic words.

"She has to go."

That was all I needed to hear. I couldn't wait to leave. Even though it was what I had wanted, it still hurt to be thrown away. I realized that she wouldn't have wanted to try and make it work if I did want to stay. I guess even the sweetest person wasn't all that they put out to be. Miriam threw me away like a piece of gum that lost its taste. That was the last of the Belts.

My second foster family wasn't exactly what I had in mind. The Walyers took me in right along with the rest of their six adopted children. I hated it. Not only was I no longer an only child, but I had to share my room with them. My personal belongings were now our personal belongings. It wasn't long before I started punking them. I had to show them that I was the boss. I started taking over everything. They all began to hate me. Four boys and four girls and I was the seconds oldest. Ciara was the first and she was their real daughter. She was fourteen. I couldn't stand how she would parade around the house as if she were so grown. She had a nasty ass gap in her mouth to match her nasty ass attitude, which almost always got us into fights. One time it got so bad to the point where I found myself choking her to death until daddy Walyer had to come pull me off of her. The bitch was purple by the time I got done with her. She always started shit for no reason and blamed me every time. Of course I always got in trouble. I was younger, I was black, and I wasn't their real child. I didn't care though. One thing was for sure, she might have been two years older, but I wasn't no punk, and I made it a point to remind her every time she fucked with me.

Next were the twins Michael and Michelle. They were eight. All they ever did was argue day and night about everything. Then there was Brianna, Sean, Josh, and Chris. They were all six and they got on my nerves every second of everyday. All of us shared rooms, except for Ciara. She had her own room. All the boys were in one room and all the girls were in one room. I guess that's why Ciara thought she was better than all of us. There were two bunk beds in each room and I had no space.

Mrs. Walyers had us cleaning that house like we was the little orphans off the movie Annie. The chores that she had us doing were totally un-called for. I didn't understand why we had to constantly spray door knobs when everybody touched them 24/7. Or why we had to mop the ceilings every other day. I had never even heard of nobody mopping a ceiling before then. I was sick of being some little house maid and I wanted to get out. That was the worst year of my twelve year old life. It wasn't hard for me to get out. All I had to do was ask and they sent me back.

Now my third foster family, they didn't last long. They were only in it for the money. They were dirty and I had no plans of staying there that long. I got on their nerves so bad that they gave me back without even thinking about it.

My last foster family were like my real family. I felt at home with the Johnsons. I wasn't the only child, but there was only one other kid in the house besides me. Mrs. Karen was so cool. I felt sorry for her because she was a widow and didn't want to remarry because she couldn't have children of her own. She adopted her sister's only child Delilah when she passed of cancer. A little chubby girl whom they called Deli. We were about the same age and she was kind of cool too. I started going to her school and she would tell all of her friends that I was her cousin and right off the bat we clicked. We had been tight ever since.

Karen had adopted me right before my fourteenth birthday and insisted that I call her mom. I secretly wished that she had been the one to adopted me way before the Belts got me, but I wasn't complaining. I was now apart of a real family. I was loved, at home, and safe…or at least I thought I was.

On Deli's sixteenth birthday Karen had taken me and Deli to get our hair and nails done. We couldn't wait to get to school and stunt. When we got back to the house, Karen had told us that her brother was moving in with us. I didn't see it as a problem. That's because I never stopped to realize that I was becoming a woman. My titties had grown and my butt was bigger than the average sixteen year olds.

Karen's only brother came to stay with us just after going AWOL. At first he came off as a loving uncle who accepted me for the niece that I tried to be. Whenever me and Deli would run off to the mall he would throw us a couple bills and we would be on our way. I began to see a change in him when he started drinking. At first, it was okay because he would kind of limit himself to a bottle a day, but then it got out of hand. He got to the point where he would drink bottle after bottle or can after can. Starting fights with Karen, not cleaning up behind himself, and leaving messes. It didn't take long for his true colors to show. It disgusted me and I began to look at him differently. I told myself that he had a serious problem and to not let it get to me, but then one night while Karen was working a night shift and Deli was asleep, he came into my room and locked the door.

"What the fuck are you doing?!" I yelled sitting up, angry that he busted into my room without knocking.

He walked over to my bed and slapped the spit out of my mouth.

"Shut up!" He said as he covered my mouth with his dirty hand.

He slid his other hand between my legs into my panties. I was still shocked from the smack that it took me a second to realize what was happening to me. "am I dreaming?" I thought to myself.

As I struggled to get his big ass off of me, he continued to hit me.

"Be still." he said as I kept on fighting him.

"Be still I said.!"

I bit his finger and he punched me in my face.

"Ouch you little bitch!"

By that time, I was weak. I couldn't fight anymore. I had given up. As I laid there crying, he continued to talk to me as if I gave a damn about what he was saying.

"You walk around this house everyday all happy go lucky with that juicy ass bouncing up and down like you tryna tease a brotha." he said squeezing my butt. "Well, I'm finna get mines."

He pulled his pants down and grabbed on to his hardened dick.

"Pull them panties down girl." he demanded.

"Kristian please don't do this." I cried.

"Shut up and do as I say!" he said.

I knew he had been drinking. I could smell the liquor on his breath. Scared to death, I slowly did as I was told. He spread my legs open wide and shoved his dick into me. The pain was excruciating. I cried out and he covered my mouth again. I couldn't understand why this was happening to me. About fifteen minutes later, he was finally done. He pulled himself out of me and pulled his pants back up. He zipped his pants and staggered toward the door.

"If you're smart you'll keep this a secret." he said turning back to me. "Ill kill you if anybody finds out."

He walked out the door and I ran to go lock it. I cried for a long time after that. I suddenly didn't feel at home anymore.

I missed my real parents. I needed for them to tell me that it would be okay. My vagina throbbed as I cried through my pain. I was confused and I couldn't figure out what to do. I didn't know if he would really kill me, but I was still scared of him. No one could help me.

3

Kristian raped me continuously after that. All the the drunken nights when Karen was at work and Deli was asleep, he would pick my lock and brake into my room. I couldn't keep him away. It got to the point where I no longer fought him off. I just laid there until he would finish.

I never wanted to tell Karen because I didn't wanna ruin her joy. She was so happy with where she was at in her life and I hated to be the one to put her down. She had her brother and two kids that she could call her own. Who was I to bring sadness back into her life? I was only her adopted child. We weren't blood. I hated the thought of her regretting bringing me into her life. I loved how she welcomed me and genuinely and sincerely loved me. I was HER daughter.

Even though Deli and I were best friends, I could never tell her what was happening to me. She was always up in my face concerned and asking questions about why I was acting so differently. Something in me just wouldn't let me come out and say it. We began to grow distant from one another which made it even easier to keep it to myself. Most nights I would come home and she wouldn't even be there. I did worry a little bit, but I managed not to think about it too much. Karen on the other hand was going crazy worried about her. I told her she was hanging around with some new friends, but that didn't seem to really matter. She would still give Deli an ear full when she would come home, whenever she woud come home.

I was finally eighteen and a senior in high school. I had met this boy named Courtney outside of a club one night. He was so cute and I knew from the way he would be watching me that he wanted to get to know me. Me, being the stubborn little chick that I was, always played hard to get when I would see him. I wasn't going to take it upon myself to talk to him because I wanted him to speak to me first. I felt like that's how it was supposed to be. One night he finally stepped to me. He was so cute and had the prettiest teeth. I couldn't help but to smile. We exchanged numbers and began kicking it outside of the club and got real close. We weren't together, he just took me out on a few dates and we often kicked it at his two bedroom apartment. He lived by himself but the extra room was for guest. He definitely had the money to do it like that. He was so different from other guys that I had met that tried to get with me. Maybe because he was older, grown man like. He was sweet and kind and gentle for the most part, but there was also this roughness that he had about him that I liked a lot.

We had been talking for awhile now and I was beginning to feel some type of way for him. I trusted him more than I had trusted any man. He made me feel special. I guess he had been noticing how I had been getting closer and closer to him and would often ask me to just move in with him. Hell, it seemed like the right thing to do seeing as that I was always over there with him spending the night anyways. The only problem was that I hated to leave Karen all alone. Delilah was never home anymore, and Kristian was a drunk. I knew she would be lonely, if she wasn't already. But at the same time back at home, things weren't getting any better for me. My relationship with Deli was no more. We barely even spoke to each other, let alone hang out. She was never at school anymore, so I barely even got to see her. I didn't know if I was the reason she was acting out or what, but I just let her do her because I didn't want her all up in my business questioning me. All it did was remind me of how dirty I felt. Even if I did tell her, I'm pretty sure she would have just run to Karen and told her everything, who probably wouldn't have believed me anyways.

On the last night that I stayed in the house, Kristian came into my room drunk as usual, ready to do what he always did. This time, I was prepared for him. I had a knife underneath my pillow and I wasn't about to play with him. I knew that this was my last night in this house and all I had to do was manage to keep him off of me for just one night.

"You know the routine little girl. Get over here and unzip your favorite uncles pants." he said, leaning up against the door.

I was scared to death but I knew what I had to do. I had already prayed earlier because I knew Karen would be working late tonight and Deli was nowhere to be found.

"I suggest you get up out my room before somebody gets hurt." I replied.

He just laughed and played with the toothpic that he had in his mouth.

"I'm confused." he said, shaking his head. "Are you threatening me?"

My heart was racing as he began to walk towards me. The liquor smell was unbearable and I could just almost vomit.

"Kristian, please don't do this tonight. I'm cramping and I'm on my period." I lied.

"I don't give a fuck!" he yelled.

At that moment, he grabbed my legs and spread them open as he got his funky ass on top of me. I knew he wasn't going to back down. I managed to slide my hand underneath my pillow and grab the knife. I raised it up to his throat and told him to stop. He stopped in his tracks and looked at me like he couldn't believe it.

"You sneaky little bitch." he said smiling, and getting up off of me. "Ill let you slide this time cause I see you MUST be having a bad day."

I sat up with the knife still pointed at him as I waited for him get out of my room. I couldn't believe that my plan actually worked. He was big enough to take the knife from me at any time but he didn't. Probably because he was too drunk to even realize.

The next day, Karen tried her best to get me to reconsider. Her tears made it even harder for me to walk out that front door, but I knew I had to go no matter how much she begged.

"Secret you know you don't have leave." Karen whined. "I really don't want you to go."

"I know mom, but its just something I have to do. I cant stay here forever." I replied.

"But you're still so young." she said. "I haven't even really got a chance to meet this boy you moving in with."

"Mama you've met Courtney plenty of times. He's like my best friend. If I wasn't sure of him taking good care of me I wouldn't be going ma'." I said.

Deli, who had just so happened to be sitting at the breakfast table, just looked at me and rolled her eyes. Without a word she just got up and went upstairs. I knew she was also mad that I was leaving, but I had made up my mind. I wasn't staying in this house for one more night.

"So I guess I gotta let you go out and be a woman huh?" Karen said.

"I'm only going to be about a thirty minutes away mama. Ill keep in touch. Don't worry." I responded.

She looked at me with dis-belief.

"I promise!" I said, hugging her and kissing her on her cheek.

When I came up from hugging her, Kristian was standing in the doorway. He kind of startled me a bit.

"Need help witcha bags niece?" He asked, chewing on another toothpic.

I started to say no, but I looked down at my heavy bags and gave it a second thought. Courtney had to work so he just gave me his car and told me to come get my stuff. I looked back up at Kristian and accepted his helping hand. As he carried my heavy ass bags to the car, he began to sweat. He looked so disgusting. I suddenly felt dirty and couldn't wait to get to Courtney's to shower and scrub myself. When he finally got done loading my last bag in the car, he took it upon himself to come around to the driver's side.

"So I take it you leaving cause of me right?" He asked, wiping sweat from his forehead and still chewing on that toothpic. I just looked up at him and rolled my window up. I didn't have anything else to say to him at that point. I fired up the engine and drove off. I took one last look at him through the rearview mirror, and had no intentions on EVER coming back to that house. Not as long as he was alive....

\\

So I had been staying with Courtney for the past couple of months. Things were going great! Even though, we still weren't considered an item, he was treating me like a princess. There was no sex involved, but it felt so much like a relationship. He liked me, true. He liked me a lot. I didn't have a problem with that, but where I came from, in order to get, you had to give, and so far, I wasn't really giving him anything. This boy was buying me jewelry, clothes, and all type of expensive gifts. I was driving his car whenever I wanted, and getting money on a daily basis. Fuck a princess, I felt like a queen.

I was kind of stuck on the fact that we had never had sex though. We had been living together for about three months and we never did it. Not once. I can admit that at first I did play hard to get, but that was only to show him that I wasn't easy. After I moved in with him I thought he would have taken advantage of me, but he didn't. Not that I wanted him to or anything, but it was just what I had expected. We would kiss and play around from time to time, but we never went all the way, even if I was the one implying it. He called himself taking it slow with me, but I called it teasing me. It was like he flipped the script and was trying to play hard to get with me. I was tired of playing it off and taking cold showers whenever I was in heat. He was so busy waiting for the right time, which I felt was never going to come. Him "taking it slow" was going a little bit too damn slow. I was fiending for Courtney. I wanted him inside me.

One night he came in and I had just finished watching Jason's Lyric. This movie always had me in heat. I took it upon myself that night to make Courtney's dick, my dick. I waited until he got into his room and took off his clothes. I knew he was going to hop in the shower because it was the same routine every night. As bad as I wanted to get in that shower with him, I didn't. I went into my room and found some sexy purple lingeri. I knew he wouldn't be able to resist. I slipt it on and crept back into his room. I slid underneath his covers and patiently waited for him to get out. It felt a little dull, so I hopped back up and turned some tunes on and lit a few candles. I heard the shower cut off and I ran and jumped back in the bed. My heart raced as I continued to wait. I was so ready for this moment.

"What's all of this?" he asked, walking into the room, looking around at all the candles.

He was standing in the doorway with his dirty clothes in one arm and a towel wrapped around his waist. I stood up from under the covers so that I could show off my features.

"I'm tired of playing with you." I replied, smiling and walking to him.

He smiled and looked me up and down admiring my body. He didn't say anything right away because I believe he was at a lost for words. The most he'd seen me naked was me wrapped up in a towel.

"Girl do you know what you doing?" he asked, still not looking in my face.

"Shhh..." I said, putting my finger up to my lips. "I got this."

I grabbed his clothes out of his arm and tossed them in his laundry basket. I then took his hand and led him over to the bed. I unwrapped his towel and let it fall to the floor as he laid back on the bed.

"Damn girl!" he said, as his dick began to stiffen. "You aint playing is you?"

I smiled as I straddled him. I kissed him from his lips, to his neck, to his chest, to his belly button. When I got to his dick, I took him in my mouth with full affection. I went to work on his penis. He couldn't handle it. It was obvious that he wasn't ready for it. All the moaning and graoning that he was doing, I knew he was loving it. He couldn't even be still. I loved that.

"Where'd all that come from?" he asked, after I was finished.

"They don't call me Secret for nothing." I replied, with a smirk on my face.

"This one hell of a secret baby girl." he replied.

He grabbed me and laid me down on the bed. He got on top of me and looked me in my eyes.

"What?" I asked confused and wondering why he was looking at me like he was.

"You are just too damn beautiful." he replied.

"Boy you need to quit." I responded, blushing and turning my head.

He grabbed my chin and turned my face back towards his.

"No. I'm serious." he said.

"Well, thank you." I said, not knowing what else to say. I was just ready to fuck. He was totally throwing me off.

"Girl you just don't know." he continued.

I giggled a little bit. "Know what?"

"What you do to me." he replied.

I looked up at him with one eyebrow raised. I was confused.

"Secret, I love you." he said. "Like, REALLY love you."

"Boy you just saying that." I replied.

"Girl you make my heart race when you laugh." he said, smiling. "My knees get weak when I'm next to you, and I still get butterflies whenever you say my name."

"Butterflies huh?" I thought. I couldn't help but to get the feeling as if he was about to propose to me or something. In my mind I prayed that that wasn't the case.

"Court, I don't know what to say." I replied.

"Wait, let me finish." he said. "I been trying to get something off my chest for a long, long time."

I could do nothing but just lay there and listen.

"Now these past couple of months aint beeen all that long, but it was just enough time for me to fall in love with you." he said. "Secret I been in love with you since the first time I seen you outside the club. I knew I had to get you shawty."

He sounded so cute that I couldn't help but to smile at him. It was so sincere and real. I almost already knew that he was about to propose or something.

"So what are you trying to say Court?" I asked, propping myself up on my elbows, not prepared for what he was about to say.

"I want you to marry me?" he said.

"Marry you?" I repeated.

"Yeah."

I couldn't believe he really asked me that.

"Don't you think it's a bit too early for marriage? I just graduated from high school Court. We barely even got our feet wet yet."

I had a lot of love for Courtney, but I damn sure wasn't IN love with him. How could he expect me to be the one for him? I was a little pissed. I think he was still gone off the brain that I had just given him.

"I know baby, but I cant help how I feel about you." he said.

I didn't have anything else to say. I was over it.

"Okay okay okay… can we talk about this later?" I asked.

"Right now, all I can think about is sex."

I didn't mean to sound rude, but I was just horny and he was totally killing my vibe.

He began to laugh at me. I knew he was laughing at how bad I was fiending for him.

"Its not funny." I responded, playfully pouting.

"Well I just wanted you to know how I felt before I made love to you." he said.

'Make love to me?' I thought. All I refered to it as was sex. S.E.X.. Nothing more, nothing less. He was starting to get on my nerves with this "love" shit. Courtney was 23 years old. Only five years older than I was. I don't think he should have been trying to settle down for good.

"FINE! I love you too Court. Are you ready now?" I asked, ready to get down to business.

He just smiled and didn't say a word. He just went to licking and kissing me all over my body. It felt so good. He took my top off just only using his teeth and then slowly pulled my bottoms off. As he got in between my legs, he gently began to bite the inside of my thighs. By this time, I was soaking wet, so when he inserted his tongue into my pussy, I could have almost told this nigga that I would marry him. As he fiddled his tongue on my pearl, I began to feel like an errupting volcano. The feeling was so good that I almost wanted him to stop. I could feel my legs bginning to shake as I was about to cum. When I came it was like heaven. When he finished he was hard as a rock and I was just ready for him to give me all of that hard dick.

By the time we were finished, I was wore the hell out. He put that dick on me so good I didn't never want to get up out his bed. I just laid there on his chest as I listened to R. Kelly's freaky ass booming out of the speakers. I was happy as hell I had finally gotten what I wanted. I looked up at Courtney to see if he was awake and he was. He smiled at me and kissed me on my forehead. Then he wrapped his arms around me and it felt so good. From this moment on, I just knew things were going to be different. Real different!

4

After that night, shit did change. We tried the relationship thing, and for awhile it worked out. I can admit that I did fall in love with him, but I still didn't want to get married. He constantly asked me and every time I shut him down. Don't get me wrong, Courtney was definitely the hubby type. He did everything to try his best to keep me happy. I just wasn't ready for that kind of commitment. I needed to live a little, get out into the world and explore. I guess he felt as if he had done that enough for himself. Clearly we weren't on the same page.

About four months into our relationship I had gotten spoiled. He was taking me out to fancy restaurants, five star hotels, movies, clubs, and doing what couples do. He was treating me like a woman was supposed to be treated. I was happy and there was no doubt about that, but for some reason I still wasn't satisfied. It felt like something was missing, I just couldn't put my finger on it. I had everything I needed as far as I was concerned, so what the hell could it be? It actually annoyed me to the point where I would take it out on Courtney, but it was never intentional. Then I figured it out one day. I was in the mist of wanting to go to the mall and I needed some more money. As I prepared to go hold my hand out for Court to put some money in it, I thought to myself. I was tired of having to ask for money. I wanted to get it on my own. It was nice not having to do shit, but that was getting boring. That was a dead issues as soon as it started though. Soon as I attempted to say anything about getting a job, Courtney wasn't having it. He said what did he look like having all this money and having his girl working a 9 to 5? He wasn't going for that. After awhile, Courtney really began to act like a real drag. He never wanted to do anything anymore. Not even come to the club with me. He claimed he was getting to old for the club scene. That pissed me off because who the hell was I supposed to go out with? I didn't have any friends to call up and go with. I pouted every time he rejected me. Slowly but surely we began to stop doing other things like going out to eat at expensive restaurants and hotels. Things had completely changed and I wasn't feeling it.

He eventually admitted that his money was starting to get low. I guess two of his main partners had gotten bumped with a lot of work and business was beginning to flop. The frustration was oh so real. I had turned into a major bitch over the whole process of riches to rags. I wasn't getting any of the things that I was asking for anymore. It was always "baby, I ain't got it right now," or "we gone have to hold that off," or "wait til' I get my money back up." I was going nuts! I couldn't help but think that this niggas money was lower than low. Obviously it was too low to share it with me. I felt like I was being punished and I wanted to punish his ass back.

I stopped having sex with him because night after night he would come home empty handed. His pockets were tight and I had become a mean, gold digging, ungrateful ass bitch, and if he couldn't give me what I wanted, I was gone get it from somewhere else. His time with me was running short and if I was gone stay with him he better had start stepping his game up. I was trying my best to play the part of a ride or die girlfriend, but shit, ain't no telling how long that would be.

"Secret,
I made you some breakfast and I put it in the microwave. I had to make a run and ill be back when I'm back.
Court..."

25

I had waken up to another one of Courtney's bullshit ass notes on the table. For the past few weeks he had been leaving every morning without me having any knowledge of where he was. I didn't care though. While he was out doing him, I definitely out doing me. I had met this guy named Lando at this strip club called Exotic Rain. The "E.R." for short. I was sitting at the bar looking good as usual and he walked up beside me. I wanted to turn and look at him, but I didn't want him to think that I was a thirsty chick.

"Yo Phil, what's up? Hit me with my usual!" he yelled to the bartender.

I had just finished my drink and I could see him checking me out from head to toe in my peripheral.

"Can I get you another drink?" he asked.

I didn't respond. I played it off as if I didn't hear anything. I wanted him to ask me again.

"Excuse me miss?" he said.

I finally turned to look at him. Damn, was he fine!

"Yes?" I asked.

"I said, can I get you another drink?" he said.

I looked down at my cup and then back up at him. "Uh, no. That wont be necessary."

I just loved playing hard to get. For some reason, playing hard o get made niggas just want you even more. I loved that feeling of control. It turned me on.

"Why not?" he asked.

"Because I can buy my own thank you." I replied, trying not to sound too rude.

"That's understandable. Independent and sexy." he said. "I can dig it."

I chuckled just a little bit.

"So you got a name?" he asked.

"Secret." I responded.

"Secret huh?" he replied, as if he didn't believe me. I didn't bother me because most people came off that way when I would tell them my name.

"Yeah, Secret." I said, leaning towards him to whisper. "So don't tell nobody."

He laughed a little.

"So, do you have a name sir?" I asked.

He reached his hand out to shake mines. "The names Orlando, but everybody calls me Lando."

After we exchanged names we sat and talked for a while, then he asked for a dance. I took his hand and went out to the dance floor. All them long islands hand me in my zone and I was feeling myself. I was dancing all type of nasty like, like I ain't have a boyfriend the first. All that grinding I was doing, I should have been pregnant by the end of the night. I drunkenly didn't care if some hating ass nigga or bitch went back and told Courtney that they seen me clowning. I was prepared to give that nigga a ear full if he even attempted to confront me. He should have had his ass in the club with me instead of acting like a old ass loser.

When the club let out, instead of putting his number in my phone like any other nigga, this nigga gave me his card. Turns out, he worked for the club. He was some kind of stripper manager. I guess he recruited strippers to be on his "team" or whatever he called it. I was kind of mad because he had potential to be my new boyfriend. I threw his card into my purse and had no intentions on pulling it back out unless I was cleaning it out. As I angrily waited for my cab to come pick me up, he came up to me.

"Do you need a ride beautiful?" he asked.

"A ride?" I slurred. "By you?... Naw I'm straight."

I was drunk as hell and wasn't no way in hell I was getting in his car. For all I knew, he would have tried to take me somewhere and fuck me. I wasn't having that.

"You sure?" he continued. "I mean, its really not a problem."

Even though he did sound sincere, what did I look like pulling up to the crib with another nigga dropping me off? Courtney would have lost his shit!

"Positive." I replied, rolling my drunken eyes. I didn't want to take any risks.

Instead, he waited til my cab arrived and made sure that I got in safe. Although, he was behaving so sweet, I still didn't plan on having anything to do with him from here on out.

Then one day, I was so bored in the house and Courtney had left me alone once again. I didn't have anything to do and I didn't feel like sitting up in the hot house all day staring at the walls. I wanted to go somewhere. I was about to go crazy. I just so happened to be searching through my purse looking for my lip balm when I came across Lando's business card. For a minute I contemplated on if I should call him or not. I didn't want him to get the wrong impression. I wasn't calling because I wanted to be one of his strippers. I was calling because I enjoyed his company that night. I just wanted to see what he was up to. So I finally thought "Fuck it! Why not?" and dialed the number. Right off the bat he remembered me. He said that anybody who could forget a face like mine, and with a name like Secret was completely foolish. I thought that was cute. I told him that I was bored and didn't have anything to do.

"Well, I got these auditions I gotta go check out in a few, but if you wanna roll with me you can." he replied.

I thought about it for a second. Did I really want to go watch some wanna-be strippers audition? Hell yeah. I was so bored that I would've went to go watch some monkey strip if that was the case. I told him that I would love to go and he came and got me within an hour.

When we pulled up to this warehouse looking place that was in the lowend off in the cut, I looked over at Lando in disgust. It was nothing that I expected. I guess I thought we were at least going to be pulling up to some club or something. It looked like some cheap shit.

"This is it?" I asked, with a look of dissatisfaction.

"Yup." he replied, smiling and noticing the look on my face.

He got out of the car and came to open up my side of the door. He held his arm out and waited for me to step out and hold on to him. He was such a gentleman. As I held on to him, I couldn't help but get lost in his scent. I don't know what cologne he had on, but he smelled so good. In my mind we looked good together. We felt good together to. I still wanted him, even though I could sense that he wasn't really feeling me all like that. I guess because there was a slight age difference. I was 20 and he was 27. Big deal!

We walked up to the place and waited for somebody to come open up the door. Some older nigga with a face full of hair came and let us in.

"Hey Papa Doc!" Lando said, greeting him.

"Hey, young blood!" he replied. "The girls were just looking for you."

"Aw, word?" Lando said. "Let me get in here and see what's up."

"Who's the pretty lady?" Papa Doc asked, referring to me.

"Yeah she is pretty huh?" Lando replied, smiling and looking me up and down. "Secret this is Papa Doc. Pop, this is Secret."

I could tell by the look on his face that he automatically thought that I was a stripper.

"No, I'm not a stripper." I chuckled. "That's my real name."

"Oh, well in that case, nice to meet you." he laughed.

We shook hands and walked farther into the place. Stripper bitches were everywhere. It was actually way better looking inside than it was on the outside. Matter of fact, the inside didn't even look like it belonged to the outside. It was clean and nicely decked out. If I didn't know better, I would have thought it was a little club or something. The girls were walking around half naked, doing each others hair, practicing dances, sitting around, chit chatting, and just all over the place. There were about 40 of them. Lando took my hand as we walked around to meet and greet some of the girls. As we walked up to the first girl, I noticed that she had a name tag on. Drip-Drop? I thought. I looked around and seen that they all had on name tags. I couldn't wait to see what the rest of their names were.

"Drip-Drop huh?" Lando said, leaning over to see her name tag.

The girl ain't have no shame in her game. She grabbed her triple D breast and shook them in his face.

"Oh, damn!" Lando said. "I can dig it."

He shook her hand as we went on to the next girl.

"What's up Undacuva?" Lando said, reading her name tag. "You got something for me?"

"You know it baby!" she replied. She was a cute little Asian and black girl. She turned around and bounced her little booty up and down. I had to admit, she was small but she knew how to work it.

"Okay, I see you." Lando said, moving along.

"Alright now Boy-Shortz, let me see what you working with!" He said.

She spent around slowly, biting down on her index finger, and slid down bouncing into a split. Even I thought it was sexy. You could tell it just came natural to her.

Lando clapped. "Now that's what I'm talking about!" he shouted, helping her up off the floor. "I'm definitely looking forward to seeing more of yo sexy ass."

She blushed and thanked him.

As we got around to the rest of the girls, they all had me going with their crazy ass names. We came across girl with names like Magic, Aquafina, Division, Juicy, Barbie, Mysterious, Tasty, Cherry, Precious, Choc-Lick, Candy, Dream, Kitty-Kat, Patience, Creamy, and Cookie Girl. That was just a few. I could only imagine what the rest of their names were. Lando had explained to me that they all were going to get picked, but based on how good they were was what determined which club they would be placed. Exotic Rain was the top Strip club of them all in the 612. Therefore, he got first dibs on picking. Even, I had not heard of Lando before I actually met him in the E.R., I wasn't surprised to find out that he had had a little rank in the streets. I just figured that I needed to get out more.

We had been there for about a hour and a half chilling and watching the strippers dance. Some of them were even having little strip battles for fun. I think they were getting a feel of what each other was capable of before the auditions started. It actually looked kind of fun. Still, I couldn't see myself getting up on a stage dancing for dollars. It just wasn't for me.

Lando had gotten a phone call telling him that he had to come downstairs for a minute. I guess the audition room was downstairs in the basement and the judges had to meet before the auditions started. It was some type of mandatory thing they had to do.

"You gone be cool up here til I get back?" Lando asked me. "I just gotta run down here and talk to these people right quick."

"So what am I supposed to do?" I asked, looking at him crazy. "I don't know these bitches."

Lando laughed. "You can chill right here. Get comfortable, I'm coming right back."

"Aight." I replied, pouting. "Come right back!"

"I got you!" he said, kissing me on my cheek. He was so damn cute, I just waved him off to go.

I sat down in my chair and continued to observe the strippers. I noticed this little skinny white girl looking over at me. She was somewhat standoffish. As I tried not to look at her, I could feel that she was still looking over at me. I began to wonder if she was trying to get my attention so I waved at her to see what would happen. Just as I suspected, that was all she needed to walk her frail ass over to me.

"Hey." she said, sitting down next to me.

"What's up?" I asked.

"Oh, nothing. Just waiting for these damn auditions to start." she replied. "I couldn't help but notice that you were sitting over here by yourself."

"Oh, no I'm not by myself sweetie. I'm with Lando." I said. "He had to make a run real quick."

"Oh okay." she said. "Are you auditioning at all?"

"Nope, just here to watch." I responded. "What about yourself."

She was so thin that I couldn't help but wish that she was only watching also.

"Yeah, this is my first time. I'm so damn nervous. I'm just ready to get it over with."

"Awww, what's your name?" I asked.

"I'm Sunny Dee" she said, sticking out her hand. "But everybody calls me Sunny."

"Well good luck today." I said shaking her hand. She was definitely going to need it.

"Thanks." she replied. "I guess I should get back over here to my spot. I just wanted to come speak."

She got up and went back over to her little table. I continued to sip my Sprite as I watched the girls prepare. I noticed one of the girls parading around like her shit didn't stank. Dy-Nasty was what her name tag read and everybody was calling her Dy. She was on the floor starting shit with everybody. I guess she was trying to throw them off before auditions or something. I watched as she walked up to some girl named Peaches and tried her right in front of me.

"Looks like you gone have to work a little bit harder on them dance moves lil mama." She said to Peaches.

"Excuse me?" Peaches relied, sitting up from stretching her legs. "Dy, please don't start with me. Ain't nobody got time for your shenanigans."

"Shenanigans?" Dy snapped. "No baby, this ain't no shenanigans. I'm serious."

Peaches stood up off the floor. "Well that's fine, but imma need you to seriously get up out my face with that bullshit."

Dy laughed right in Peaches's face.

"Dice, come here girl!" she yelled over to her friend Paradice. "You hear this bitch?"

Dice got up from her table and ran over to Dy. "What she over here talking about?"

Peaches just shook her head. "Both of you bitches are miserable. Always starting shit."

I was at the edge of my seat because I knew some shit was about to pop off.

"Miserable?" Dice asked. "Bitch, what's miserable is them cut up tights you got on with that cheap ass weave in yo head. Now that's miserable."

It was clear as day that Peaches's outfit was way cuter than Dy and Dices outfits put together. And to top it off, I think Peaches was wearing her real hair, which was in a long dangly ponytail. The bitch was just hating on her. What Dice needed to do was turn towards her friend Dy, who was looking tacky from head to toe. She needed to tell her about herself.

Peaches just laughed and crossed her arms. "Now that's funny. You two are too much for me."

"Bitch, get slapped!" Dy yelled.

Peaches stopped laughing and got serious. "Try me!"

As soon as Dy swung and missed Peaches went to work on her. Her fist were moving so fast that Dice didn't stand a chance jumping in. Her best bet was to step back and that was exactly what she did. Peaches had Dy on the ground by her hair and was kicking her dead in the face. Some of the girls were yelling "Beat her ass!" while Dice was yelling "Dy get up!" I was just watching like damn ain't nobody gone break it up. Then all of a sudden two big niggas came rushing in and snatched the two of them apart. Peaches was calm while Dy was still trying to get at her. I never did understand those type of bitches. Why did they always try to run back up if it was clear that they didn't stand a chance the first time. Oh well, it was always entertaining to watch. While Dy was still yelling and screaming, Peaches was grabbing her belongings and getting ready to leave.

"I see you catching you a little action up here." Lando said, walking up behind me.

"How could you leave me up here with these crazy bitches?" I laughed.

"I promise I had no idea." He replied.

"Stupid Bitch!" Dy yelled, as we turned our attention towards her and watched as one of the security men struggled to keep her calm.

"Man let her ass go Steve!" Lando yelled. "Chill yo ass out up in here shawty!"

"Lando that bitch put her hands on me!" Dy yelled.

"Word is, you been the one startin' shit with everybody up in here."

Dy glanced around at everybody then back at Lando.

"So that's the word huh?" She said. "Well fuck it then! Gimmie my shit! I ain't gotta take this shit. I'm outta here!"

Some of the girls chuckled and laughed. Nobody cared that she was leaving except her little flunky Dice. As soon as Dy ran out the door, she quickly grabbed her things and followed behind her.

"Man, these bitches be trippin'." Lando said turning his attention back to me. "You good?"

"I'm great." I responded.

"Alright, come on ladies! Auditions are about to start!" Lando shouted. "I need everybody to head downstairs in an orderly fashion!"

I watched as the girls struggled to hustle down the stairs in their 6, 8, and 10 inch stilettos. I had to give it to them because neither one of them fell. The way they were running down them stairs, even I would have taken a dive.

When we got down there, Lando tapped me and said he would be right back. I shook my head okay and went to sit down in the back. The stage was way up front and the judges table wasn't to far from it. The girls had to line up outside the door til their names got called. As I sat and waited for Lando to come back, my phone began to vibrate in my purse. I looked, seen it was Courtney, and slid my phone back into my purse. He never answered for me when I called him so I was going to treat him the same way. There were rules to this shit. I knew that he was probably tired of me bitching to him all the time, but so what. I was tired of putting up with his broke ass. He should have never spoiled me in the beginning like he did and expected me to know how to act when I couldn't get what I wanted anymore. He called about four times back to back. He was just gone have to learn the hard way.

About five minutes later, Lando had made it back downstairs. Not only was everybody waiting on him, but he was accompanied by Peaches. I guess he had ran and went to get her from wherever she had dipped off to. If I didn't know better, I wouldn't have thought that she even got into a fight. She wasn't scratched or anything. She had a smile on her face like she hadn't just Laila Ali'd a bitch not even twenty minutes ago upstairs. She just fell in line with the rest of the girls.

"Auditions are starting!" One of the other judges yelled. "Lets get this show started."

Soon as Lando took his seat they called the first three ladies in the room. There were three poles up on the stage so there were three girls auditioning at a time. I watched as Swirlz, Ices, and Magic strutted their asses up there. When they got to the poles, they all had their own little poses and positions that they started off with. Soon as they cued the music, the girls did their thang. They all were actually really good. I had a hard time focusing on just one of them. They were doing all type of tricks within their little minutes that they had. The music was booming and I couldn't help but to move in my seat. It took a minute for me to realize that my phone was vibrating again. I felt myself getting annoyed hoping that it wasn't Courtney again. I was going to answer and let his ass have it. I finally found my phone and it wasn't Courtney. To my surprise it was Karen. I started not to answer, but I had been ignoring her calls for the longest and something was telling me that I needed to pick up. I quickly ran into the bathroom and answered.

"Hello?" I said.

"Baby girl, I'm so happy that you finally answered." She said, sounding frantic. "Please tell me that you've heard from your sister."

"No ma. Is everything okay?" I replied, getting worried just by the way that she was sounding.

"I hope so baby." she said. "I haven't heard from her in about a week. I'm starting to get worried."

That was just like Deli though. To run off for days and not let anybody know where she was at. I guess it had gotten worse since I had left.

"Ma don't let that girl get your blood pressure all high. You know Deli. She'll turn up soon." I replied, trying to get her to calm down.

"Yeah, but she usually calls or stops in real quick to grab something and leaves back out and I'd be fine with that, but it hasn't been none of that. Nobody's seemed to have seen her in the last past week. I feel like something bad has happened." She said, beginning to cry.

"Don't cry ma. You always let her get you like this. Don't worry about it. Deli always does what she wants. You know that."

"But Secret she came in here about a week ago with a bruised up, bloody face like somebody had just put their fist in my baby's eye over and over again. When I asked her about it she cursed me out, packed a bag and left again." She sobbed.

That's what threw me for a loop. Deli? A bloody face? That shit didn't sound right at all. What the hell was she out here doing in these streets? Obviously something that she ain't have no business doing. Deli wasn't the type to have no enemies. Shit wasn't adding up.

"Okay ma, imma look into that." I informed her. "But for now just call and report her missing. She's probably just out staying with a friend or something and doesn't think your looking for her. You don't need to be worrying too much. Its not good for you."

"Alright baby girl. I sure do hope your right." she said.

"Okay ma. I love you and ill call you later." I said.

"Love you too baby." she replied as we both hung up.

"What the hell Deli?" I thought aloud to myself. Now Karen was going to have me worrying about this girl. I couldn't let this mess up my night with Lando. I pulled myself together and went back in the audition room. The girls were still in there getting it in up on stage. While they were calling in the next three girls, Lando looked back at me and mouthed the words "where'd you go?" I held up my phone and mouthed to him that I had to take that phone call. He shook his head "okay" and turned back around and got to work.

By the time the auditions were over, it was going on 7:30. I realized that I had been with Lando all day, so when he asked me if I wanted to do dinner I hesitated to say yes. I knew Courtney was going to wring my fucking neck when I got in. I didn't care. I liked hanging with Lando. Even if I couldn't have him, he was still a cool ass nigga.

"So whatcha think?" he asked, as we sat down at the table waiting for our food to come.

"Think about what?" I asked.

"The auditions."

"Oh." I said, not ready to go where he was going with this conversation. "It was pretty cool."

"No, I'm asking could you ever see yourself doing something like that?" he replied.

"Not really." I responded nonchalantly.

"Well, why not?" he asked smiling. "I mean, don't get me wrong, but you have the perfect body for it."

"Is this your way of trying to recruit me or something?" I asked. "If so, I'm not interested."

"Do you feel as if I'm trying to recruit you?" he asked, still smiling at me.

I looked at him blatantly, but didn't say anything.

"Okay, you right. I guess I gotta work on my recruiting skills, but I'm just saying. It would definitely be worth your while. Especially with a body like yours. I guarantee that."

"Its not about my body being perfect. Its about me getting up on a stage naked in front of strangers while old ass men throw their wrinkly ass dollars at me." I said. "Doesn't that sound a little trashy?"

He laughed. "Only when you put it like that."

"Well, that's the only way I know how to put it." I replied.

"Naw sweetheart, theres so much more to this shit that you don't even know. Talk about having your own. Cars, clothes, a crib, money. Not depending on anybody. Not mommy, daddy, boyfriend, or baby daddy. Just your damn self." he said. "Independence sounds lovely don't it?"

Once again I didn't respond. It all did sound good but I don't think I was quite ready to be completely on my own. Even though I wasn't getting everything I wanted, Courtney was still taking good care of me. I liked having him around and plus I did love him. I couldn't just up and leave.

"Tell you what," Lando said, interrupting my train of thought. "Ill let you think about it. If you haven't made a decision by the end of the night, that's fine. You have my card. If you ever decide to cross over to the independent side, give me a ring. If not, you can still give me a ring. I enjoy your company."

The waitress brought out our food and we continued the rest of our date without conversing about strippers. It was really nice. Lando was such a gentleman and I was sure that he was going to make some little bitch real happy one day. It was just too bad that it wasn't going

5

The next couple of weeks went past and Deli still hadn't shown up. She was really nowhere to be found. The police claimed that they would keep looking for her, but I was pretty sure that they had given up. They were good for nothing anyways. All of her closest friends said that she had been starting to act real different days before she went missing. Even her best friend Ashley told me that she thought Deli was doing drugs. When I asked about her bruised face she said that she had been fooling around with some niggas that were no good and she always showed up with different kind of marks on her from time to time. I couldn't believe Deli was out here like that. She was acting totally out of her character. Drugs, bad boys, runaway? What was really going on? Where the hell was she at? All these questions were running through my head over and over. I prayed that wherever she was, that she was safe. The last thing I wanted to hear was that she was somewhere dead.

I was sitting in the living room one night watching TV., eating chicken and macaroni that Courtney had cooked. I had just gotten off the phone with Karen from calming her down, who was once again crying about Deli. Something told me that Deli wasn't coming back home but Karen just didn't want to believe it. She just needed to get that there was a possibility that Deli might just be gone. I couldn't say those words to her, but I just wanted her to know. I hated to hear her cry. Half the time I didn't even want to answer the phone, but I guess I just felt a little obligated to do so. I had became overwhelmed and frustrated with it all. When I hung up from with Karen, Courtney had gotten out of the shower and came in the living room butt ass naked. All I could do was laugh.

"Boy, what are you doing?" I asked.

I guess he wanted some because I had put his ass on restriction.

"You ain't had daddy dick in a long time girl." he said.

I laughed again. "So what that mean?"

"So, lets go in this bedroom so I can put this on you." he replied.

"Naw, I'm straight." I lied, with my panties soaking wet.

"Or, I can come get it on the couch." he said. "Its up to you baby."

I don't know what got into him, but he was ready to play. I cant even lie, I did want some sex, but I wasn't going to give in that easily. He was going to have to take it.

"Courtney, its not happening so just forget about it." I replied.

He walked over and stood in front of the TV.

"So you telling me you don't want this?" he said, holding his arms out and looking down at his penis.

I started clapping my hands. "Bravo! So you do get it!"

We both started cracking up.

"Why you playing with me girl?" he asked. "You know you want me to taste that."

"You the one playing!" I shouted. "Get from in front of the TV."

He shook his head and came to sit next to me on the couch.

"I see we gone have to do this the hard way."

I looked at him like he was crazy. "Don't start playing and shit."

I knew exactly what his next move was. He was determined to irritate the hell out of me til I decided to give in. He put his arm behind me and propped one leg up on the table expecting me to tell him to move. I completely ignored him. We sat like that for about five minutes before he began to try something else.

"Bae, let me see the remote." he said.

"No. Cant you see I'm watching something?" I replied.

"Don't nobody wanna watch no damn Rush Hour." he said.

"Well, clearly I'm watching it." I said.

Next thing I knew, he was diving over me reaching for the remote.

"Get off of me!" I yelled, tussling with him.

He didn't stop. I tried my best not to let him get the remote. He was naked as hell all over me.

"Move!" I yelled again.

He had put all his body weight on me. "Gimmie the remote first."

I didn't give his ass shit. I had the remote down in my bra and he couldn't get to it.

"I'm not giving you shit!" I yelled.

"Oh, you not?" he asked, sounding like he was about to fuck me up.

All of a sudden he picked me up and turned me over and slammed me down on the couch. I tried to get up but he had me pinned down by my arms. I was loving the aggressiveness.

"Didn't I tell you to stop playing with me?" he asked.

He leaned down and started kissing my neck as I kicked my legs trying to get him off of me. It wasn't working. The more I struggled to get up, the more aggressive he got.

"Let me go!" I shouted.

"Girl shut up. You ain't going nowhere." he replied, continuing to forcefully kiss me. He slid one of his hands between my legs and played with my wetness. As bad as I didn't want to give in and let him win, I did anyway. I couldn't help it. It felt so fucking good. He began to lick and suck all over me as I moaned loudly. He spread my legs and his tongue worked its magic.

"I knew you missed daddy." he said, as he continued to lick me. "You couldn't resist."

The shit was feeling so good that I couldn't even respond. I just held my head back, bit down on my bottom lip, and enjoyed his tongue in me. After I came, I made him fuck me real good. Nice, hard, and long. I needed it. Something had to take my mind off all the stress. If not forever, at least for a little while.

The next morning, Courtney was gone AGAIN. I started to call him but I had noticed that he'd left his damn phone on the dresser. I really didn't too much care because I was still feeling good from the night before. I was feeling so good, that I decided to get up and clean up. I cleaned the living room, dining room, bathroom, and the kitchen. The place was spotless by the time I got done with it. After all that, I was hot, sweaty, and dirty so I hopped in the shower. When I got done, I went into the bedroom to lotion up and put on some clothes. As I was lotioning up, I noticed Courtney's phone was blinking. I got up and went to go look at it. It read "5 missed calls." they all were from the same number. Some nigga named Roe. I wondered what was so important that he had to call five times in a row. Then I thought that it could have been Courtney looking for his phone. I decided to call the number back to see what was up. It rung about three times before someone answered. To my surprise, it wasn't a nigga on the other end.

"Hey baby." A female voice answered.

"Baby?" I replied, chuckling. "Now ain't this some shit?"

For a minute, she didn't say anything. She knew she had fucked up.

"This must be Secret." She finally said.

"Right, cause you know me huh?" I replied. "Who the hell are you?"

"Look, I was looking for Courtney. Its obvious that he ain't around, so ill just call back later." she responded.

"Naw, don't hang up." I snapped. "You know me so well, why cant I know your name?"

"I ain't tryna start no problems. I'm just gone call back later." she said.

"Just like that?" I asked. "You do know that Courtney is my nigga right?"

She laughed.

"Excuse me?" I said. "Something funny?"

"How old are you again?" she asked. I could hear the tone of her voice changing.

"I don't recall discussing my age with you." I replied, as I felt my blood beginning to boil.

"Oh that's right, Courtney's the one who told me you were a baby. Not you."

I looked down at the phone like the bitch was crazy.

"A baby?" I snapped. "Bitch you don't know me."

"I know enough." she laughed again.

Just then, I heard the front door slam. Courtney had walked in just in time.

"Baby!" he yelled out to me from the living room. I didn't respond.

"Oh, we finna see how much you know right now." I said to Roe as I waited for Courtney to come into the bedroom.

"Secret!" He yelled again.

"I'm in here!" I yelled back.

"Babe, have you seen my…" he stopped in his tracks as soon as he seen his phone up to my ear. "Why you on my phone?" he asked.

"So, this what you been doing Court?" I snapped, throwing his phone at him. "You out here fuckin' other bitches and telling them my business?!"

He picked up the phone and seen Roe's name across the screen.

"Damn, man. Let me call you back." he said, hanging up.

"Call that bitch back for what?" I shouted. "You got me fucked up!"

"Man, it ain't even like that." he said. "You trippin'."

"Oh, I'm trippin' Courtney? You got some other bitch on the phone laughing in my face, but I'm the one trippin'?" I said.

I turned around and took a deep breath because I could feel myself getting ready to fight him.

"What you doing' all up in my phone anyways?" He asked. "You got your own damn phone."

I turned back to look at him like he was stupid. "You really gone go there with me after I done caught yo ass red handed? Just be straight up. Clearly she ain't just some chick Court. Who the hell is she?"

He shook his head and sat on the bed as I stood there with my hand on my hip waiting for a reply. He was wasting my time not saying shit.

"So what's up? Its clear you fuckin' this bitch. And what? You wanna go be with her?" I asked.

"Baby, I was gone tell you bout her sooner or later." he said. "I met her a while back at JT's crib when he had that lil shindig for his birthday. We was drunk and she just threw herself at me like it was nothing."

I stood there and listened to every last word coming out of his mouth, trying my hardest to keep my hands to myself.

"For a long time after that I swear I ain't touch that bitch." he continued. "I ain't even see the bitch for a long time after that."

I looked at him in disbelief.

"For real bae. We ain't have no communication." he said.

"So why is the bitch calling your phone talkin' bout hey baby and shit? Ain't nobody stupid."

He took a deep breath and put his head down in his hands.

"Hello!" I shouted, not giving a damn how bad he felt. "I'm waiting."

"She's pregnant." he mumbled.

My heart skipped a beat.

"Excuse me?" I said, holding my ear out to make sure I heard him correctly. "What did you just say?"

"She's pregnant!" he shouted, jumping up in my face. "Aight? It was an accident."

My eyes filled with tears as I looked into his eyes. I was enraged!

"You got this bitch pregnant?" I said. "Are you fucking serious?"

"Bae, I didn't mean to. It just happened." he said trying to grab and hug me.

"Get your fucking hands off of me!" I shouted, pushing him away. "So, that's where you been going every day leaving me in this house?"

He put his head down in shame.

"You a bitch!" I snapped. "I hate you."

As I tried to push past him and walk out of the bedroom, he grabbed my arm. Before I knew it, I had slapped the shit out of him.

"Don't fuckin touch me!" I said, as he grabbed the side of his face.

The first slap felt so good that I wanted to do it again. He wasn't going for that though. He grabbed my arm before my hand reached his face. I quickly snatched out of his grasp.

"You ain't never gotta worry about me again." I informed him. "As far as I'm concerned, your dead to me."

I rushed in the other room to finish getting dressed. All I could do was cry. Even though I was spoiled and could be a major bitch at times, I did love Courtney. Even though he didn't have any knowledge of it, he was my savior. He rescued me from that hell house and in my heart I will forever be thankful of him for that. I knew he probably didn't mean any harm in what he'd done, but he did it. There was no coming back from that. He was about to have a baby with another woman and there was no way that I would dare put myself in that position. What did I look like having to fight with his side baby mama for the next 18 years? I couldn't see myself being that bitch. From this point on, Courtney and I were over. No matter how much he begged me to stay. As I sat there trying to figure out what my next move was, reality hit me. I had nowhere to go. I had no friends, no family, no money, and I damn sure wasn't going back to Karen's. As far as I was concerned, there was only one person left for me to call.

6

Exotic Rain turned out not to be so bad. Dancing for money was actually kind of fun. Lando was right. Making my own bread did feel good. It changed me. I was developing into a new woman. No longer would I have to ask for anything. I was able to get my own shit.

Three months into the game, I was on top of my game. I found me a nice apartment that I had decked out really nice. Rent was fair, and money was never a struggle after the first. I was living the good life. I hadn't bought a car yet, but transportation wasn't really a problem for me. I got to and from where I needed to go with no problem.

Karen had practically disowned me because she didn't approve of my new lifestyle. She said that I was better than this and no daughter of hers was going to be shaking her ass for dollars when she stood in church faithfully every Sunday praying and praising the Lord. She didn't want anything to do with me as long as I was stripping. At first, she wouldn't accept the money I would send her and would send it right back. Then, she stopped calling to check on me. Sometimes, I would call her and she wouldn't even answer the phone. She eventually changed her number in the process. For a while, I was hurt. I couldn't understand why the people that claimed that they loved me kept betraying me. I began to feel like I had an expiration date for everybody who loved me. I quickly learned how to not give a fuck anymore. As long as I loved myself, that was all that mattered.

In the club, I was my own boss. Lando might have ran the club, but I did what the fuck I wanted to do. I could do what I wanted, say what I wanted, and the fellas still threw money at me. My body was power, something else that Lando had been right about. Lap dances paid the most, even though I hated them the most. Men always tried to talk me into sleeping with them afterwards like I was some type of hoe. I constantly had to curse the thirsty motherfuckers out. The niggas ranged from little creepy dudes, to highly paid ballers. As long as I had a drink or two in my system, I had no shame in my game.

I had met this girl named Nyprii. She worked in the club to. We had somehow gotten real close. She had been working there a few months before me and let me know the scoop on everybody in the club. At first it was kind of hard for me to really just trust this stranger, but she eventually grew on me. When we met, I was nineteen and she was twenty-one. We had had so much in common. She became the big sister I never had. Her mom put her out when she had gotten pregnant with her three year old son Na'Priice. Her sons father was killed when she was just seven months pregnant. Na'Priice was all she had. She had been on her own ever since he was born, trying to make a living for the both of them. Just as I did, she had met Lando in the club and he put her to work.

A bunch of the girls envied me for the way that I was put together. I was young, sexy, with a head full of my own hair, with a body filled out very nicely. Which I was not able to say about too many of them. The E.R. was a home for most of these girls. This bitch named Princess had been there longer than most of us. For some reason she felt as if she had some kind of rank. She was always popping off at the mouth with somebody. Nobody ever seemed to really say anything back to her either. Not even Lando and she always had smart shit to say to him. I found that quite awkward. Other than that, everybody pretty much got along. It took awhile for me to really get comfortable, but I eventually became equipped.

7

A day after my 21st birthday, Lando had called all the girls in to work early. It was some kind of mandatory meeting. I guess he had something important to tell us. All of the girls were sitting and conversing in the back room, when Lando walked in.

"What's up ladies?" he said.

"Hey Lando!" we all replied.

"Now, I know yall been getting tired of dancing in the same spot night after night. Right?" He said.

"Hell yeah!" shouted this girl named Peanut.

"And I know yall tired of seeing the same faces and dancing for the same dollars. Am I right?" he said, looking around at all of us.

We all shook our heads in unison.

"That's why I've decided to give you all a break from the E.R.." he replied.

We all looked around at each other confused about what was going on.

"Um… excuse me, but Lando honey, some of us cant take no breaks. We got bills and shit." Said this girl named Keisha.

"Right!" her friend Crystal agreed. "And I got kids to feed."

Some of the rest of the girls chimed in agreeing with them.

Lando laughed. "Okay okay. Calm down." he said. "Here's the surprise."

I sat up straight in my chair and prepared to hear what the surprise was.

"I'm taking you all to Vegas." he said. "On me."

"Vegas?" Crystal said. "Why Vegas?"

Lando opened up his briefcase throwing rolls of money at each one of us.

"That right there is a thousand dollars for each of you." He said. "I need you all to go out and get yourselves some new costumes and fits. We talking big money in Vegas so I need my girls to be top notch."

"How long we gone be gone for? I gotta find my son a babysitter." Nyprii asked.

"Just a week." Lando replied. "So yall get them babysitters on deck, get them fits right, and come prepared."

"So we just going down there to dance?" Missy asked.

"No. I entered yall into a competition." Lando replied. "I need yall to go down there and show'em what we bout."

"A stripping competition?" Princess laughed. "Well yall mind as well give me my prize now."

Princess was so full of herself. Always thinking she was better than somebody. I didn't even know why she was still here. Nobody liked her. I had no idea as to why Lando was keeping her here, but something didn't sit too right with me about the two of them.

"Okay, so here's the deal." Lando continued. "For this first week coming up, I want you all to go shopping for everything your going to need. Make-up, clothes, smell goods, the works. The week after that I don't want you doing anything but resting. Your gonna need it. By the end of this two weeks you should be ready to go. If not, oh well. Stay here and make money in the club while the rest of us go have fun."

With that being said, Lando closed up his briefcase and walked out of the room. The girls got hype slapping each other fives and talking about what stores they were going to be shopping in. I was dazed because I had never even been out the state of Minnesota. I was excited to see how different things would be. I guess Nyprii had kind of noticed.

"You ready girl?" she asked, waving her hand in front of my face.

We left out and went to go pick up Na'Priice from her friend Shanell's house. She was Nyrii's on call babysitter. They had known each other since they were younger, but had fallen off when Nyprii found a sex tape of Shanell and Na'Priice's dad in the back of Shanell's car a long time ago. I guess since they had had so much history, they continued to be cool after he had gotten killed. From jump, Shanell lead me on to believe she was sneaky. I didn't trust the bitch.

Shopping week was fun. Prii and I had found a bunch of cute and sexy shit. I still couldn't believe Lando had threw out a thousand dollars to each of us. That nigga was definitely a boss. I knew he had it like that, but it was just still shocking to me. The week after shopping week, rest wasn't even a factor for me. I was too damn anxious and excited to sleep. My mind was stuck on Vegas. I was so ready to go. I couldn't wait for our plane to take off.

We got to Vegas and it was nothing like I had ever seen. Lights were everywhere, buildings were everywhere, and people were everywhere. I couldn't wait to explore. I had gotten sick from the plane ride, but I didn't care. I was just ready to go sight seeing.

We were staying in some hotel called The Mirage and I had never been in a hotel as big as this one. I felt a little bit like royalty. Lando assigned two girls to each room and he of course, had his own. He gave us our room keys and told us to go get settled in. we were to meet back in the lobby the next morning at around 11:00. Prii and I hurry up and headed up to our room. We were on the third floor which wasn't really that far from where we were in the lobby. We were so excited, we ran in and immediately started jumping on the beds like two little ass kids. The rooms were nice as hell and very spacious.

"Girl you know we gotta make this a trip to remember." Prii said, jumping down off her bed.

"Who you telling?" I replied, jumping down after her. "I cant wait to act up."

Prii laughed. "Girl do you see this TV?" she said, walking over to it.

"If only it could fit in my purse."

We started cracking up. For some reason, black people always had to take something from hotels. No matter what it was. Soap, lotion, hair dryers, towels, bibles. Whatever it was, if it was small enough to fit in a bag, it was going home with whoever.

While we were still cracking up, we had gotten a knock on the door. For no reason at all, we both got quiet and just looked at each other. They knocked again and Prii punched me in the arm.

"Bitch go open it!" she whispered, laughing.

I walked over to the door to see who it was.

"Who is it?" I asked.

"Room Service." They responded.

Room service? I thought. We didn't order any room service. I looked back at Prii confusedly. She shrugged her shoulders.

"Just open it." she said.

"Hi." I said opening the door.

"Hello. I have a special delivery from a Mr. Orlando Johnson." the man said.

He dug into his little cart of goodies and pulled out a bottle of Moscato with a note attached to it. I grabbed the note first.

It read ;

"Ladies,

Have as much fun as you can tonight, because tomorrow we got work to do. Stay with your roommates, be careful, and don't get lost.

Lando…"

I grabbed the bottle, thanked the man, and closed the door. Nyprii snatched the bottle out of my hand.

"Hell yeah! Lets pop this bitch open!" she yelled.

I laughed. Prii was like a kid in a candy store. I could tell she hadn't had this much fun in a long time. She was ready to kick it. She was acting a fool enough for the both of us. I didn't mind though. It felt good to see her enjoying herself.

After we got done sipping on our drinks, we went to go explore the hotel. It was so big that we didn't know where to start. We decided to go check out the casino first. Neither one of us had gambled before, so we just walked around and observed. People we playing all type of games. While we were walking around checking out all the different games, a Jamaican man had caught my eye.

"Girl, look at his fine ass." I said, nudging Prii.

She turned and looked as we both began to stare.

"Ladies." he said nodding and sitting down at the table next to us.

Embarrassed, we smiled and slowly turned around.

"Did you see him smiling at me?" Nyprii asked.

"Bitch, you know them pearly whites was all for me." I laughed, pulling her arm to our next spot.

We left out of the casino and walked over to the bar. We sat down and ordered a few drinks. I just so happened to look over my shoulder and seen Mr. Jamaica walk in.

"Girl look who just walked in." I said to Prii.

She turned around and got excited. "Bitch you better go talk to him before I do." she said.

"Now?" I asked, thinking that I didn't want to look thirsty.

"Duh! Not later. Go head." she replied.

I started to get up and go, but my pride made me sit back down. I hadn't had enough drinks in me yet. Prii looked at me like she wanted to slap me.

"Ugh, you so simple. Come on." she said, throwing the bar tender a tip. "I'm ready to go swimming."

We got upstairs, changed into our bathing suits, and went down to the pool. Unexpectedly, they were walking around serving drink on the poolside. I grabbed me a few more before I decided to get in. Prii on the other hand ain't waste no time hopping in.

"Would you put that drink down and come on?" she shouted over to me. "The water feels great!"

I finished the last sip of my Bahama mama and went to go join her. She was right, the water did feel great. After we got done in the pool, we went to go relax in the Jacuzzi. I felt like I ain't ever want to get out.

"Girl, this is life!" Prii said, resting her head on the ledge with her eyes closed. "If my baby wasn't back in Minnesota I would never go back home."

I laughed as I held my head back and closed my eyes. It was so relaxing. I was feeling myself and couldn't nobody tell me nothing.

"You ladies mind if we join you?" asked a familiar voices towering over me.

I opened up my eyes and there he was, Mr. Jamaica, glistening and looking just as tasty as he wanted to be. Prii and I both waved at the same time. It took me quite a second to realize that he had had somebody else with him. A younger looking man, light skinned, but also Jamaican. He was a sexy one too.

"Hello boys." Prii said, greeting them with no shame in her game. "Come on in."

They both smiled and stepped into the Jacuzzi.

"I'm Prii and this is my girl Secret." she continued, holding her hand out. "And you two are?"

"I'm Quam, and this is Rasaan." Mr. Jamaica replied, as we all shook each others hands. So there we were, sitting in the Jacuzzi with two sexy ass men. Rasaan was more of a baby face, while Quam on the other hand was more than just my type. Dark-skinned, well toned body, had two sexy ass dimples in each cheek, with the perfect smile to go right with them. He had these dreads that hung down to his shoulders that were looking oh so yankable. God had definitely put in work when he created him.

"Quam, if I'm not mistaken, I would like to think that you've been following us." I chuckled.

"Well, can you blame him?" Rasaan asked. "You two are beautiful."

"Awwww that's sweet." Prii replied. "Where have you been hiding? We haven't seen you at all today."

"I've been out and about. I just got in not too long ago." Rasaan responded.

"Aw okay." Nyprii said.

As they went on in conversing, me and Quam were in our own conversation.

"So, what brings you pretty ladies to Vegas?" he asked.

"We're sort of here on a business trip." I replied, not sure if I wanted to tell him that we were strippers.

"Oh?" he said.

"Yeah, we're dancers." I replied.

"Dancers?" he asked, as I unsurely nodded my head. "I like that."

He knew exactly what kind of dancers I was talking about.

"So what brings you and Rasaan here when you can be in beautiful ass Jamaica?" I asked. "I would just love to go there one day."

"Oh, well he lives here in Vegas and I'm here visiting him." he replied. "I usually come visit often."

We went on talking for about fifteen minutes. Nyprii claimed that she had gotten too hot and her and Rasaan had gotten out and went to get back in the pool. While they were over there playing like kids, my pussy was on some other shit. I don't know if it had been the liquor that had me hot or what, but I was ready for some sex. Quam wasn't making it no better looking the way he was looking, and I swear if he would have licked his lips at me one more time we were going to have some problems. As he was in mid-sentence talking about some shit that I wasn't even paying attention to, I spun around to the front of him and sat on his lap on some slick shit and leaned in.

"You wanna come up to my room?" I whispered in his ear, hoping that he was on the same thing that I was on.

I thought that he would have been shocked, and acting all weird about it but he was actually pretty laid back.

"Where did that come from?" he smiled.

"You tell me." I chuckled, grabbing his hand and placing it in my bottoms. "I wanna show you how wet I can get outside of this Jacuzzi."

I drunkenly, looked around the room as he played with my clit up underneath the Jacuzzi bubbles. Luckily we were the only ones in there because as he fiddled his fingers, I quietly moaned to myself. He began to whisper shit in my ear with that Jamaican accent that he had that was making me want him more and more.

"Girl, you are bad." he whispered, as I nibbled on his ear. "But I like it."

I reached down into his pants and he was hard as a rock. I wanted to put his dick in me right there in the Jacuzzi but I knew that would have been doing too much.

"Secret, if I didn't know better, I would say that you were trying to seduce me." he whispered again.

I giggled. "That ain't all I'm trying to do."

We stood up, grabbed our towels, and headed towards the door.

"Ooooooh, where yall going?" Prii yelled, splashing water at us.

"We'll be right back." I lied, winking at her.

"Yeah, right." she replied laughing, as we walked out the door.

As we headed for the doorway, an annoying voice called out to me. I wanted to keep walking but Quam had already stopped and turned around. It was Princess.

"Hey Secret." she said. "I was just wondering if you've seen Lando by any chance?"

"Nope, haven't seen'em." I replied grabbing Quam and preparing to walk off.

"You don't waste no time do you?" she said giggling.

I started to go back and slap her, but instead I just stopped and took a deep breath without responding.

"Remember, what happens in Vegas, stays in Vegas." she yelled again as our elevator doors were closing.

We got up to the room, went in, and didn't even bother turning on the lights. I pulled his swimming trunks down and he picked me up as I wrapped my legs around him. We laughed as we hit the dresser on the way over to the bed because it was pitch black and we couldn't see a thing. He was kissing me all over my neck until he finally laid me down on the bed gently. He turned me over on my stomach and untied my bikini top. Then he turned me back over and slowly pulled my bottoms down. I just laid back and let him do whatever he wanted to do to me. As he played with his tongue between my thighs, I couldn't help but to play with his dreads. I pulled and yanked on his hair until I came all over his face. When he finished, I thought it was my turn to do him, but he turned me over onto my stomach, into my favorite position.

"You got a condom?" I asked, hoping it wouldn't fuck up the mood.

"No. Do you?" he replied.

I reached down into my purse that was on the floor beside me and felt around for one. I was tipsy and horny, but I wasn't no fool. I always kept condoms in my purse for emergencies, such as this. I handed him the condom as my pussy cried, waiting impatiently for him to struggle and put it on in the dark. When he got it on, he slid his hard dick into me from the back and I could have just started singing. It was so fucking big and it felt so fucking good. He was definitely a pro. He grabbed on to my ponytail as he entered in and out of me with long hard thrust. All I could do was moan loudly as he let my hair go and began to smack my ass. I buried my head into the pillow and screamed as he held on to my waist and fucked me nice and good. When it was my turn, I turned over and pushed him down on the bed, sliding down onto his dick. Courtney used to say that his dick was the biggest that I would ever come across. I could have almost thought that he was telling the truth, but no. He obviously hadn't seen a Jamaican dick. Quam's shit was huge! I rode that dick til I couldn't ride no more. It was beautiful as we both came together. As I laid there next to him after we had finished, I secretly wished that I could pack him up and take him with me.

"Damn girl, you don't play around do you?" he said, catching his breath.

"You ain't so bad yourself." I replied.

In the mist of us talking, I had somehow fallen asleep. I was awakened by the sound of a high pitched voice.

"Secret,
I had a great time last night. Looking forward to spending time with you again before you leave.
Quam.."

Nyprii was sitting up reading the note that Quam had left for me on the nightstand. I sat up and wiped the sleep out of my eyes.

"You little whore!" Nyprii said, throwing the note at me. "Well, I guess I don't have to ask what you two did last night."

"Huh?" I said, sitting up and pretending as if I wasn't comprehending.

"Huh my ass!" she said laughing. "I know you gave Mr. Jamaica some ass last night. Don't play."

I laughed too. "Well since you think you know all my business, I don't recall you coming back to the room last night miss thang."

She started to say something, but began stuttering instead. We both laughed knowing damn well that she was on the same shit that I was the night before. We shared stories with each other detail for detail. She told me that Rasaan's had a big dick too. She joked talking about she wanted to switch, but I could have slapped her. She wasn't getting a piece of my Jamaican Mandingo. That was all for me. By the time we had finished talking, we hadn't even noticed the time. We had forgotten all about meeting up with Lando. I had began to wonder what the other girls nights were like, and then it dawned on me.

"Oh my God!" I said, hopping up butt ass naked. "What time is it?"

"I don't know, but you need to put some clothes on?" she laughed.

"Did you forget we gotta go meet Lando at 11:00?" I asked, digging for my cell phone to see what time it was. Safely, it was only 10:30, which meant we needed to hurry up and get dressed. We managed to quickly do it, seeing as though we both had to get in the shower, do our hair, and do our make-up.

We got down to the lobby to see nobody but Keisha, Jasmine, Peanut, and Tiffany. I was so worried about me and Prii being late, when some of the other girls weren't even ready yet. Not to mention that Lando wasn't even around. We sat down for about twenty minutes before I started blowing up his phone. He wasn't answering.

"Has anybody seen Princess?" Michelle asked, walking into the lobby. She was one of Princess's little minions. Always following up behind her and kissing her ass. It took for Princess to find a her a little white girl to boss and push around.

Most of us shook our heads no, while others just didn't respond. Nobody really cared for Princess and didn't mind her staying absent.

"I haven't seen her since last night." She replied.

"Well ain't she yo roommate? Yall was supposed to stay together." Peanut said.

"Princess is probably out with somebody's white husband thinking she finna up his money." Keisha chimed in, as the rest of us started laughing.

"Actually, Princess is right here." Princess blurted out, walking into the lobby with Missy.

We all laughed because she knew it was true. Princess was always up in somebody's mans face.

"Its nice to know that my name is always in you bitches mouths." She said. "Sounds like I have a fan club."

She giggled as her and Missy slapped fives while the rest of us took her as a joke. Missy was the youngest of the bunch. She was freshly 18 and didn't hesitate to let us know it. Childish and always had something to say. She portrayed Princess as if she were her God, following up behind her and doing whatever she told her to do. That is, if she didn't have Michelle doing it first. An irritating little bitch is what she was. I couldn't stand her.

"Keisha honey, you should fix those tracks before you mention my name." Princess said. "Its not a good look."

I looked over at Keisha because I knew she was about to explode. Everybody knew Keisha was crazy and not to say shit to her, even Princess. I guess Princess thought that since we were in a different state that Keisha wasn't going to do shit to her. Keisha was one of those girls who wasn't too pretty, but she looked like she had some kind of potential to be. It was clear that she didn't have it all up there. She never really thought things through. She had a bad ass temper that you would never want to come across. When she was mad, she didn't give a fuck about right or wrong. She just did what she wanted to do. Ain't no telling how many times she done went to jail either. You could just tell that she had had a rough background.

"What you say?" Keisha replied, standing up out of her chair.

Princess just chuckled. Everybody was on the edge of their seats because we just knew what was about to happen.

"Don't even let her get to you Keish." Peanut said, hoping it would make Keisha sit back down.

"Yeah Keish." Princess said. "Don't let me get to you."

Keisha looked back at Peanut, then at everybody else in the room, then back at Princess.

"Bitch who you think you talking to?" Keisha snapped, charging at Princess. "You got me fucked up."

Before she reached Princess, Peanut grabbed her.

"Keisha calm down! This ain't the place for all that!"

"I know Keisha, don't let her fuck up our trip on the first day!" Tiffany yelled.

"Fuck that Bitch!" Keisha shouted. "Ill kill that hoe!"

Keisha was small so Peanut didn't have a problem holding her back. Being that Peanut was taller and thicker than her.

"Beat her ass when we get back to Minnesota. We on a business trip right now."

Princess was just standing there as if she wasn't the one to egg her on. She knew if Lando would have found out they both would get kicked out the club. He didn't play about his image. He brought us out here on business in his care and he would have found out that these bitches were in here fighting and making his name look bad, it would have been off with their heads. Hopefully these people standing around and watching from the side wouldn't go back running their mouths. It seemed as if Peanut had gotten Keisha to calm down a little bit.

"Keisha you good?" she asked, still holding on to her.

Keisha shook her head yeah, panting and trying to catch her breath.

"I'm finna let you go. Be cool." Peanut said, slowly releasing her grip.

I took a minute to make sure things were back calm. When I realized that Keisha was no longer in a rage, I told them that I was going to call Lando and see where he was. I was so relieved when he finally answered the phone.

"What's up?" He said.

"Hey." I replied, trying to sound like everything was cool. "Where you at?"

"I'm on my way to yall. I'm running a little late cause I had to go talk to some people about the schedule for today." he said. "Be there in five minutes."

"Oh, okay. I was just checking. See you when you get here." I replied as we hung up.

I walked back into the lobby and the girls were still cool, calm and collected.

"Lando said he'll be here in about five minutes ladies." I said, informing them.

I looked out the corner of my eye at Keisha, who was obviously still mad for some reason, mugging me like I was Princess. I just looked away without saying anything to her. I didn't have time for her crazy ass.

By the time Lando arrived, all the girls were ready. He came in with a big smile on his face like he had some good news for us. Hopefully, nobody would mention the little altercation that had just went down just minutes before he got there. That's all we needed was for somebody to just fuck up Lando's day.

"Aight, listen up!" Lando shouted. "Its time for us to head on over to the strip club, catch a feel of the place, and check out some of the girls that you're gonna be up against."

We all stood up ready to leave. I couldn't wait to see how different things were going to be compared to back home. I imagined it to be super huge. I was anxious to get in there and see what was up.

"So how long does this competition last?" Peanut asked.

He informed us that the competition was going to last til the end of the week, and that it would be best if we did as much stretching as we could. I began to wonder what type of girls we were up against. They could have been some muscle bound, flexible ass, gymnastic bitches. I felt myself beginning to worry a little bit, but I immediately shook that off.

8

We got to the strip club, which was right down the street from the Mirage hotel. It was definitely big, just as I had expected it to be. There were about seven stripper groups other than us, and by the looks of it, we were the only all black girl group. I underestimated white girls though. Growing up, the only white girls that I ever came across were skinny, sadiddy, proper, and well kept. Some of these girls were ghetto, sleazy, rough looking, and had bodies of black girls. They didn't too much come off to me as competition, but there were a few groups that looked like they weren't here to play any games. I knew we definitely had to bring our A game to the table.

Everything was going great and girls from all different groups were getting along. Even Princess was going up to girls and introducing herself. I spotted a girl from one of the groups who looked familiar. I just couldn't recall where I knew her from. I started to walk up and speak to her, but I had gotten distracted by the competition director.

"Okay ladies!" he said. "Today will be the first day of competition."

He was a big hefty guy, standing about 6'2 with a head full of curly red hair. Not attractive at all. He actually looked pervertish. This job was probably the most action he had ever received. Directing a bunch of half naked bitches, on poles, shaking their asses. I'm pretty sure he enjoyed every minute of it.

"Its starts at 7:30 and I'm going to need you all here by 6pm to receive your numbers." he continued.

"Numbers for what?" Somebody in the crowd asked.

"So you can know when its your turn to come up to the stage." he replied.

He went on and on about the rules and regulations, while all I he had to say was no fighting or touching of the other components or else we would be disqualified. All the rest of the shit he was talking about was irrelevant. It was still early and my stomach was growling like crazy. They were serving little snacks to us, but that wasn't doing anything for me. I was ready to get out of there and find some real food. It was obvious when he finally sounded as if he was trying to wrap it up. I think he would have been done, but people kept asking him questions, making him take longer. I was beginning to become impatient. When I heard him say "Now, if there will be no more questions, have a good evening and ill see you all tonight" it was like music to my ears.

On the way back to the limo, the girls were excited and conversing about the night to come. Unfortunately, I couldn't join in on the fun. I had my mind set on this pizza place back at the hotel.

"You aight Sii?" Nyprii asked, noticing that I was being antisocial.

"Girl yeah. I'm just hungry." I replied.

"I'm hungry too!" Tiffany said.

"Well there's plenty of restaurants for you to eat at when we get back to the hotel." Lando said. "Just don't eat too much. You guys don't need to be dancing on full stomachs."

After I finished eating my delicious California styled pizza, I headed back up to the room to take a little nap before it was time to go back to the club tonight. I had totally stuffed myself, not remembering that Lando said that we shouldn't dance on full stomachs. Hopefully, I could sleep some of it off in time. Shortly after I laid down, Nyprii came in, plopping down on my bed.

How in the world did she find me?! I thought to myself, pulling the covers over my head.

"What are you doing?" she asked, pulling the covers back from over me.

"As you can see, I'm trying to take a damn nap." I said, snatching the covers from her.

"Uh, no your not!" she yelled, pulling the covers all the way off of me this time. "We're supposed to be making this trip memorable remember?"

I took a deep breath and sat up, knowing she wasn't going to let me get any sleep.

"That's what I'm talkin' bout!" she said, turning to get something out of her purse. "Look what I got for us."

She held up a bag of weed, and shook it in my face.

"Bitch where you get that from?" I asked.

"Girl, Rasaan hooked us up." she replied.

"Rasaan?" I said. "Girl, you gone die trying to smoke that Jamaican ganja."

"Bitch please! I smoked three blunts of this shit with his ass last night." she replied. "I was definitely fucked up, but I'm still alive."

We both laughed.

"Trust me, this some good shit."

Even though I didn't smoke as much as she did, I let her talk me into smoking that shit with her. I only smoked a blunt with her because we only had a few hours til the competition, and I didn't want to be too fucked up trying to dance.

The club was super packed! I took a glance around the club and seen so many fine looking men. It was like I had x-ray vision because I could see their fat wallets right through their pants. It was only a matter of time before they would be sharing all of that money with me.

Back in the strip room, it was always hectic before work. Clothes were always missing, girls were always fighting, or somebody was always missing. Not today though. Lando wasn't having it. He made sure everything was perfect. His motto was "Stay focused, no mistakes." He wanted us to be on our best behavior. As we were changing, some lady came in, giving instructions and handing Lando our numbers.

"Please pay attention to the stripper caller." she said. "New numbers are going to be called after every song."

"Do we have to stand there and watch the other girls on stage, or can we work the floor until its our turn?" Princess asked.

"That's fine. Just as long as you listen for your numbers after every song." she replied.

She left out and we all went back to getting dressed and fixing our hair and make-up. I couldn't wait to get out on the stage and make this money. I just knew the cash flow was going to be lovely.

"Girl did you see them sexy ass niggas out there?" Prii asked, sitting down beside me, combing her hair in the mirror. "I cant wait to get out there."

"Hell yeah I seen'em." I replied. "I seen them fat pockets too!"

"Hello!" she shouted in agreement as we slapped fives.

"Ten more minutes ladies!" said another white lady, bursting into our strip room and leaving right back out.

"Ten minutes?" Prii shouted, panicking.

"Chill out girl. We got this." I said, sitting her back down in her chair.

"Girl I gotta pee I'm so nervous." she said running off to the bathroom.

I just laughed and shook my head. When I got done with my hair, the same white lady came back into the room.

"Time ladies! Its time!"

As we lined up in an orderly fashion, Lando handed us each our numbers. I was lucky number seven. In the land of gambling and taking peoples money, I couldn't believe they picked me to be lucky number seven. I felt good about my number.

"Prii what number are you?" I asked.

"I got third." she replied, showing me it.

Her eyes were a little too low and I just knew she had smoked again.

"Bitch is you high?" I whispered to her.

She just looked at me and smiled.

"Lando gone kick yo ass!" I whispered again. "Stay focused, no mistakes remember?"

"Girl I'm more focused than ever now." she replied.

I couldn't believe this bitch really had smoked again. She was number three and I just knew she was gone get up there and fuck up. Oh well, it was her money and if she wanted to get up there and fuck it all up then so be it. Prii was my bitch and everything, but work was work. I just prayed that she knew what she was doing. I didn't want her to mess this up for the rest of us.

I walked around the club, flirting and giving out lap dances. Them boys had me banked. For the most part, majority of the crowd was black men. I had no idea that this many niggas would be in Vegas. Well, this many with all this money. As I was having fun making my ends, I heard the stripper caller call Nyprii's number up to the stage.

"I need all my three's to the stage!" he shouted.

I watched as she walked up to the stage like a pro. She was completely confident. As soon as the music blasted out of the speakers, my girl did her thang. I guess she was right. She really was more focused than ever now. She danced on that pole like there was no tomorrow.

"Excuse me miss, but can I finish getting my dance?" said the man who I had just got done dancing on.

"Ill be right back." I lied, rushing to the strip room to put up the money I made and to use the bathroom.

When I came out the stall, the same familiar looking girl from earlier, was at the sink washing her hands. I tried to get a good look at her face but she had her head down. She got done, dried her hands, and rushed out of the bathroom before I could even say anything. I couldn't quite put my finger on it,

67

but I knew I knew this girl from somewhere. It was starting to bug me.

I headed back out to the floor and stood next to one of the strippers. She was bobbing her head to the music when I noticed that her number was seven too.

"They working it up there ain't they?" she said, without looking at me.

"Yeah, they're pretty good." I responded. "I wonder what their basing the competition on."

"Its pretty much the same thing every year." she said. "They keep track of which ever group does the most tricks, gets the most money, and has the best costumes."

"Oh?" I replied.

"Yeah, and if there are any ties, they do a trick-off."

"A trick-off?" I asked. "How so?"

"Its when they line up the tied and whoever does the most trick in a certain amount of time, wins."

She spoke as if she had been doing this for years or something. She didn't really sound too enthused about it. She finished explaining it to me and went back to bobbing her head to the music.

"Secret!" I heard Nyprii yell.

I turned towards her direction as she waved for me to come over to her.

"What's up?" I asked, approaching her.

"How'd I do?" She asked, wiping herself down with a towel.

"Bitch you killed it." I replied. I thought yo ass was gone get up there and clown, but you snapped."

"Thank you." she laughed.

We went to take a seat and watch the rest of the girls til it was my turn. A few minutes later, I heard my number.

"NUMBER SEVEN!" The number caller yelled. "I need all my sevens to the stage."

"Go get'em bitch!" Prii said, slapping me on my ass as I got up.

I took a deep breath as I walked up to the stage. Me and the rest of the sevens strutted up to the poles and got into position. The girl that I had had a conversation with looked at me and winked her eye. I smiled, and mouthed "Good luck" to her. She said thank you and we both got back focused. As soon as they cued the music, I took off dancing. I was doing everything I could in those couple of minutes we had up on that stage. I felt like I was up on that stage by myself.

When I got done, I was so out of breath and hot that I had to go get me some fresh air. Nyprii followed shortly after.

"Bitch, when you learn all them tricks?" She shouted, coming out of the door.

"Girl I have no idea." I said. "The music came on and I felt like I was somebody else."

She started laughing. "Bitch, we gotta win after that."

She went on imitating my moves that I did on stage and had me cracking up. Prii knew she ain't have no sense. She always kept me laughing. While she was in the middle of a sentence, the door opened up and bumped her.

"Oh excuse me." Said the familiar looking girl, coming out.

"Damn girl." Prii snapped. "You in a rush or something?"

"I'm so sorry. I didn't mean to." she said.

"Slow down." Prii said, as the girl looked up and saw me.

Just then I knew that she knew me. I could feel it just by the way she was looking.

"Don't I know you?" I asked her.

"I don't think so." She lied. "I'm not from around here."

Prii looked at me then back at her. "We ain't from around here neither. Where you from?"

"Minnesota." she said, as I then realized exactly who she was.

It took a minute for me to notice the nasty ass gap that she had in her mouth. It was my evil older foster sister.

"Ciara?" I shouted. "Bitch you do know who I am."

She just rolled her eyes. I'm guessing she was really hoping that I didn't remember her.

"Daddy's little princess is stripping now?" I asked laughing.

"Oh, stop! I see your quite the little dancer yourself." she replied. I could tell that she was still just as stuck up as she used to be.

Prii just stood there looking confused.

"So, how have you been?" I asked.

"I've been doing well." She replied, rolling her eyes again.

"Why were you running from me earlier?" I asked.

"Running from you?" Prii asked. "What the hell is going on?"

"I'm pretty sure you remember we weren't quite the best of friends when we were younger." Ciara responded.

"So what? You thought I was gone fight you?" I asked. "Bitch we're grown now. And anyways, if I can remember correctly, you were the one always starting shit with me."

"No, I was avoiding you because I didn't want to have to do the small talk like we're doing now." Ciara snickered. "I don't really care for it."

"Oh, that's fine." I said, shooing her away. "I'm not keeping you here. Keep it moving."

She shrugged her shoulders and chuckled.

"Secret, who is this bitch?" Prii snapped.

"A nobody." I said, grabbing Prii's arm. "Come on, before I let her mouth get us kicked out of Vegas."

We left her ass outside and went back into the club. Nyprii just wouldn't give up until I told her who Ciara was. She jus HAD to know. When I finished explaining to her who she was, we went back into the strip room.

"Where yall been at?" Missy asked.

"Minding our own." Nyprii replied.

"Alright ladies, you did good out there." "Lando said walking in, and clapping. "I got some good news and I got some bad news. Which do your prefer to hear first?"

All of the girls shouted for the good news first. I personally didn't care which one he said first.

"Okay, the good news is that there was a change of plans and tonight was the only night for completion. Which means, we get the rest of our vacation to do whatever." he said.

Everybody sighed with relief as we waited for the bad news. "The bad news is, we're not going to know who the winner is until the end of our trip." He said.

"What?" Missy asked. "Why not?"

"Because that's just how they do it. We just gotta be patient." Lando replied.

"That's so stupid. They should just tell us." She said.

Nobody paid attention to her while she whined and pouted. I hated that her young ass even had to come here with us.

All of our girls had finished competing for the day. Some of the other strippers were still competing because their groups were larger than ours. I didn't care though. I was ready to go back to the hotel and shower up. I was hot and sticky.

"So, do we gotta stay here an finish watching them?" I asked.

"If you want to that's completely fine. If not, you don't have to." Lando replied.

Some of the girls stayed back to make a few dollars and watch the other girls. Prii and I went back to the hotel to freshen up and find us some business to mind. We ended up running back into Rasaan and Quam on the strip and they decided to show us around a little bit. Then they took us out for some drinks and to dinner. They were the perfect gentlemen. We needed some of these back home.

On our last night in Vegas, I had met Quam back in his room for one more night of Jamaican lust. The next morning, I woke up first and decided to leave him a note on his nightstand. I didn't want to wake him, so I quickly wrote it and headed out.

"Quam,
Thanks for the trip to Jamaica. I had a lot of fun with you.
Maybe we will meet again someday.
Secret…"

I went back up to my hotel room and hopped in the shower, and for some reason, I couldn't wipe the smile off of my face. Quam had really done my body right. It had been a long time since I had had some good dick like that. I woke Nyprii up so that we could pack our things and head on down to the lobby. Even though we didn't win, I had made so much money just working the floor. I couldn't wait to get back and go shopping.9

We had been back home for a couple of weeks and business was kind of down. It took awhile for our customers to start rolling back in because there had been rumors going around about the club being closed down. I was happy when it began to pick back up.

Lando had ended up firing Keisha when we got back. Turns out somebody snitched about her and Princess's little fall out in Vegas. Once again, Princess had won. But shortly after that, Keisha had came back up to the club and whooped her ass. Princess should have seen it coming. As she sat in the bathroom crying and wiping blood off of her face, nobody comforted her. Not even Lando.

One night after the club, Nyprii's car had gotten a flat tire right in front of my apartment.

"Damn man!" She yelled. "I'm too tired for this shit."

"Want me to run in and call somebody?" I asked.

"Naw, ill just spend the night. Ill deal with it in the morning."

"Okay, but what about Priice?" I asked again. "Who gone go pick him up?"

"Girl imma just call Shanell and see if he can spend the night." she replied. "I'm sure she wont mind."

She picked up the phone and called Shanell who wasn't answering her phone. After about six tries, she finally answered. When Prii got the okay that she would keep him, we took our asses to sleep.

The next morning we called around looking for somebody to come fix the tire. Lando answered and said that he would call us right back. While we were standing outside waiting for Lando to call us back, a tow truck pulled up.

"I hope he don't think he finna tow my car." Nyprii said, looking at the truck.

We waited for him to step out the truck. I felt my phone vibrating in my pocket. It was a number that I didn't recognize.

"Hello?" I answered.

"Is Nyprii around?" They said.

"Who's calling?" I asked, already knowing who it was.

"Her babysitter, Shanell." She replied.

"Can I have her call you back because she's doing something?" I asked.

I could hear her irritatingly sigh. "Yeah, just tell her don't take all day." she replied hanging up.

"Rude ass bitch." I said aloud to myself. I walked back outside and the tow man was already bent down taking her back tire off. I guess he wasn't towing it after all.

"Prii that was your rude ass friend on the phone." I said, smirking.

"What she say?" Prii laughed. She knew I couldn't stand that girl. "She said for you to call her." I replied.

"Excuse me ladies." The tow man said standing up and turning around. "I need the spare."

He was gorgeous! Despite that it was cold outside and he had on a big ass dirty jump suit.

"Oh yeah, its in the trunk." Prii replied, walking to open up her trunk.

"How you doing?" he asked, probably wondering why I was staring at him like I was.

"I'm fine, and you?" I responded.

He nodded and rubbed his hands together. "I'm good. Trying to keep warm."

I just smiled and agreed with him.

"Can you come help me with this?" Prii asked.

"Oh, my bad." he said, rushing over to help her.

"Prii ill be in the house if you need me." I yelled shivering.

While I was in the house preparing to make breakfast, Lando called back to see if we still needed him. I told him that it was alright and that we had gotten some assistance. After about ten minutes, I heard Prii come rushing in.

"Bitch you got it smelling good up in here." She said. "and I'm definitely hungry right now."

"I ain't cooking for you." I lied, playing.

"Yeah right!" she replied. "But anyways, I hooked you up girl!"

"Hooked me up?" I replied. She was always trying to play cupid. "Bitch, hooked me up with who?" I asked.

"Girl, the tow man." she said with a big ass smile on her face.

"You play too much. What you done did now?" I asked.

"I ain't do nothing." she said, with her hand on her chest.

I looked at her in disbelief.

"I'm serious!" She said. "Girl, he asked me if you were single and I told him yes."

I shook my head. "Now why would you do that?"

"Don't you want a man in your life?" she laughed. "I'm just helping you out."

"Bitch, you don't even have a man." I replied.

"Actually, I do." she said. "He's five, and he's all the man I need."

I laughed. "So what did you say to this tow man?"

"I kind of to told him that you would be interested in going on a date with him." she replied nervously, squinting her eye.

"Prii!" I shouted, shoving her. "Why would you do that?"

"Because he was cute and because I wasn't his type." She said cracking up.

"Well, too bad because I'm not going." I said.

"Yes you are."

"No I'm not."

"Yes you are."

"No I'm not."

"Yes you are!" She finally shouted. "You have to go."

"And why is that Prii?" I asked.

"You cant your make your bff look bad now can you?" she replied, batting her eyes. "And plus, I already gave him your number."

She snatched a biscuit and ran towards the door. I could have wrung her damn neck. How dare she give this nigga my number. The sneaky little bitch.

"I'm finna go pick my baby up! See ya later girl!" she yelled, leaving out the front door.

In the mist of my chuckling at her, my phone rung. It was her ass.

"What you want girl?" I answered.

"Oh yeah, I forgot to tell you his name is Stephan." she said, hanging up.

Prii was something else. She always called herself trying to hook me up with somebody. She didn't know this nigga from a can of paint. He did look good though. I cant even lie. I guess it couldn't have hurt to find me a new little guy friend. After all, it had been a couple weeks since Mr. Jamaica and my needs could use a little satisfying. I just hated that Prii made me come off as desperate or something. I wasn't at all desperate. I didn't care to have a man in my life. And who was to say, he probably wouldn't even call me anyways. I don't know what I was getting myself all worked up about it for.

As I was in the middle of my thoughts, my phone had rung again. I thought to myself that it better not had been Prii again. The number across the screen had been another unfamiliar number. It took a minute for me to answer because I thought that it could have been Shanell again, but I doubted it. Being that Prii had left to pick Priice up already. I'm pretty sure she had called from her phone.

"Hello?" I answered.

"What's up baby girl?" said a familiar voice.

"Kristian?" I screeched.

"Yeah, girl. What's up?" He replied.

"Why are you calling me?" I asked.

"A brother cant call and check up on his niece?" he replied. "I miss you girl."

"Your niece huh?" I replied. "Oh, you must mean me right? Well, I'm not your niece. How the hell did you get my number?"

"Girl did you think you was hiding from me or something?" he asked.

My heart began to race.

"Baby girl, you mines. So you don't ever forget that." he said.

Before I could say anything, I closed my phone and hung up. I sat there for a minute in thought. I couldn't believe that his ass had the audacity to call me. I hadn't seen or heard from him in about three and a half years. All of a sudden I had felt dirty again. I could feel him on me. I ran to get in the shower and wash him off of me once again. I couldn't believe that he still had had that affect on me. After all these years, I found myself still crying and washing him away. All the soap in the world wasn't good enough. When I got out of the shower, I got in my bed and continued to weep. I realized that I was still afraid of the rapist bastard. As I laid there hugging my pillow tight, I drifted off to sleep. A couple hours later, I was awakened by somebody ignorant bamming at my door.

"Who is it?" I yelled, dragging my feet to the door.

"Bitch its me! Open up! Its cold out here!" Prii shouted.

I opened up and she came rushing in in with Na'Priice in her arms.

"Here, take him." she said, tossing him to me. "I gotta pee!"

As she rushed off to the bathroom, I took Na'Priice into the living room and took his coat off. I didn't understand why she constantly carried the boy. He was definitely small for his age, but the boy was five years old. He was to old to still be getting carried. He walked perfectly on his own, but I guess that was her baby.

"Look tete." he said, showing me his owie on his arm.

"Ouch! How'd you do that?" I asked.

"I fell at Nell's house." he replied.

"Awww, let tete kiss it." I said, kissing his little scratch. "Feel better?"

He shook his yeah and went on playing with the toys that he brought over with him.

"Phew! Girl I feel a hundred pounds lighter." Prii said coming out of the bathroom. "That Taco Bell went right through me."

She laughed and came to sit next to me on the couch as I plugged my nose.

"You stink." I said.

"Oh shut up." she said, pushing me. "So what was you doing earlier? I know you seen me calling you."

"Girl I been sleep all day." I replied.

"So that explains why you look like shit." She laughed.

"Oooooh, mommy you said a bad word." Na'Priice said.

"I know baby. Mommy sorry." she replied, hitting herself on the mouth.

"So anyways, did he call you yet?" she asked, turning her attention back to me.

"No Prii. And I'm still mad that you gave that man my number." I said.

"I didn't want it to have to come to this, but I got his number for you too." she said, pulling out her phone. "I just thought it would be better if he called you first."

"Girl, I am not about to call him." I laughed. "You are a mess."

"You are about to call him. Not now, but right now." she said.

"And say what to him Prii? I don't even feel like talking to him right now."

"Why not?" she asked.

"Because I just don't."

"Not a good enough answer. You're calling." she replied, grabbing my phone off the table.

"Prii, ill call him on my own time." I said, still laughing at her.

"Your own time?" she asked, looking at me crazy.

"Yeah, like when I'm by myself or something." I replied.

She laughed. "Girl please! You don't get your own time with me. I thought you knew that by now."

She dialed the number, let it ring a few times and tossed it to me when he answered.

I mouthed the words "Imma fuck you up!" to her as I put the phone up to my ear.

"Hello?" I heard him say.

"Hello." I replied, nervously. "Is this Stephan?"

"Yeah, this me. Whose calling?" he asked.

"This is Secret. Remember me from earlier?" I chuckled, as Prii held her ear up to the phone so that she could hear.

"Aw yeah, I remember you." He said. "I was thinking bout calling you but I didn't want to seem like a creep calling so quickly."

I laughed embarrassed. "So am I creeping you out by calling you first?" I asked.

He laughed to. "Naw, you good." he said.

"Aw okay." I replied. "So were you sleeping?"

"Nope, not at all. What you up to?"

"Damn girl, he sound even sexier on the phone." Prii whispered.

"Nothing much. Just sitting here watching a little TV. You?" I replied, getting up and moving away from Prii before he heard her loud, non whispering ass.

"I'm okay. I just got off work not too long ago."

"That's cool." I said. "At least you get to stay in and warm up. I still have to go back out in this shit."

"Work?" He asked.

" Yeah. I'm a dancer." I replied, as Prii threw a couch pillow at me.

I guess she was mad at the fact that that would probably scare him off, but I didn't care. He was gone find out about me anyways so why not keep it one hundred from jump?

"Oh, a dancer huh?" he said. "I can dig it."

"Yeah, I work at Exotic Rain." I said.

"Exotic Rain?" he asked.

"It's a strip club." I said.

"Oh, that's cool." he said.

"Is it really? Or are you just saying that because you don't know what else to say?" I asked.

He chuckled. "Naw, its cool. Just as long as you out here handling yourself right. If you got talent then use it. I just think its dangerous because some people get too caught up into that lifestyle you know."

"You right." I replied. "Everybody doesn't think about it like that."

"Like what?" he asked.

"It being a talent." I replied.

"Aw yeah. But I guess that's just people though."

The whole time we were on the phone, Nyprii was so anxious to know what we were talking about. We had been on the phone for about thirty minutes before hanging up, but not without setting a date for him to take me out. He said he wanted to take me out and treat me real nice. It was only right to accept his invitation.

"So...?" she said, walking over to me. "What he say?"

"Nothing really." I lied.

"Now I know you're lying." she said, looking at me blatantly.

"How?" I laughed.

"Is he taking you out or what? I know he is." she said.

"Damn, you nosy." I yelled. "All he said was that we needed to kick it."

I didn't want to tell her everything because she was too nosy for her own good. I knew once I spilled the beans that she would be more up in my business than I was.

"When?" she asked.

"Girl, I don't know. I guess whenever we both get some time off work." I replied. "And speaking of work, its about time to go."

I jumped up and went to go get ready to head on down to the club. I threw my hair into a ponytail and figured I'd do something to it when I got there.

"Hurry up secret! We still gotta go drop my baby off at Shanell's." Prii yelled rushing me.

"I'm coming!" I yelled back.

I finished freshening up and rushed out to the car. I instantly had a funny feeling about something, but I couldn't quite figure out what it was. I start to wonder if I was forgetting something, but it seemed as if I had everything I needed. I guess I was just trippin'.

"You alright?" Prii asked. I guess she could tell that something was bothering me.

"Yeah, I'm good. Lets go." I replied.

We got to Shanell's house and the bitch had the audacity to not be home. I was mad as hell. We were already on the verge of running late and now this shit.

"Where the hell she at?" Prii snapped. "She not even answering the phone."

"Imma call her from my phone." I said, knowing that Shanell was probably not answering for her on purpose. I picked up my cell and dialed the number.

"Hello?" She answered.

Before I could even say anything, Prii had snatched the phone out of my hand.

"Bitch where you at?" she said. "I'm sitting in front of yo crib."

"Girl, I'm at my nigga crib." Shanell said.

"Yo nigga crib?" Prii asked. "Did you forget that you was supposed to be watching my son tonight?"

Shanell got quiet.

"Hello….?" Prii shouted into the phone.

"Damn Prii. I completely forgot. I'm sorry girl." Shanell finally said.

Prii just sat there for a minute. I was about ready to snatch the phone out of her hand and let Shanell have it, but I decided that Prii had to learn one way or another. Shanell was always dogging Prii around, but Prii continued to fuck with her.

"So , now what am I supposed to do Nell?" Prii asked.

"Girl, you know if I could, I would be there in a heartbeat, but I'm all the way out in Blaine." Shanell replied.

That was all I needed to hear. I had heard enough of her bullshit. I reached over, snatched the phone and hung up. I guess Prii was at a loss for words as we sat there in silence in front of Shanell's crib for about ten seconds.

"Now what?" she asked, shaking her head.

"I'm suggesting we call Lando and tell him that Priice is coming in to work with us once again." I said, knowing that she hated the thought of that.

She turned to look back at Na'Priice, who had somehow fallen asleep in the mist of everything.

"Man, I hate bringing my baby down to that ratchet ass club." she said. "He don't need to be around all of that."

"I know Prii, but what other choice do we have?" I replied. "We gotta get a move on it."

She started the engine and pulled off. She knew she ain't have no choice but to bring him with. I did feel bad about the whole situation. Her having to bring her son to the strip club where she worked was embarrassing, but stripping wasn't the only job out there. It was just an easier job. Prii was smart, sexy, and very talented. She had what it took to be out here doing something way better then this shit. Hell, so did I, but I was fine with what I was doing. I didn't have any kids to worry about.

We pulled up to the club, and I had already called Lando to let him know what was up. He sounded cool on the phone, but knowing him, his attitude all depended on how his nights were going. Hopefully, it was going good because Nyprii hated for him to be mad at her. We walked in side by side as she held Na'Priice in her arms. Lando approached us with a smile on his face as if everything was still cool.

"Ladies..." He said, greeting us.

"Man Lando, I'm so sorry. This wont..." Nyprii started as Lando cut her off.

"Shhh... Don't even sweat it." He said. "Just give me lil man so I can go lay him down."

Prii was stuck as Lando grabbed Na'Priice from her arms. She couldn't believe how cool he was being. He snapped on her before about this same shit, but for some reason he was being real nice tonight. As he turned to walk away, we both just kind of stared.

"Girl, pinch me. I think I'm dreaming." Prii said.

I turned and I pinched the hell out of her.

"OUCH!" She whined.

"Well, you told me to pinch you." I replied, as we both laughed and walked into the strip room.

When we got in, I instantly got a weird vibe from Peanut and Tiffany. They were acting all weird and secretive like they knew something that Prii and I didn't. I started to let it bother me, but I brushed it off and sat down at my mirror.

"What you two over there whispering about?" Prii asked. "Is there a problem?"

They just laughed.

"Trust me, the problem is definitely not with you Prii." Peanut said, looking over at me.

"Oh, it must be with me then, right?" I asked, chuckling.

"You said it, not me." Peanut replied, smirking.

"And what is that supposed to mean?" Prii snapped.

Peanut just snickered and looked over at Tiffany.

"You'll hear about it sooner or later." Tiffany said, smiling and turning back around to her mirror.

"Whatever. I'm not worried bout none of you bitches." I replied, turning to my own mirror.

As I was fixing my hair, I overheard one of them whisper something about snitching. I had no idea as to what the hell they were talking about. I didn't really get the whole scoop, but I was for certain that they couldn't have still been talking about me. Secret McKay Adams ain't have a ounce of snitch in her. And even if I did, what the hell could I have possibly snitched about? Them hoes were always starting up some mess.

I finished getting dressed and went out to the dance floor. I still had that crazy gut feeling from earlier and I couldn't shake it. It was really starting to annoy me. I noticed myself starting to take it out on my customers, so I went over to the bar and took a few shots of patron. It was definitely what I needed. I quickly got in my zone and got back to work. The rest of the night I was good. That gut feeling was gone and I had forgotten all about the bullshit that Peanut was talking about. I was shaking my ass, making money, and not giving a damn who was hating on me.

When it was time to leave, I was exhausted. I couldn't wait to get home, take a shower, and jump in my bed. As we were leaving, Lando came walking down the stairs with Na'Priice walking next to him.

"Hey tete!" Priice shouted, waving at me.

"Hey boo boo." I replied.

"Look mommy." he said, holding up the sucker that Lando had given him.

"Oh lord." Nyprii responded, looking up at Lando. "You done messed up the churches money."

"What? That's my lil dude right there." Lando replied. "We was chillin' all night."

"Well, when yo lil dude get to bouncing off my walls, be expecting me to drop him off so yall can finish chillin' tonight." She replied, sarcastically.

We all started laughing.

"Naw, but thanks again Lando for letting me slide with this shit for another time." Prii said. "My babysitter be trippin.'"

"Don't even worry about it. You good." Lando said. "Yall make it home safely."

"Goodnight Lanno." Priice said, leaving the D out of Lando's name.

"Goodnight shorty." Lando replied.

We pulled up to my apartment and I was so ready to just get inside. I was too tired. I said my goodbyes, got out the car, and walked up to my door. I was shivering from the cold and it was taking me forever to find my damn keys. I was still drunk so when I finally found them, it took me a minute to realize that my door was slightly cracked open. "What the hell?" I thought, as I slowly opened up the door. I reached into my purse and grabbed my mace, praying that there wasn't anybody inside. I crept in quietly, trying not to make any noise. It was pitch black and I couldn't see shit. As soon as I turned the corner to my room, BAM! It was over. Somebody had hit me in the head with something that I'm pretty sure was a bat. When I hit the floor, they continued to punch, kick, and stomp on me. I could feel the blood leaking from my head and I was for sure that I was about to die. The person kicked me in my head one last time and ran out of my apartment without making a sound. I could barely move as I tried my hardest to reach for my purse and dial Prii's number.

10

A few days later, I woke up in the hospital. At first, I didn't know where the hell I was, or why I was even there. I was bandaged up from damn near head to toe. I started to sit up, but got a sharp pain in my side. That's when I remembered what had happened to me. I began to panic. Out of anger I began to scream. My head was already throbbing and I had just made it worse. The nurse, Prii, and another nurse had came rushing into the room. Prii rushed over and held me.

"I'm so happy your awake." She said, as I cried hysterically. She began to cry to. "Its okay baby."

At first, the nurses just stood there. I believe they were trying to give Prii a minute to calm me down. I couldn't understand why some shit like that had happened to me. I was a good person. I had a great heart. Why the hell was I laid up in the hospital beat the fuck up?

"Prii...!" I cried, screaming. "Why me?!"

"I don't know baby." she replied, crying and rocking me. "I just don't know."

"How are you feeling Ms. Adams?" One of the nurses asked. "I mean, how's your pain?"

I didn't answer her. I couldn't answer her. I knew she meant physically, but emotionally I just wanted to die. There wasn't any way of describing how bad I was hurting.

"Ms. Adams, we're going to give you a few sedatives." The other nurse replied.

I really could care less what they were about to do.

"Sii, do you know who did this shit to you?" Prii asked.

I didn't answer her either. I didn't want to talk. I just wanted to finish crying my eye's out. Whoever had done it, they should have killed me. Who could be so heartless? As the nurses injected the drugs into my arm, I laid there lifelessly.

"This is all my fault." Prii cried, as she stood up off the bed. "I should have stayed and made sure you got in safely."

As tears continued to run down my face, I found myself drifting off to sleep. I could feel the drugs beginning to kick in fast. After a few moments, I was out for the count.

When I awoke again, there were two policemen standing at the head of my hospital bed with Nyprii, asking her questions. As I came to, I watched as Prii just stood there and shook her head, not being able to answer the questions. She didn't even know shit to even try to attempt to answer. The only thing she knew was around what time it had happened because she had dropped me off.

"Oh, she's awake." Said one of the policemen, noticing that I was just laying there listening.

"Secret, they wanna talk to you to see if you remember anything." Prii informed me. "Do you feel up to it right now?"

I shrugged my shoulders and rolled my eyes. Not at her, but just because.

"I guess." I replied.

"Ms. Adams, I'm Officer Cleon and this is my partner, Officer Smith." The policeman said, walking over to my side. "We just want to ask you a few questions."

I shook my head okay.

"Now, do you have any idea who could have done this to you? Do you know of anybody that has an issue with you?" he asked.

I took a minute to think, but nobody came to mind.

"No, I don't." I replied.

"Okay." he said, as Officer Smith began to write in his little notepad. "Is there anything you can remember about the night you were attacked?"

I swallowed hard and tried not to cry as I began to speak.

"Well, I remember my door being cracked when I got home." I said, taking a deep breath. "I remember it being dark and quiet. I guess I figured if anybody had broken in, they had to be gone by now."

The two policemen just shook there heads as the three of them continued to listen to me.

"Although, I figured that they were gone, I immediately pulled my mace out." I said. "I remember walking to my room and as soon as I turned the corner, I got attacked."

"Why didn't you call 911 before you walked in?" he asked.

"I didn't think about it." I replied. "I was drunk and I just wanted to get in and go to sleep."

"Do you know if it was a man or woman that attacked you?" Officer Cleon asked. "I know you said that it was dark, but did they happen to say anything to you that you can remember?"

I shook my head no. "I really don't remember anything after that. I think I passed out."

Officer Smith continued to write in the notepad.

"I don't even know how I got here." I said.

"Secret you called me and I couldn't make out what you were saying, so I rushed back and found you laying there in a pool of blood." Prii said, jumping in the conversation. "I thought you were dead."

She wiped her tears as she sat down in her chair and didn't say anything else.

"Ms. Adams, thank you for your help. We're going to try our best to catch the monster that did this to you." Officer Cleon said.

"Yeah, we don't need those kind of people out on the streets." Officer Smith added. "If you remember anything else, I don't care how unimportant you might think it is, just give us a call."

"Thanks." I replied, as they handed me both of their cards and walked out of the room.

"Secret, I am so sorry." Prii said, apologizing again after they walked out. "I feel like shit."

"Its not your fault." I replied, not wanting her to feel at fault. "You could have easily been laying next to me on a hospital bed, had you'd stayed."

Knock knock knock...

Prii got up to go see who was at the door.

"How she doing?" I heard a mans voice say.

"Not too good." Prii replied.

As he walked in, I could have almost lost it. What the hell was Stephan doing here? Who was he to see me like this? Who was he to even care? I was pissed. A complete stranger was what he was.

"What is he doing here?" I snapped.

"Secret, Stephan been coming to check on you since you've been in a coma." Nyprii replied.

"For what?" I asked. "I don't know this nigga. He needs to leave!"

"Secret, I ain't even mean to come up here and upset or disrespect you. I was just concerned. That's all." Stephan said.

I was furious! For all I knew, he could have been the one to do this shit to me. Stephan handed Prii the bouquet of flowers that he'd brought with him and stepped back out of the room.

"Secret, I know your mad, but you taking it out on the wrong person." Nyprii said. "You see all of this shit? He got you all this shit."

She was referring to all of the balloons and flowers that were everywhere. I didn't care though. I wasn't trusting it. I didn't know him. How coincident was it that we had had our first phone conversation just hours before I had gotten attacked? I had even told this man that I was on my way to work. He knew I wasn't going to be home that night. There wasn't really any motive, but whose to say that he wasn't just crazy and done it for no reason? I just didn't want to have anything to do with his ass at this point.

"I don't care about this shit." I replied. "Do you see my face Prii? Somebody did this shit to me and I don't know who the hell it was. Until I find out who did this shit, I don't have time to be playing get to know each other with nobody."

Prii rolled her eyes. "He cares about you."

"That nigga don't even know me Prii." I replied, irritated. She acted like she ain't hear shit I just said.

"I still think you should give him a chance. He's been here comforting me this whole time." she said.

I looked at her as if she was crazy.

"Well, you know what Prii, you can go fuck him then if he's that important to you." I snapped. "Matter of fact, you can leave. I shouldn't have to explain shit to you."

I knew she couldn't believe the words that were coming out of my mouth, but I didn't care. She wasn't the one laying down in a hospital bed with fractured ribs, a busted head, and a bandaged up body. I was. She couldn't even dare imagine how the hell I was feeling. I was mad, my feelings were hurt, and I wasn't about to filter my mouth for nobody. She looked at me as if she wanted to throw that bouquet of flowers at me. Instead, she sat them down and walked out of the room. As she was walking out, a nurse was walking in.

"Hey, how ya feeling?" she asked.

"Exactly how I look." I replied.

"I understand." she said. "Are you ready for some more meds?"

I shook my head yes, as the pain in my ribs throbbed.

"Okay." she said as she injected me with more morphine.

"I also have to redo your bandages." she said. "This should only take up a few moments of your time."

I thought about how bad my ribbed felt and dreaded the thought of her touching me.

"Is there anyway you can wait til the medicine kicks in and I fall asleep?" I asked, hoping she wouldn't shoot me down.

"Sure thing." she said, smiling. "Ill be back to check on you in a little while. By the next time you wake up, you should have new bandages."

A few seconds after she walked out of the room, Prii came back in. She had tears in her eyes.

"I'm sorry Sii." she said. "You're right. I was in the wrong for bringing him up here to see you like this."

She walked over and stood next to me. "You forgive me?" She asked.

"You get on my nerves." I replied, smirked. "I guess."

She climbed up in the bed next to me. She didn't say anything else and neither did I. She just held my hand as I let the morphine take over. If I'm not mistaken, I believe she fell asleep too.

11

About 4 weeks later, I was back home and back on my feet. Well, not exactly all the way back on my feet, but I was moving around a little bit. I was too fucked up to go back to work, and Lando told me that he didn't think it would be a good idea to come back anyways. I know he was just looking out for my best interest, but I had bills and shit. I planned on coming back as soon as I was healed. As of right now, him and Prii was holding me down. That was cool and all, but I didn't want to get back used to people taking care of me.

Through my healing process, Prii had been taking me to this gym workout place. There was this therapy class there that she had me attending to get back right. I hadn't even heard about it before and had no idea as to how she even knew about the place. But let her tell it, she was miss know it all. She knew every damn thing. I had been going there for about a 2 weeks trying to get my shit back together. So far, I hadn't seen or ran into anybody that I knew there. Then, one day she just so happened to drop me off. Usually, she stayed until I was finished, but this particular day she all of a sudden had some "business" to go handle. At first, I didn't think nothing of it. It seemed normal. So I went in, got stretched and hopped on the treadmill. With my headphones in, I started of walking into a slow jog. As I let the music in my ears take me away, I held on the handles and closed my eyes. Minutes later as I was humming the words to Monica's "So Gone," and felt the treadmill began to slow down. What the hell? I thought, opening my eyes.

"Hey beautiful." Stephan said. "I didn't know you came here."

I couldn't do nothing but shake my head and chuckle. That sneaky little bitch Prii had set me up. Handle some damn business my ass. Prii knew exactly what she was doing. I decided to play it off and act as if I didn't know shit. Apparently, the both of them must have thought that I was boo boo the fool or something.

"Yeah, I've been coming a couple weeks." I replied, trying to keep it short.

I didn't even understand why he was even talking to me, being that the last time I seen him it wasn't too good.

"That's pretty cool." He said. "I usually come here, but I haven't been in a while cause of my job and shit."

"Yeah, I was just finna say I haven't seen you here before." I replied.

I guess he really expected me to believe that shit.

"So, how have you been holding up?" he asked.

"I've been doing pretty good." I replied.

I still wasn't too sure about his ass. Although, in my heart I knew he probably really isn't have shit to do with it, I still didn't want to trust him.

"Yeah, you lookin' good too." he said, smiling. He was so damn sexy and his bare chest wasn't making it no better.

"Is that game you spittin'?" I asked, thinking that that line was so cliché.

"Is it wack?" he asked, sarcastically.

"Just a little bit." I replied, laughing. "But thanks for the compliment though."

Somehow in the middle of our conversation, he managed to hop on the treadmill next to mines. For the next hour, we talked and joked and worked out together. We never brought up the whole hospital situation, in which I was kind of happy about because I was enjoying myself.

"So what time you leaving?" he asked, as we came to the end of our workout.

"I don't know." I said. "I guess until Prii brings her ass to pick me up."

I looked down at my phone and seen how much time had past. I was so busy laughing and joking with Stephan, that I hadn't even noticed the time. I dialed her number and waited for her to pick up.

"Hello?" she answered.

"Hey what's up?" I said, playing it cool so she wouldn't know that her little plan had worked. "I'm ready when you are."

"Okay, give me thirty minutes." she said.

"Thirty minutes Prii? Really?" I said, not wanting to wait that long.

"Yeah, I'm still handling some business. Ill be there as soon as I can." she replied.

I just rolled my eyes. "Well just hurry up!" I shouted.

"Damn bitch okay." Prii said, as we hung up.

"That didn't sound too good." Stephan joked, walking up behind me.

"So I see your nosy to." I replied.

"I'm not nosy. I just got good hearing." he said.

"Whatever." I laughed.

"But if I'm not mistaken, I think I overheard that you weren't getting picked up for quite a while now, right?" he asked, as I shook my head yeah. "Well, I have two suggestions for you."

"What?" I asked.

"One, I can stay here with you until your ride comes. Or two, I can give you a lift to wherever you need to go. Whichever you're more comfortable with. Its up to you." he said.

"Or three... neither." I replied. "I'm a big girl. I can wait here by myself."

He just chuckled. I knew he thought I was crazy or something. It was hard for me not to be so stubborn. I guess I wasn't ready to be too comfortable with him. Although, I did enjoy myself for this little time that we were together. It was fun while it lasted.

"You sure?" he asked. "Its really not a problem."

I shook my head. "No, its okay. I don't need your help. I'm fine."

"Woman!" he snapped. I guess I struck a nerve. "I know you don't NEED my help, and I'm pretty sure everybody in here with good eyesight can see that you're fine. I just wanna help you out."

I smiled thinking that he was so cute. "Well, I'm sorry, but I don't want your help Stephan. Ill be okay. Don't take it personal."

He threw his hands up and walked back to the men's locker room. I knew by now that he had to be fed up with me. It kind of sucked that such a good time ended on a bad note, but oh well. I had to do what I had to do. I couldn't let my guard down for this stranger. Especially right now. I was skeptical about everything and everybody. After he showered and got dressed, he came back over to me. I tensed up a little bit. I figured he was coming back over to snap on me again. He wasn't. He just held his arms out.

"What?" I asked, confused.

"Can I at least leave with a hug or something?" he asked, smiling.

I didn't get this nigga. He was too nice. If I was a guy and a girl treated me the same way that I treated him, I would have been done with her ass. There were plenty more fish in the sea. He just wasn't letting up.

After I hugged him, I guess he felt satisfied enough to leave. I sat there waiting for Prii to come and get me. When she pulled up, I couldn't wait to get in the car. I had some words for her ass.

"Damn, yo weave sweated all the way out." Prii laughed. My hair was so long she always joked about it being weave.

"Bitch shut up." I replied, laughing. "I see you just got jokes out the ass today huh?"

94

She made a guilty face.

"What you mean?" she asked, laughing.

"Don't play stupid. You know that little stunt you pulled today." I replied.

She continued to laugh as I looked at her sideways. I wanted to punch her.

"I don't have a clue as to what you're talking about." she said, trying not to look at me.

"Prii, why you tell Stephan to come to he gym today?" I asked, letting her know exactly what I was talking about since she wanted to play dumb.

For a second she didn't say anything. She just sat there with a smile on her face as I stared at her.

"Okay okay okay..." she said. "I wanted to surprise you."

"Surprise me?" I shouted. "Prii, I cant stand yo ass."

She laughed. "Well, did you have good time?"

"What you think?" I asked.

"No?" she asked.

"Yeah, Prii. It was cool." I replied, smiling.

"Awwww, I'm so happy!" she shouted, reaching over to try and hug me.

"Whatever." I said, pushing her away. "I still cant stand yo ass."

"He better had showed you a good time or I would have broke his neck." she laughed.

"Whatever. You still isn't have to have me waiting on yo ass all day." I said. "I'm starving!"

"Damn, I said I was sorry bitch. What else you want me to say?" she shouted.

"You isn't gotta say shit. Just pull up into this Mc Donald's so I can eat."

We went through the drive-thru and ordered a bunch of shit off the dollar menu. She said we were on our way to pick up Priice, so we ended up ordering him a kids meal. I was pretty sure Shanell isn't feed him. He always came home complaining about how hungry he was.

"Call Shanell and tell her we on our way." Prii said.

I picked up my cell, dialed the number, and some little kid answered.

"Hello?" he said.

"Hey, is Shanell around?" I asked.

"She isn't here right now. He replied.

"Where she at?"

"I don't know."

"Did she take Na'Priice with her?" I asked.

"Who is that?" He said.

"The little boy that she was watching." I said, getting frustrated.

"Oh him?" he said. "No. He right here."

"Okay, let me talk to a grown up." I said. "Who's watching yall?"

"Nobody." he replied. "Its just us."

"Alright." I said, hanging up. "Girl did you know some little boy is watching your son?"

"Oh, that was probably Don-Don." Prii said.

"Who is Don-Don?" I asked.

"Her fifteen year old nephew." she said.

"Fifteen?" I snapped. "Hell naw. This little boy isn't sound like he was no fifteen. More like nine or ten."

"Girl please. Shanell crazy but she isn't that crazy." Prii said, sounding so sure.

"Yeah whatever." I replied, rolling my eyes. "I wouldn't put it past her."

We got to Shanell's and the front door was wide open. There was really no need for me to go in, but I did anyway. I guess I wanted to look around and be nosy because I had never been inside her crib before. We walked in and just as I suspected, it was a little ass boy sitting in front of the TV on the floor.

"Is that your Don-Don?" I asked Prii sarcastically.

Nyprii cut her eyes at me and then back at the little boy.

"Excuse me little boy." she said, trying to get his attention away from the cartoons.

He was so stuck, he didn't even bother to acknowledge the fact that we had walked in. "What's your name?"

"CJ." he replied.

"CJ honey, why are yall here by yourselves?" Prii asked.

I looked over at Na'Priice, who was fast asleep on the couch with his thumb in his mouth.

"Nobody. Nell told me to watch him over there." he said, pointing to Priice.

"But how old are you sweetie?" Prii asked.

I could tell she was trying to keep her cool.

"Seven." he replied, innocently.

Prii and I just looked at each other.

"See, I told you that hoe couldn't be trusted." I whispered.

"I cant believe this." Prii said, walking over to the couch. "The bitch left my baby in the house with another baby."

CJ just sat there looking like he didn't have any idea as to what was going on. He turned his attention back to the cartoons.

"Priicy baby, wake up." Prii said, shaking him a little. "Put your jacket on. We finna go bye bye."

She quickly put his stuff on and picked him up. He was still half sleep as he rested his head on her shoulder. He actually looked a little sick, but I guess Prii was too mad to notice.

"CJ baby, how long have they been gone?" Prii asked.

He shrugged his shoulders. "I don't know."

"A long time?" She asked.

He just shook his head yeah.

"Did she at least feed yall?" I asked.

He shook his head no.

I looked at Prii like this shit was crazy. I didn't even want to ask the boy anything else. I was getting pissed by the second.

"So is Shanell your aunty or something?" Prii asked.

"No. That's my daddy girlfriend." He said.

That was it. I had heard enough. I went back out to get in the car. I couldn't believe she left Na'Priice up in the crib with some little ass kid who needed to be watched his damn self.

I honked the horn to let Prii know that I was ready to move around. About five minutes later, she came out the house with both kids.

"Where you finna take him?" I asked, as she was putting them in the car.

"He going with us." she said, strapping them in their seatbelts.

I looked back at CJ and then back at Prii.

"Don't you think they gone be a little worried when they get back and he isn't here?"

"They cant be more worried than I was when I walked in and seen two little ass kids watching themselves." she replied. "If she's smart enough to check her messages, she'll know where he is. I'm not leaving this baby here by his self."

We went and grabbed CJ something to eat and headed back to Prii's crib. Na'Priice didn't eat his nuggets and was acting really weird. He didn't want to eat, play, or talk to anybody. He just kind of laid around and whined.

It was going on midnight and Shanell still hadn't called or answered her phone. For a second, I stopped to think that maybe something could have happened to her, but I just knew that wasn't the case. Prii and Na'Priice were in the room sleeping, while CJ was wide awake, laying down watching cartoons on a pallet. I was on the couch trying to fall asleep, but couldn't because I had to pee really bad. I had been holding it for the longest because I didn't feel like getting up. After a while I just got up and went because I knew that that was the only way that I was going to be able to sleep. As I was sitting on the toilet, Prii came screaming and banging on the door.

"What's going on?" I asked, cracking the door.

She was talking so fast that I could barely make out what she was saying. Out of all of her rambling, all I heard was Na'Priice and hospital. I quickly wiped, washed my hands and went into the bedroom where Na'Priice was gagging and throwing up blood.

"Oh my god!" I shouted. "What happened?"

"I don't know." Prii said, on the verge of tears. "He just woke up out of his sleep like this."

Na'Priice was crying and kept complaining that his stomach was hurting. I knew that something was wrong with him. He wasn't being himself at all.

"Can you come hold this on his head while I get dressed so we can go to the hospital?" Prii asked, handing me a cold towel.

As I watched her nervously scurry around to put on some clothes, I couldn't help but to think that this shit had Shanell's name written all over it.

"Come on. We gotta go." Prii said, as she put her shoes on.

My heart was beating as he sat on Prii's lap in the passenger seat screaming, crying, and throwing up into a plastic bag. I had never seen him like that before. We rushed into the emergency room and Prii wasn't cutting them no slack. She was on it.

"Excuse me! We need help. My son is throwing up blood." She said to the people at the front desk.

They must have known that she wasn't about to play no games with them.

"Okay, Ms. We're going to try and get you seen as soon as possible." One of the ladies said. "We just need you to fill out these forms."

Nyprii knocked the papers out of her hand. "I didn't ask for these damn forms. My son is sick. I asked for help. Somebody needs to find me a damn doctor right now!"

I picked up the forms and filled them out as fast as I could to the best of my ability. I knew we wasn't gone get nowhere by her yelling so I went ahead and handled that. She was so busy fussing that she didn't even notice that I had filled them out until I handed them back to the lady. She told us to take a seat and that somebody would be with us shortly.

I watched as CJ just stared and looked around at all the different sick people. He really had his eye on a man with a missing leg. Na'Priice had finally stopped gagging and just laid on Prii's chest as we waited for the doctor. About ten minutes later, the doctor came out.

"Na'Priice Williams!" He yelled.

Prii got up and launched to the door with Na'Priice in her arms. I grabbed CJ's hand and we quickly followed behind them to the room.

"So what seems to be the problem?" The doctor asked.

"I don't know." Prii said. "He woke up out of his sleep throwing up blood. It scared the hell out of me."

"Oh, that cant be good." he said, taking out his stethoscope and placing it up against Na'Priice's chest. "Can you take a deep breath for me?"

Na'Priice was doing really good. He cooperated with the doctor like he was supposed to.

"His breathing seems to be fine." The doctor said. "Can you tell me what he ate?"

Na'Priice didn't respond. He just stared at the man.

"CJ you sure yall didn't eat nothing at Shanell's house?" Prii asked. "Breakfast, a snack, anything?"

"No. we didn't eat nothing all day until you came." He said, as I caught the doctor kind of frown up at his response.

"Hmm…" the doctor said. "Do you think you can get him to urinate into a cup so that we can run some test?"

Prii shook her head yeah. "Yes, I can do that."

The doctor went into the drawer, and handed Prii a container and a little gown.

"Ill be back shortly." he said.

As the doctor left out the room, she changed Na'Priice into his gown. He began whining again, sounding so miserable.

"Mommy my tummy hurts." He cried.

"I know baby. I know." Prii said. "The doctors gone make it all better kay."

"Okay." he replied.

She got his gown on and went into the bathroom so that she could get him to pee in the container. Soon as he finished, the doctor came knocking on the door.

"Need a few more minutes?" He asked.

"Naw, we ready." Prii replied.

"Well, that was fast." He said.

"Yeah, he's a big boy." Prii said, handing him the container.

"I see. How old is he again?" he asked.

"He just turned five." Prii responded.

He wrote something down on the little clipboard that he was carrying.

"Alright, you all can come with me." He said.

"You're moving us?" Prii asked.

"Yup, to a different room." he said.

I didn't understand. We got into the new room and it was no different from the other one.

"Okay, sit him up on the table for me." The doctor said.

Prii did as she was told and Na'Priice had stopped whining. He just sat up on the table with his thumb in his mouth. He behaved like a big boy as the doctor checked his vitals. When he finished, he did a rectal temperature check and informed us that Na'Priice had had a high temperature of 103. We had already known that he had a fever. We just didn't know it was that high.

"Well, I'm going to drop this urine and another doctor will be right with you." he said, walking out.

"Its gone take forever for them to come tell us what's wrong." Prii said.

As we sat and waited, and sat and waited, there was still no doctor. "Right with you my ass." I thought aloud to myself. CJ had fallen asleep and Shanell still hadn't called for this boy. Prii had climbed up on the table next to Priice and was on her way to sleep too. About a half an hour had past and I had gotten bored. I couldn't get comfortable and fall asleep, so I decided to get up and go find the vending machine. As I walked out and turned the corner, there were two doctors, a policeman, and a heavyset lady in a blue dress all standing in a circle having a conversation.

"Excuse me." I said interrupting them. "Does anyone know where I can find a vending machine?"

One of the doctors instructed me out past the two doors to the left. When I found it, there were two snack machines and a soda machine. I felt as if I had hit the jackpot. I grabbed a few snacks and a juice. As I was walking back, I overheard the doctor who had instructed me to the vending machine, say Na'Priice's name. What about Na'Priice? I thought. Why would he be talking to the cops about Na'Priice? I walked back past them as if I didn't know anything. When I hit the corner to where they could no longer see me, I stopped and listened in on their conversation.

"Well, we still have to go in and talk to the mother. From what I heard about her when she first came in, its probably not going to go so well." the other doctor said. "Either way, he's not leaving with her tonight. We have to be prepared for her to blow up."

The policeman said that he was going to be right outside the door just in case things got crazy.

"Does everybody know the procedure?" the doctor asked.

I didn't understand what was going on, but I knew that we had to get the hell up out that hospital. I hurriedly made it back to the room and shut the door.

"Girl get up!" I yelled pulling on Prii's arm. "Bitch we gotta get outta here."

Nyprii jumped up, in a panic. "What? What's going on?" she asked, looking around.

"I don't know, but I think they tryna take Priice from you." I said. By the look on her face, I could tell that she was confused. I didn't have time to explain though.

"Ill tell you everything in the car, but bitch right now we need to hurry up."

As I picked up CJ who was still sleeping, I peeked out the door to see if the coast was clear.

"Come on, lets go." I whispered to Prii.

We left out the door looking for the nearest exit. When we finally seen one, we darted for the door. It was way across the room, so we had to make a run for it.

"There they are!" we heard the policeman yell. "STOP!"

Prii and I both came to a halt. I was so mad because the exit was so close. Its funny how we almost made it.

12

"This some bullshit."

I thought aloud as the policeman instructed me to wait in the waiting area. I sat there shaking my head as they hauled Nyprii and Caprice off to the back. What could have been going on? What could have happened just that fast? I wondered if it was something that they found in Na'Priice's pee. Why was it taking so long for me to find out anything? My thoughts were on a hundred as I impatiently waited.

I told CJ, who was now wide awake, to go play over at the little toy table. I glanced around the room and noticed that the man with one leg was still waiting. He had fallen asleep and I wondered if he hadn't heard his name get called or something. I thought about waking him up, but I quickly decided against it. A vision of me tapping him and him rolling over dead popped into my head. It freaked me out a little bit as I shook the image out of my mind.

Time was going by so slow. I got up and went to the receptionist. She was on the phone, but I didn't care. I interrupted her anyway.

"Excuse me." I said, tapping down on the counter.

She turned and signaled for me to hold on, then turned back around in her chair.

"Yeah girl," she said, continuing her unimportant conversation. "So like I was saying, how did Raiyjah catch Diamond messing around with Chris?"

I stood there in disbelief as I listened to the unprofessional ass receptionist have a conversation about some bullshit ass drama over the phone.

"Hell yeah!" she continued. "And I seen that hoe Diamond up in Juicy's last Saturday with Tanisha's man... mmmhmm. She was getting it in too. Puttin' in extra work if you know what I mean."

Her friend was just as ignorant as she was. I could hear her laughing just as loud as this ghetto ass receptionist was. I couldn't help but to wonder how this lady even ended up with a job here. It was just like two hoodrats to be gossiping.

"Excuse me." I said again, tapping a little louder this time. I was beginning to get annoyed.

She stopped in mid-laugh. "Look, I said ill be with you in a minute."

"Well, can you tell me how long that's gonna be?" I asked.

She rolled her eyes and shook her head like she was fed up.

"Girl, let me call you back before I have to hurt somebody up in here." she mumbled into the phone.

"Bitch please." I thought as I smirked at her. I started to go off but I just laughed it off. It wasn't the time or place for all that.

"Now, how can I help you?" she asked.

"I was wondering if you could let me know what's going on with my nephew Na'Priice Williams?" I said.

She looked me up and down as if I belittled her or something.

"Let me see what I can do." She said. "How you spell it?"

"N A P R I I C E." I replied. "Williams. Do you need me to spell that out too?"

She looked at me and smiled fakely, turning back to the computer. Just as she was about to fix her lips to tell me some bullshit, the emergency doors to the back opened up for a nurse to walk through. I heard Nyprii crying and screaming like somebody had died or something. Before I knew it, my feet transported me back there with no hesitation. Two policemen had her down on the ground in handcuffs, while another stood by. Prii was cursing and letting the whole world hear her call them every name in the book. Pigs, crackers, slobs, white trash, honkies, and hill billies. She was on a rampage.

"What's going on?" I asked, damn near shouting my damn self.

"Excuse me Miss, but you cant be back here." A doctor said, trying to grab my arm and lead me back towards the waiting area.

I snatched away from him. "Get off of me. This is my sister. What the hell is going on back here?"

I looked up and saw the heavyset white lady that was wearing the blue suit, struggling to hold Na'Priice in her arms as he tried to get away from her. To my beliefs, she was social services or something. I headed for the lady, but the cop standing next to her pulled his mace out and told me to step back.

"Is this your family?" The doctor asked.

"I just told you that she's my sister." I snapped. "Somebody better tell me something before I tear this damn hospital up."

He pulled me to the side. "There is an investigation going on that has to do with your sister and your nephew." he said.

"Investigation?" I shouted. "What are you talking about?"

"We found alcohol in your nephew's system." he said.

"Alcohol?" I said. "As in liquor?"

"Yes." he said. "Either you nephew is an alcoholic, or somebody has been giving him excessive amounts of alcohol to drink."

A alcoholic? I thought. Was he trying to make a joke as if this was something to play about?

"Are you trying to be funny?" I asked.

"No ma'am." he said. "This is more serious than you know."

I turned to look at Prii, who they had now let up off the floor. Her lip was busted and her clothes were all stretched out and hanging off of her. She looked a hot ass mess. She was finally calm, but Na'Priice was still yelling and screaming. I wasn't understanding why they still had him even around her in the facility. They could have at least took him somewhere. He didn't need to see his mom like that.

"Please don't take my baby from me." she cried. "I would never give him alcohol. Ever!"

Patients were all out of their rooms being nosy, trying to figure what all the commotion was about.

"Everybody needs to go back into their rooms! There's nothing to see here!" One of the policemen shouted, as they all scattered.

"Excuse me, but why is she handcuffed? She didn't give him any alcohol." I said.

"Well," the fat cop said with a smirk on his face. "Seems like your sister thought it was okay to assault an officer."

"Fuck you!" Prii spat. "I never touched you."

"Prii just be quiet." I said, not wanting her to get into any more trouble.

I watched as they hauled her out of the hospital, and into the back of the police car. The doctor who had been explaining everything to me was still standing there.

"So, what about my nephew?" I asked. "What's going to happen to him?"

He informed me that Na'Priice was going to have to stay overnight so that they could run some more test and give him what he needs. They had to make sure that there was no internal bleeding caused by the alcohol. I shook my head and sighed because it was just all too much for me. This shit had Shanell's name written all over it. Either he drank it on his own at her house, or she gave it to him at her house. Whichever it was, it had to have happened at her house.

"So, lets say he drank it on his own. Does that change things?" I asked.

"Maybe, but in most cases no because its still neglect." he said.

As those words came out of his mouth, I suddenly remembered that I had left CJ alone in the hospital lobby alone.

I ran back out there and to my surprise, he was sitting down in the chair waiting patiently. When he saw me, he ran up to me.

"Hey!" he said hugging me.

I smiled and hugged him back. He was so sweet.

"Ready to go?" I asked.

He shook his head yeah.

We got in the car and drove to my house. It was going on 3:15 am and I was exhausted. By the time we pulled up in the driveway, CJ had fallen back to sleep. I didn't want to wake him up so I carried him in the house. He was under weight and quite small for his age, so it wasn't a hassle to carry him in. As I laid him down on the couch, I felt a warm wetness on my side. "I know this boy isn't pee on me." I thought, as I looked down and smelled my shirt.

"Yuck!" I said. No doubt it was pee.

I quickly made him a pallet to lay on because I isn't want him pissing on my pillows. He could pee on the covers because those could easily be washed. After I laid him down, I pulled his wet pants and boxers off. Spiderman was pissy as hell. I threw them in the washer for a quick run and tossed them in the dryer. I laid some plastic bags underneath his butt like my second foster mom used to do to Michael.

After I got him situated, I went in my room to call Shanell again. I wasn't understanding why she hadn't called for her mans son. And plus, I knew she was the reason behind this alcohol shit. To my surprise, she answered.

"Hello?" she said, in a sleepily manner.

"Shanell?" I said, shocked that she answered. "Is that you?"

"Yeah, this me." She said, clearing her throat. "Who is this?"

"I'm going to need for you to get up." I said.

"Man, do you know what time it is?" she said. "Call me in the morning."

She hung up right in my face. Not even caring to ask about her boyfriends son. What the hell kind of shit was that? They both were some deadbeats. Its clear that he obviously didn't give a shit about him being gone either. I felt so bad for CJ. I wondered where his mother was. I wanted to call her back so bad, but I knew it wasn't going to get anywhere. I just told myself to wait until tomorrow. I put on some pj's, went to go check on CJ one more time, then climbed up in my bed. It took a while for me to finally fall asleep because I had about a million thoughts running through my head. I finally was able to relax my thoughts and close my eyes.

The next morning, I got up and the first thing I did was call Lando. For some reason he always knew what to do or say. I told him the situation and we was very calm about it. He told me not to worry about Prii and to just go check on Na'Priice at the hospital. When he said that, I just knew he would take care of everything. Lando was just that type of guy. And plus, I secretly knew he had a thing for her.

"Hey…" I said, trying to catch him before he hung up.

"What's up?" he asked.

"I was thinking about coming back into work when all this shit is over." I said.

"You sure that's what you wanna do?" he asked.

"Positive." I said.

"Well, we'll talk about it later then." he said. "For now, just go check on lil man at the hospital. See what's up with him and keep me posted."

We hung and I got up and got dressed. When I waked into the living room, CJ was sitting up on the couch staring into space.

"Good morning." I said.

He didn't respond.

"CJ?" I said, walking over to face him.

He looked up at me with tears rolling down his face.

"What's the matter?" I asked.

"I didn't mean to pee on myself." he said.

I looked down at the little puddle of piss that sat on top of the plastic bag.

"Aw, its okay sweetie. It was just an accident." I said. "You don't have to cry."

I grabbed his hand and took him into the bathroom to wash up. As he washed himself up, I went into the kitchen and cooked breakfast. He came out, got dressed, we ate and headed out the door. We pulled up to Shanell's house and it looked pretty dead. I guess because it was still kind of early.

"Well, it don't look like anybody's here, but come on." I said, unbuckling my seatbelt.

We began walking up towards the door and before we could even touch the first step, she came running out the house yelling and screaming.

"CJ get yo ass in here! Who told you to leave out this house?"

CJ quickly let my hand go and ran inside. Shanell was standing there in a robe, with house shoes on and a black eye.

"At least you knew where he was at!" I shouted. "That's why you wasn't calling to get him back. And what's wrong with you leaving these babies in the house by themselves? Are you crazy?!"

"First of all, CJ ain't no damn baby." she said, rolling her neck. "And who is you to be all up on my property questioning me about somebody else's kids? Where Prii at?"

I looked at her like she was half stupid. She isn't have any knowledge of what was about to hit her. Between me, Prii, and the charges she was about to get pressed against her, the bitch was definitely stuck in between a rock and a hard place. She had nowhere to run.

"Bitch, you should know!" I snapped. "You the one got her locked up."

She chuckled. "How did I get her locked up?"

"You been giving Na'Priice alcohol and he got sick last night." I said. "Are you fucking stupid? How could you do that?"

"Alcohol?!... Ain't nobody give that boy no damn alcohol!" she yelled, folding her arms, looking guilty. She knew she gave him that shit. "I advise you to go on back to wherever it is you came from with all that bullshit."

Just as I was about to take off on her, a half naked man came out the house. Off top, I knew he was CJ's daddy. He looked just like him.

"What the hell is going on out here?" he yelled

"Nothing bae. She was just leaving." Shanell said, looking at me with a slight smirk on her face.

"No, I wasn't actually." I said. "Yo bitch been giving Na'Priice alcohol. She need to own up to some shit."

"Bitch I ain't owning up to shit I ain't do!" she said.

"My bitch isn't give that little ass boy no alcohol. Shanell get yo ass in this house!" he snapped.

Before she could even turn around fully, I grabbed her by the back of her shirt and swung her to the ground. With all my might, I reached back and flew my fist into her face over and over. She was swinging her arms and kicking, but wasn't getting nowhere with that shit. I finally stood up and caught my breath.

"Get up bitch!" I yelled, as I watched her struggle to her feet. "What's up?" I shouted. "I been waiting to get in that ass."

Her nigga started shouting at me as Shanell wiped the blood from her nose and lip.

"Bitch is you crazy?!" He said. "Get the fuck from round here!"

"Oh, you can hit the bitch but I cant?" I asked, assuming that he was the one to give her the black eye. I was on a roll.

"Fuck you and this bitch!"

"Bitch, you got me fucked up!" she yelled, walking towards me.

Her nigga started walking down the stairs to grab her as I waited to see what she was going to do. He held on to her telling her to calm down. He knew what was good for her. I was gone definitely tag that ass again if he would have let her go. I laughed.

"Let her ass go!" I shouted.

"Bitch move around!" He said. "That's enough."

As I continued to run my mouth, my phone rung in my pocket. I didn't pay it any mind.

"Ain't you gonna get that?" Shanell asked, being sarcastic.

Something instantly came over me, and I charged at her like a raging maniac. Her man had no choice but to step back and let her go. I must have startled him a little bit for a minute. I pounded my fist into her face some more. I couldn't stop. It took me a second to realize that her boyfriend was pulling me up by my hair. As he pulled me, I pulled her, and we both were dragging across the yard.

"Get this crazy bitch off of me Chad!" Shanell shouted, as she struggled.

"Let her go before I knock yo ass out!" he yelled at me.

I didn't care about his threats. I just kept punching and pulling on her until he finally was able to brake us apart.

Just as I was about to charge at her again, CJ came to the window crying.

"Daddy!" he shouted, scared.

"Junior get yo ass out the window!" Chad snapped.

CJ just stood there crying as if he didn't hear what his dad told him.

"Oooh, bitch you lucky that baby in the window." I shouted, calming down and catching my breath again. "But this isn't over and you can believe that!"

"Fuck you!" she shouted, as I began walking to the car.

"Bitch shut up and get in the house!" he shouted, pushing her roughly towards the steps.

I got in the car, stuck my middle finger up, and sped off. I was hot! I wanted to just turn back around and finish, but CJ was there. I isn't want to do all that in front of him. She was so lucky. As I calmed myself down, I drove to the hospital.

"Excuse me?" I said to the lady at the desk. "Can you tell me which room to find Na'Priice Williams in?"

"I sure can." she replied.

She gave me the directions to the room and I went on up. I knocked on the door and went in without anybody telling me to come in. Even though he was in there chilling, watching cartoons and eating ice cream, I could have cried when I seen those I.V.'s in his arm.

"TETE!" he shouted, when he saw me.

"Hey boo boo!" I said, walking over to him. "How you feeling?"

"I feel better now. The doctor fixed me." He said, smiling. "Where's mommy?"

"Mommy had to go out of town for a little while." I lied. "She'll be back."

It was the first thing to come to mind because I didn't want to tell him she was in jail. He would have had a fit. I quickly changed the subject before he got to asking too many questions.

"They treating you nicely in here?" I asked.

"Yes." he replied. "They have a lot of ice cream."

I laughed. "Is it good?"

He shook his head yes, with a huge smile on his face.

Just as he was about to start showing me all of his stickers, a nurse walked in.

"Oh, I didn't know you had company Na'Priice." she said smiling, with apple juice and cookies in her hand. "Is this your sister?"

"No, this my tete." He said, correcting her.

"Oh, okay." she chuckled. "Well, nice to meet you tete."

I thought that it was so cute.

"You too." I said, shaking her hand. "So, how's he doing?"

"Oh, he's doing great." She said. "His little body responded very well to the medication."

"I get to go home now?" Na'Priice asked. "I really wanna go home now."

"Maybe." the nurse smiled.

"Can I talk to you in private?" I asked

She shook her head yeah, and we walked into the hall. I got straight to the point.

"So, tell me what's next for him. Is he able to come home with me or does he go into foster care or what?"

"Well, to my knowledge, I believe the police is still investigating the case, which means he's probably going to have to go into social services until they get to the bottom of everything."

"Well, when does he leave the hospital?" I asked. "I would like to know his whereabouts at all times."

"I'm not authorized to give out that information ma'am." she replied.

"Please?" I begged. "I have to know. What if this was your son?"

She paused for a moment and put her head down. I knew she was thinking about it. Nobody would have to know that she had told me anything. I just wanted to know what was going to be going on with him. Prii would have done the same for me. She finally held her head back up and sighed. She looked around to see if anybody was listening.

"Okay look," she whispered. "All I can tell you, is that social services is supposed to be picking him up tonight or tomorrow morning. That's all I know."

She pulled a pen out of her scrubs, wrote down a number on a piece of paper and handed it to me.

"What's this?" I asked.

"Social Services." She said. "Call that number tomorrow and they should be able to answer anymore of your questions."

I thanked her an she nervously scurried back into the room.

13

The next day, I kept calling Social Services to see if they would just let me keep Na'Priice, but they turned me down. I sat in my living room waiting on a phone call from anybody. I was getting tired of not knowing what to do next. Lando hadn't called to update me on anything that he had done. Even though, none of it was really my business, I felt like all of it was my business. Prii had been there for me since the day I met her and I felt like I was letting her down by letting those people keep Na'Priice. I needed somebody to call and let me know something, anything. Just as I was starting to really get impatient, my phone finally rung. I quickly answered it like it was my last phone call.

"Hello?" I said, almost yelling.

"You have a collect call from Prii." To except, press eight." said the operator.

I pressed eight and waited for us to be connected.

"Hello?" Prii said.

"Bitch imma kick yo ass!" I yelled into the phone. "Why you just now calling me?"

"Girl, its been crazy in here!" she said. "They ain't been tryna give a bitch her one phone call."

We laughed.

"How's my baby doing?" she asked.

"Girl," I said, pausing for a second. "As far as the alcohol in his system, he's doing great! The doctors said he's going to be fine. But, they took him Prii. They wont give him to me until they finish investigating."

"Yeah, I figured they were gonna do that much." She said.

"Yeah, I keep calling them people but they ain't saying shit I wanna hear. All they keep talking about was the investigation."

"They ain't investigating shit, because if they was, I wouldn't be sittin up in this funky ass cell. They need to investigate that dirty bitch Shanell. I cant wait to get my hands on that hoe."

"Girl I done already went over there and handled that." I said, laughing.

"For real?" Prii shouted.

"Hell yeah. Just yesterday." I said. "But I ain't gone say too much over this phone. Ill tell you about all that later."

"Aw damn, okay." She chuckled.

"So when the hell you coming home?" I asked. "I miss you."

"Girl I don't even know. I been working with this lawyer guy named Adam. I guess he's a friend of Lando's, but he's tryna help me get these assault charges dropped."

"Damn, Lando's actually doin his part." I said. "I just hope this lawyer knows what he's doing. Assaulting an officer is pretty big Prii."

"Yeah, I know. The thing is, I barely even touched him though." She said. "All I did was smack his hands away when he tried to grab Na'Priice out of my arms. He told them I did way more than that."

"That ain't right." I replied. "They can't keep you in there for that bullshit."

"You have 60 seconds remaining on this phone call." said the machine.

"Hello?" Prii said.

"Yeah girl, I'm still here." I said.

"Okay, well, imma get off this phone before they cut me off. Imma try to call you tomorrow." She said.

"Okay Girl. I love you bitch."

"Love you too." she said. "And don't stress about Priicy. Just wait til I get out so we can make them investigate the case right together."

"Alright. Call me later."

We hung up and I laid down on the couch. I didn't have anything to do. I had the urge to smoke, but I didn't have any weed. I decided to call Lando instead.

"Nigga just go watch that front door." he yelled, answering the phone, talking to somebody in the background. "Hello?"

"Hey." I said. "What's up?"

"Shit. Sitting up here tryna school these niggas on how to be a bouncer." he replied.

"Aw, you must've got you some new niggas working up in there." I said.

"Naw, its just Sammy ass actin' a damn fool." he said. "But what's up with you though?"

I sighed. "Nothing much really. I just got off the phone with Prii."

"Word? What she say?"

"She said that her and that lawyer you hooked her up with are working on getting them assault charges dropped."

"Yeah, that's what's up. He be on point so she should be out soon." he said. "What's up wit lil man?"

"He's good too. They let'em out the hospital but Social Services snatched him up."

"Aw yeah, we ain't gone see him til she out." he said.

"Yeah, I know. Imma go talk to the investigators and tell them about Shanell."

"Don't even worry about all that." He said.

"What you mean don't worry?" I asked.

"All that's being taken care of. All you need to do is relax. I got yall."

"But I'm tired of relaxing." I whined.

"Go out or something." He said, sounding like a big brother.

"How can I go out and my best friend is locked up? It wouldn't feel right." I said.

"I know you got a male friend somewhere." he said. "Why not go out on a date or something. No need to sit around and mope."

"I'd rather just come back to work." I said, trying to slide that in there, knowing that it was the real reason that I had been calling.

"Naw, how bout you come back when Prii comes back." he said. "Yall work better when yall together anyways."

"Why?" I whined some more.

Now he was laughing at me.

"You ain't ready to come back yet."

"Well, fine then! I'll just sit up in this fucking house and die of boredom." I shouted, as he continued to laugh.

"You'll find something to do." he said, as his lined beeped. "Oh, that's my other line. Imma hit you later."

For the rest of the day, I was bored as shit. I found myself cleaning up things that didn't even need to be cleaned. I was falling asleep and waking back up over and over not knowing what to do with myself. 8:30 came and I had gotten fed up. I cooked, ate, and ran me some bathwater. I went and got some candles and put them around the tub. Lando had told me to relax so that's exactly what I was going to do. I put Usher's Confessions CD in and pressed play. I slid down into the hot bubbled water and tilted my head back. I closed my eyes and listened to Usher's sexy voice sing to me. My song 'Burn' was playing and I couldn't help but to sing the lyrics.

"Its gonna burn for me to say this,
But its coming from my heart,
Its been a long time coming,
But we done been fell apart,
I really wanna work this out,
But I don't think its gonna change,
I do, but you don't,
think its best we go our separate ways.."

Usher did his damn thang in that song. Now the song 'Confessions', that was my song too, but it pissed me off. Him cheating and getting the side bitch pregnant, and begging to stay was a no no. What bitch in her right mind would take him back? Second of all, when I realized that this was the exact same reason I left Courtney for, it pissed me off even more. Niggas could be so out of line sometimes.

By the time Usher got done crying at the end of Burn, I was so relaxed that it took a minute for me to realize that my phone was ringing.

"Hello?" I answered, not recognizing the number.

"What's up stranger?" They replied.

I immediately knew who it was, but I played it off.

"Umm, who's calling?" I asked.

"Oh, its like that?" He chuckled. "I know you ain't forgot about me already."

A smiled splashed across my face. I cant even lie. I was happy that it was Stephan on the other end of my phone.

"Sorry, but this number isn't saved in my phone stranger." I said, slightly laughing.

"Oh, my bad." he said. "This my new number, but I know you know my voice by now."

"Okay you got me." I said laughing. "What's up Stephan?"

"Who the hell is Stephan?" he said.

I got quiet for a minute, feeling stupid.

"I'm just playing." he said. "This me."

"See, now I should hang up on yo ass." I said, cracking up. "You play too much."

"Okay okay okay…" he laughed. "I had to get you back for acting like you ain't know it was me."

"So you got jokes huh?" I said.

"Just a little humor." he replied.

"Right." I said. "What's up sir?"

"Nothing much. Just off work and had somebody on my mind." he said

"Oh really?" I asked.

"Yeah girl. A nigga cant miss you?" he snapped.

"Not if the nigga don't know me." I shot back.

He chuckled. "You really are a tough one to crack, but I think that's what I like about you."

"Well, I guess that's nice." I laughed.

"Why you laughing? I'm serious." he said.

"Oh, I'm sorry. I thought we were still stuck on this humor thing." I said laughing.

"That's funny." he said, laughing.

"I know." I replied.

"So what you doing on this lovely late night?" he asked

"Its not that late." I said, not wanting him to think it was too late to come over.

I picked up my towel and made a little splash so that he could hear.

"You taking a bath?" he asked.

I chuckled. "Maybe."

"Can I join?" he asked, chuckling.

"Sorry. This ain't a Jacuzzi." I said.

"Well, I'm pretty sure you could use some company when you get out." he said.

"Oh, you wanna come chill with me?" I laughed.

"If that's fine wit you." he replied.

"I guess I can handle that." I said, knowing that chilling wasn't all we were going to be doing.

I had something else in mind.

"Aight, well should I come over in an hour?" he asked.

"That'll work." I replied.

"Aight, well, imma get cleaned up and be on my way to you." he said.

"Okay, ill be waiting." I replied.

"I know." he said, as he hung up the phone.

I just smiled. He was something else.

I put my phone down and continued my relaxing bath. For some strange reason, I couldn't wipe the smile off of my face. It wouldn't go away for nothing. I guess it was because I kept thinking of what I wanted to do to him when he got here. I hadn't had sex in a long time and I was determined to have some tonight.

I finished my bath and threw on some cute pajamas. Everything was clean so I didn't have to worry about straightening up. I went into the living room, sat down on the couch, and kicked my feet up. I had popped in 'What's Love Got To Do With It' and chilled. At about 10:35, he called and told me he was outside. I was so excited as I jumped up off the couch and went to go open up the door. He got out carrying something that looked like a bag of goodies. I was anxious to know what was in it.

"What's up?" He said, as he approached me.

"Hey." I replied, as I let him in.

He came in and sat down on the couch as I sat across from him on the love seat. I immediately went into focus on the bag that he had with him. I had to know what was inside.

"I see you in here getting ya little Tina Turner on." he said.

"What? You don't like Tina?" I asked, frowning up at him.

"I mean, this movie aight. Its more of a chick flick." he laughed. "My mom can watch it all day long."

"Which means your mom has good taste." I said.

"Well, maybe its just a woman thing." he said.

"Or maybe you just have bad taste." I said as we both laughed. "So, what you got in the bag?"

The bag had been just sitting there staring at me. I just had to ask.

"Don't worry about it." he said. "It's a surprise."

"Oh, you just got the whole night planned out right?" I asked, smirking.

He smiled and winked at me. My panties began to moist. I was ready for whatever he had planned.

"I figured you ate already, so I only brought dessert." he said. "I hope you like strawberries."

Little did he know, we could have skipped right passed dessert too. I just wanted to taste him. If it wasn't for my pride,

I would have grabbed him by his shirt, brought him to my bed, and fucked the shit out of him.

"I love strawberries." I said. "What you got in store for me?"

"Chocolate dipped strawberry cheesecake." he replied.

"That sound good." I said. "I didn't know you could cook."

"Yeah, I'm pretty good with my hands." he said, as he reached into the bag and pulled out the ingredients for the cake.

I took him into the kitchen so that he could get started. I pulled out all the things he needed to cook with. I went and sat back down on the couch and finished watching my movie, which was at the part when Ike and Tina were in the back of the limo fighting. This was my favorite part of the movie. Tina had Ike in the back of that limo screaming like a little bitch. Not too long after that, the movie was over. Stephan must have been in the kitchen doing his thang because I was loving the aroma already.

"Damn, you got it smelling good up in here." I said, carrying the strawberries into the kitchen.

"Thanks." He said, smiling. "I'm a pretty decent cook."

"Oh, you just think you pretty good at everything huh?" I joked.

"I told you I'm good with my hands." he said.

"Well, let me be the judge of that." I said, trying to pick up one his chocolate covered strawberries.

"Not yet!" he said, tapping my hand away. "You gotta wait. Its almost done."

"Ugh, fine!" I said, pouting. "Well, what can I do?"

"You can go relax in that chair right over there." he said, pointing to the kitchen table.

I mimicked him and went to go sit down. As I sat down and observed him, I watched as he carefully decorated the strawberries. I looked him up and down from head to toe, and if I'm not mistaken, I might have even been licking my lips. When he finished decorating the strawberries, he pulled the cake out of the oven. It took him about ten minutes to finish preparing the cake. When it was done, it looked so good. He grabbed two saucers, a knife, and two forks and brought them over to the table. Then, he carried the cake over, which looked professionally made, and sat it in the middle of the table.

"This looks really nice." I said, as he finally sat down.

"It's a lil something something." he said, smiling.

I picked up the knife and cut a slice. I dug my fork in and took the first bite. It was so good that I could have just melted right there in my seat.

"So?" he said. "What you think?"

I completely forgot that he was sitting across from me for a second.

"Oh, uh… its alright." I replied, smiling, trying not to let him know that I probably just had had a mini orgasm off of his cheesecake.

"Just aight?" he asked.

"Naw, its really good." I said, digging my fork into my piece of cake. "So, where'd you learn to cook like this?"

"My moms." he said. "She hooks shit up."

We sat at the table eating cake, talking, and getting to know each other a little better. Turns out, we actually had a lot in common. Way more than I had expected. Both of our birthdays were in February, we both were an only child, and we both pretty much raised ourselves. He had been in and out of foster homes between the ages of nine and thirteen, while me on the other hand, had been in foster care damn near my whole life. The only difference was that he still had his biological mother. He did mention that his father had passed when he was about nine, and that his mom turned to alcohol and drugs to deal with the pain. He said that somebody called child protection on her and they came and took him away. When he was about twelve, his mom met a guy named Michael, who cleaned her up and helped her get back on her feet. They married and had been together ever since. Stephan praised him for it. It all took me by surprise because if he would have never told me any of this, I wouldn't have suspected that his life was any better than mines. I can tell by the way he reacted, that he was just as surprised to hear about how crazy my life had been. I left out the part about Kristian because I vowed to myself that I would take that secret to my grave. When I told him about how my parents passed, he couldn't believe it.

"Man, no wonder you're so hard core." He said. "Yo parents were some real gangstas."

"Oh, you think so?" I asked, with a slight attitude.

I guess he had struck a nerve or something.

"Like a modern day Bonnie and Clyde." he said, enthused.

"Yeah, except Bonnie and Clyde ain't leave a child behind." I replied.

I knew he was only joking, and that I was probably messing up the mood, but I guess his little joke had hurt my feelings. For about a second, there was awkward silence. My guess was that we both were trying to figure out what to say next. As I stared down at my empty dish, hoping that I didn't just ruin my night, he spoke.

"Damn, I fucked up didn't I?" he said. "I ain't mean to go that far."

"Naw, it ain't your fault." I replied, looking up at him. "It just still hurts because I never really had any closure."

"Yeah, I feel you." he said. "Feels like something's missing?"

He was exactly right. There was definitely a void, and my life was just so incomplete. He continued talking and telling me about all the different feelings and emotions he went through when his dad died, and how much counseling he had to get to help him through it. I guess his mom wasn't the only one who had taken it hard. He suggested that I try and get some counseling.

"Well, I don't know about all that." I said.

"Why not?" he asked.

"I just don't understand how talking to a complete stranger can help me with my problems." I replied.

"Yeah, it sounds pretty crazy at first, but if you go through with it, you'll feel a lot better."

"Better like how?" I asked.

"I guarantee you wont be walking around feeling as empty as you do now." he said.

I just smiled. Him caring so much just turned me on even more. I just wanted to say "Well why don't you counsel me then" but I didn't. I just told him that I would take it into consideration.

We finished up talking and trying to figure out each others lives, and out of the blue, he rose up out walked over to me. I looked up in his eyes and we just kind of felt one another. Then he leaned into my lips and kissed them gently. My heart raced as he took my hand and we went into the bedroom. I was so anxious and ready. I had been waiting on this moment all night. Or at least I thought I had been.

I kicked off my slippers and climbed into the bed. I watched as he removed his button up and wife beater, and while I tried not to squirm, I quickly took my clothes off too. The bulge in his boxers had already gotten my full undivided attention. We walked over and mounted me with his muscular body and kissed me long and hard. It was rough and I was liking every bit of it. He went down to kissing and licking on my neck and stomach. Just when I knew he was about to go lower, he stopped.

"What you doing?" I asked.

"Hold on real quick." he said, climbing off of me.

"Hold on for what?" I whined, not wanting him to stop.

"Ill be right back." he said, walking out of the room.

I sat on the bed, folding my arms and pouting. What the hell was he doing? I thought to myself. After about two minutes, he came back into the room with his bag of goodies. No longer was I pouting. He emptied the bag into the chair next to the bed, and asked me if I wanted to play a game.

"What game?" I asked, confused, noticing that there was some kind of rope involved.

He chuckled. "Its called 'Can You Handle It?'."

"Never heard of it." I replied, sitting up and getting nervous. I wondered if I had let some crazy, psycho person into my crib.

"The rules are pretty simple." he said. "One of us lays there, while the other does everything to please you."

I looked at him like he was crazy.

"So you telling me you wanna tie me up?"

"Yeah." he laughed. "What? You don't trust me?"

"Uh, not enough to let you tie me up nigga." I said.

He was cracking up.

"I figured you'd say that." he said. "Its actually really fun."

I just shook my head and couldn't take my eyes off the rope.

"We can do this the easy way or the hard way." he said, still laughing.

"Aw, shit. He finna kill me" I thought.

After all this time, I had finally let my guard down for this nigga and he wanted to do some shit like tie me up. What the hell was this shit about? I didn't know whether to get ready for some crazy ass sex, or fight for my life. I relaxed and decided to play it out. I mean, I liked the whole kinky and extra freaky thing, but me getting tied up was some new shit.

"And what is that supposed to mean?" I asked.

"Oh, you know exactly what it means." he said, walking over to me with the ropes in his hands. "So you gone let me do this or what?"

"How bout you let me tie you up first?" I said, jumping up in his face.

"Naw, ladies first." He replied, smiling.

Before I could even do anything, he picked me up and slammed me on the bed. As I tried to fight him off, he sat on top of me and grabbed one of my arms. I tried with all my might with my other arm, but it was no use. He was strong as hell. I was getting turned on by the second. After the first knot was tied, I just gave up and let him continue to tie the rest. I was still talking shit though. As soon as his lips touched my body,

I ain't have shit else to say. He started at my neck and once again, worked his way down. This time he went further and licked and squeezed my inner thighs. He let his tongue play in and around my pussy, while his hands caressed my breast. I was tied up, so all I could really do was moan and squirm until I came. I wanted so badly to touch his body. This shit was definitely torture. As I laid there helplessly, unable to move my arms and legs, I had no choice but to let him do whatever he wanted to do to me. It was feeling so good. He stood up on the bed towering over me and pulled his rock hardened dick out of his boxers.

"You ready for this?" he asked.

I bit down on my bottom lip and nodded my head yes. Just by looking at it had me soaking up the sheets. I wanted it so bad, I tried to break out the knots, but they weren't budging.

"You sure you want this?" He asked, getting on his knees in between my legs.

"Yes, put it in!" I moaned.

He teasingly rubbed the head of his dick up and down against my clit and pussy lips. It felt so good that I could have just cried.

"Naw, I don't think you ready for that yet." He said, putting his dick back in his boxers.

"Oh my god!" I said, getting frustrated.

I pulled and yanked and tugged and pulled some more trying to get out of the ropes. I believe I was only making them tighter as he just laughed and watched me.

"For real? You gone do me like this?" I asked.

"Huh? What you talking about?" he asked, sarcastically.

He really thought that the shit was funny. I was pissed. Nothing about the situation was funny to me. I couldn't take this torture.

"Untie me Stephan." I demanded.

"Why?" he laughed.

"Because, I don't like this game." I said. "Just untie me."

"Nope!" he said, grabbing the baby oil and pouring it all over my naked body.

I liked that a lot.

"You still want me to untie you?" he said, licking and rubbing on my toes and feet.

I moaned and shook my head no. Tilting my head back, there were so many tingles going through my body.

"I hate you." I said, as he got done massaging , licking, and sucking on my toes and worked his way up to massaging my legs and inner thighs. He began to massage my pussy with the oil, using just his fingertips. The shit was wondrous. I guess he wasn't lying when he said that he was good with his hands. He went up to my stomach and breast and massaged my front in a way that it had never been touched before. I think I was falling in love with this mans hands. I hadn't even had the dick yet and this by far was some of the best sex that I had ever had in a long time.

When he got done playing with the baby oil on my body, he got up and dropped his boxers to the floor. He was finally going to give me what I had been waiting for. Without warning, he went down to the end of the bed and untied my legs. He got up on the bed, tossed my legs over his shoulders, and slid his dick in my wetness. He stroked in and out and in and out until I couldn't almost take it. He grabbed my legs and spread them wide as he began to pound me. As the music of both of our sounds filled the room, I felt myself coming to a climax. I held on to the ropes that had my wrist tied as he held on to my legs and continued to pound.

"Oh my god! Oh my god!" I moaned.

It felt so good that I almost wanted him to stop. Suddenly, I felt something in me erupt. I began to squirt everywhere. I couldn't control it as he continued to stroke. Finally, he stopped as he also came to a climax. I was so happy because I don't think I could take it any longer. He climbed off of me, untied both of my wrist, and my arms just dropped to my sides. He had completely wore my ass out. He knew exactly what he was doing. There was no way in hell that I was going to be able to tie him up and do him next. He had wore me out on purpose. I wasn't complaining though. That shit was like something that I had never even experienced before. I wanted to marry his ass after that. It was over with for me. He got back in the bed and laid down behind me.

"You want me to stay or leave?" he whispered in my ear, noticing that I was dozing off.

I grabbed his arm and wrapped it around me.

"Stay with me." I replied, snuggling up closer to him.

He kissed me on my cheek as we both then just fell asleep. He had surprised me in many ways tonight, so I was happy, and my vagina was even happier. And just like that I was STUCK! There was no way I was letting this nigga get away from me that easy.

14

"Girl, tell me everything!" Prii said, jumping in the car, as I went to pick her up from jail.

The judge had let her go because her lawyer was able to get some witnesses to come forth and say that Prii had never touched the cop. As we drove off to her crib for her to get cleaned up, I told her about everything that she had missed out on. From me jumping on Shanell, to Lando playing like super save a hoe, to me and Stephan slowly becoming an item. I told it all. She couldn't believe that I had went over to Shanell's and whooped on her. She was happy, but she was mad at the fact that she wasn't there to do it herself. Then Prii informed me that Lando had the investigators at Shanell's door and she was due in court sooner than she thought. The bitch was getting exactly what coming to her.

"So, what's up wit Na'Priice?" I asked. "I know you've talked to somebody about it since you been in there."

"Girl they said that I could come see him, but I could only visit. They said it wasn't safe for him to leave yet." She said. "I started to go off, but I ain't wanna get no more jail time."

We pulled up to her crib and it took me a minute to realize how quiet she had been during the majority of our ride. I looked over at her and it looked like she had had a lot on her mind. I figured we be talking each others ears off since we hadn't been able to really speak to one another. Prii was being a little too antisocial for my liking. We got in the house and I tried to small talk her.

"Girl, you see how well I took care of yo whip while you was in there?" I asked, sarcastically.

She slightly laughed and plopped down on the couch without saying anything back. Now I was really getting frustrated. I knew she was sad, but when she had first got in the car she was so excited to be out. She was laughing and talking and everything. Her mood just died down the rest of the way. I wasn't feeling it.

"Okay, talk to me!" I whined, plopping down next her. "What's on your mind?"

She took a deep breath and still didn't say anything.

"Prii, if your worried about Na'Priice, you know we're going to get him back. We just have to let the police do their job and be patient." I said.

"Naw, it ain't that." she said, leaning back on the couch.

"Then what's wrong?" I asked.

"Its just..." she sighed.

"What?" I asked. "Just say it."

She sighed again.

"Okay." she said. "What did you say your sisters name was again?"

"Delilah?" I replied, as she shook her head yeah. "What about her?"

I couldn't help but think as to where Prii was going with this. Delilah was dead to me. She was dead to everybody. The only one that I'm pretty sure didn't believe it was Karen. How could Deli have anything to do with anything.

"I met her." Prii said. "I know you said she was dead, but I just know this girl was your Delilah."

"It couldn't have been her." I said, not wanting to believe her. "Deli is dead."

"Secret, just think about it." she said. "You said you weren't positive about her being dead. She just disappeared. There was never any confirmation. I know this girl was her. It had to be."

"What makes you so sure?" I asked. "You've never even met her before."

"Girl, she went on talking about her adopted mom who was really her biological aunt. She was just so comfortable talking to me and telling me about her whole life. About how she ran away and got into the streets and how her life just went down the drain after her sister left. She didn't say her sisters name, but in my heart I just knew she was talking about you." she said, looking at me with serious eyes. "As I was sitting there listening to her, it all seemed so surreal."

As she was speaking, chills ran through my body at the thought of Deli really being alive after all this time. It wasn't making any sense. Why had she been hiding? I dropped my head in my hands in disbelief. I didn't know what to think.

"Girl, I ain't know how I was gone just come out and tell you." Prii said, comforting me as I began to drop tears. "Its been on my mind since the first time I talked to you on the phone."

It had been almost five years since Deli's disappearance. Even though they never found her lying dead anywhere, or even pronounced her dead, in my mind she was very much not alive. I couldn't understand why the police hadn't informed us that they had found her. They just didn't care. It hurt because for a while I grieved after she went missing. It took forever for me to get passed the fact that she was gone. I used to pray for the day when she would just come back, but I never thought it would ever happen. Especially after all these years.

"So, now what?" I asked, coming up from my train of thought. "What do I do now Prii?"

"I think you should go see her." Prii responded.

"Go see her? In jail?" I asked. "I wouldn't even know what to say to her."

"Well, I think you should just go. Don't worry about trying to figure out what to say to her. It'll come to you when you get there."

So many thoughts were racing through my brain. I thought about it not even being Deli when I went to visit, or if it was her, she'd be gone when I got there, or if I did see her what she would say to me? I was nervously anxious. I finally just sucked it up and decided that I would go for it. The next day, Prii drove me all the way back down to the jail and waited for me outside. As I waited for my turn to visit, I was nervous as a sinner in church. I felt my palms beginning to get sweaty, as I wiped them down the sides of my jeans. After what seemed like forever, it was finally my turn. 'This is it' I thought to myself. As I walked in I noticed the little inmate bitches eyeing me and trying to get me to give them some attention. It made me a little bit uncomfortable. I walked down to the last booth and there she was. Even though she was no longer the Deli that I used to know, I could still recognize her. As I stared down at her, she stared back up at me, and I slowly sat down in front of her. We both picked up the receivers at the same time but neither one of us spoke right away. Then I realized that we didn't have that much time to talk, so I moved my lips.

"Damn, you look different." I said.

It was the first thing to come to mind. She wasn't chubby little Delilah anymore. She was small and sickly looking. She sucked her teeth and chuckled.

"You got some nerve coming up in here. You know that?" she replied.

"What?" I asked, confused.

"Did you really think that when you waltzed up in here that it was gone be all smiles, hugs, and kisses?"

"Deli, why are you so mad?" I asked. "I couldn't be more happy to be sitting here with you right now."

"Sorry to rain on you little parade, but sweetheart, I never wanted you guys to find me. I was doing fine on my own."

"What happened to you?" I asked. "How could you just leave and disappear like that?"

"If I'm not mistaken, you left to." she said. "You never came back."

"That's not the same." I said. "Nobody thought I was dead Deli."

"You could have fooled me." She replied. "Because you were dead to me. As far as I'm concerned, you all are dead to me."

I couldn't fathom her words. They hurt so bad. She was so angry and I was so confused. She couldn't have been this mad just because I left. She was tripping. Even though her words cut right through me, and as bad as I wanted to slap her through the glass, I just couldn't snap back at her. I knew she was hurt and I knew it was partially my fault, but she wasn't the only one mad and hurt. She made us suffer the thought of her being dead. No one had ever heard from her. She didn't call, write, or try to even get in contact with us. Deli was being so inconsiderate.

"Why didn't you call?" I asked. "We were so worried about you D."

"Worried?" she asked. "About me? How did you find me anyways?"

She chuckled.

"My friend told me you was up in here." I replied. "Why does it even matter?"

"Because," she said, tearing up. "You would think that after all these years that I could forgive yall, but I cant."

As those words left her mouth, I found myself completely thrown off. Everybody loved Deli. She was Karen's little star. I seen no reason as to why she hated us so much. She was always the center of attention. A spoiled little brat was exactly what she was. This wasn't adding up to me.

"Why Deli?" I asked, irritable. "Just tell me what went wrong?"

She put her head down.

"Is this all because I left?" I continued.

She shook her head no.

"I ran away because yall stopped caring. Nobody paid attention to me anymore." she said.

"So you decided to never wanna be seen again?" I asked. "Deli, that's selfish."

"Oh really?" she said. "Well how selfish was it for you to leave me there in that house?"

"But Karen..." I started, but she cut me off.

"And Karen..." she chuckled. "That bitch ain't care about nothing after you left. She was so busy being mad and trying to keep up with you, that she forgot that I was even around. So, just like you, I went out and found someone to take me in."

"Where were you all this time? Why couldn't we find you?" I asked.

"All of that don't even matter." she replied. "Boppa took me in and I ain't have shit else to worry about."

"Boppa?!" I said. "You let that junky motherfucker take you in? What's wrong with you?"

I couldn't believe her. Boppa was a good for nothing drug dealing pimp. He didn't give a shit about this bitch or the next one. I had heard that he even murdered a few bitches down the road. He was a cold hearted man. In the beginning, most niggas were scared to cross him. He ran a lot of corners. Just as quick as he was to slap a bitch, he was even quicker to kill a motherfucker that crossed him. He eventually became his best customer and fell off. A junky ass pimp who was still trying to keep hope alive.

"He took care of me!" she yelled. "The only person that gives a fuck about me."

I shook my head.

"He don't care about you D." I said. "That man don't care about nothing but himself."

"You don't even know him." She yelled into the receiver. "That man loves me."

"Deli, if you out here selling your body just so he can make a buck, how can you call that love?" I asked. "That crackhead motherfucker don't love you."

As I spoke, she held her head down in shame. She knew I was right, but she was too damn stubborn to admit it.

"Whatever." she said. "He took me in and put me first. I was his number one. He gave me and showed me things that nobody else could or would. So I don't care what you say. I love him."

"Yeah, well, look where you at now." I replied.

I was feeling so sorry for her. We weren't blood sisters, but blood couldn't make us any closer. I couldn't take anything that was coming out of her mouth.

"Oh, and don't think I don't know about you either." She continued. "How's your stripping going?"

"What?" I asked confused. "What does me stripping have to do with your situation?"

She chuckled. "You just don't get it do you?"

"No, I don't actually. Why don't you enlighten me." I replied.

"Bitch you was just sitting up here trying to tell me that what I'm doing is so bad, when you ain't stopped to check ya damn self." She snapped. "Or is it that maybe you think your shit don't stank? Is that it?"

"What are you getting at?" I asked.

"Exposure." she laughed. "We're both in the same damn game baby."

As I sat there confused, trying to take in everything that she was saying to me, I still couldn't make sense of it all. I could feel that there was something that she wasn't telling me. I knew there was something she wasn't saying. I just didn't know what the hell it was.

"Ladies, about two minutes left." One of the guards yelled.

"Look," I said trying to get to the point, since we were running out of time. "You're still my sister and I've missed you so much over the past couple of years. When I heard you were alive, my heart fell to my feet. I came here to make things right. All I wanna do is help you if you just let me D."

"Well, its too late for all that." she said, standing up with tears filling her eyes. "You ain't wanna help back then, so don't worry about me now. I'm grown now. I don't need nobody's help. Thank you for resurfacing all of my pain by making this visit. You've outdone yourself."

"What pain?" I asked, dropping tears. "Talk to me!"

"KRISTIAN!" She yelled, slamming down the receiver, giving me one last stare, and walking away.

At that moment, I was at a loss for words. I almost couldn't move. I swallowed hard. Tears began to just flow from my eyes uncontrollably. I now understood why she hated me so much. I mean, hated all of us for that matter. We both had been victims to the same man, under the same roof, and I had never even noticed. I was so busy being scared for myself that I never stopped to think that it could have been happening to Deli. I began to think that everything was all my fault. That maybe if I would have just paid her a little more attention, gave her a little bit more of my time, then I probably would have noticed something wrong. I just up and left her behind in the house with that monster. She must have been so afraid.

As I walked back to Prii's car, I felt this rush of adrenaline coming over me. As I continued to walk, my hart began to race. I tried to keep calm and just breathe, but something was really wrong with me. My ears began to muffle and my heart was beating faster and faster by the second. I began to feel weak. I sat down in the middle of the parking lot, feeling as if I could no longer walk anymore. I couldn't even speak, let alone yell for help. I just knew I was dying or something. I laid down on the pavement and closed my eyes. There was nothing else that I could do.

After what seemed like forever, I woke up in the emergency room. Prii was sitting next to me in a chair holding my hand.

"Oh my God!" She yelled, noticing my eyes opening. "Bitch you scared the hell out of me."

"What the hell happened?" I asked, not quite remembering.

"Girl, I don't know." She replied. "I was taking a nap in the car and woke up when I heard the loud ambulance sirens going off. Next thing I know, I look up and it's a crowd of people surrounding somebody on the ground. Me being nosy, I get out to go see what was up, and its you passed out. I ain't know what the hell to think."

"What the hell!" I thought, wiping my eyes. "This ain't never happened to me before." I said.

"That shit was crazy." Prii said, getting up and walking to the door.

"Where you going?" I asked.

"They told me to let them know when you woke up." she replied.

I sat up as she walked out the door. I couldn't believe that I had passed out. What was my world coming to? Deli had been alive after all this time. Now she was locked up for prostitution and mad at the world because Kristian had been raping her just as he'd been doing me. My head was still spinning. All of this was just too much for me to take in at once.

"Hey Ms. Secret." said the nurse walking in.

"Hey." I replied, sitting up a little more.

"How are you feeling?" she asked.

"To be honest with you Ms….?" I said, stopping to read her name tag.

"Tonya." she said. "You can call me Tonya."

"Well, to be honest with you Ms. Tonya, I really don't know." I replied with a slight chuckle.

Even though I knew she was probably talking about physically, I was referring to my mental state.

"Understandable." she said. "Can you tell me what was going on just before you passed out?"

I explained to her how I couldn't breathe, my heart was racing and my ears were muffled. I told her how it was one of the scariest things I had ever encountered. When I finished explaining to her, she informed me that I had just encountered my first anxiety or panic attack. Usually brought on by being overwhelmed by something. That was exactly right. As she began to go over the procedures of what to do if it were to happen again, I began to wonder where Prii went. Prii never came back in with the nurse. I turned my attention back to

Tonya when I heard her say something about prescriptions. She told me to only take them if needed. When she got done explaining everything to me, she gave me my papers and told me to pick up the prescription at the front before I left. When she left out pf the room, I walked over to my purse to call Prii.

"Where you go?" I asked.

"I'm out here in the lobby." she said. "You done?"

"Yeah, here I come."

"Okay." she said hanging up.

I gathered all my belongings and got myself together. The stopped and got my prescription first since the prescription desk was close by. I got my pills and went out to the lobby to meet Prii. To my surprise, I found Stephan sitting across from her.

"Hey baby." he said, walking over to me. " You aight?"

He kissed and hugged me tightly.

"Yeah, I'm good." I replied.

"What did they say?" Prii asked.

"I guess I had an anxiety attack or something." I said. "I guess finding out about Deli put a lot on me."

"Damn boo." she said. "I'm glad you okay girl."

"Well, all that matters now is getting you home and getting some rest like the doctor ordered." Stephan said.

He had no idea who Deli was. I had never spoke of her to him the whole time that I had been seeing him. I knew he was just as confused as the next stranger would be. He didn't bother to ask any questions though. He just walked me out to Prii's car.

"Make sure you take her home Prii." he said, closing my door.

"Don't worry. I am." she replied.

"I'm coming over tonight when I get off work boo." he said, kissing my cheek.

"Awww, look at yall." Prii said cheesing. "Ain't yall cute!"

I blushed and rolled my eyes as he grabbed my chin and kissed my lips.

"Straight home Prii!" Stephan said reminding her.

"Yeah yeah yeah…" Prii said, nodding her head and starting up the engine.

"So….. You wanna talk about it?" Prii asked, cuddling up next to me on the couch.

We had just got done eating ice cream and sipping on strawberry daiquiris.

"Talk about what?" I asked, already knowing what she was referring to.

"Your visit with Delilah."

"What is there to talk about?"

"Whatever's fucking with you. I know when something's bothering you Secret. I'm your best friend remember?"

"I'm fine Prii. Honestly. Deli's alive and that's all that matters." I just wanted to drop the subject.

"No that's not all that matters. Something else is bothering you. What did she say to you in there?" Prii continued.

"How you figure she said anything to me?" I asked.

"Because, you're not yourself. You're different from when you went in there to see her. I figured that when you came out that you would be all smiles with tears of joy. I'm not getting that. So tell me what's really going on?"

I chose not to respond. I wasn't ready to talk about this shit. It was too much.

"Oh, so its like that?" she said, looking up at me.

"I told you that there isn't anything to worry about." I replied.

"Well, gone and keep your secrets then Secret!" she said getting up. "You need anything before I go?"

"So you call yourself being mad now?" I asked.

"Shouldn't I be?" she asked. "But naw, I gotta get up early to go see my baby in the morning."

"So why not spend the night so that I can go with you?"

"Because your boo is coming over here and I'm not to big on threesomes." she chuckled.

The liquor had completely let me forget that Stephan was coming over.

"So, you just gone dip on me?" I replied.

"Yeah, unless you just really want me to stay." she said.

In a way I did kind of want her to stay until Stephan came, but who knows how late he'd be and I didn't want to keep her up.

"Naw, I'm okay." I said. "Just make sure you call me in the morning before you leave."

"You sure?" she asked, putting on her coat.

I nodded my head yeah.

About three hours had passed since Prii had left and it was almost two in the morning. I had gotten tired of waiting up. I finished watching Training Day and decided to go to bed. As soon as I got up to turn off the TV., my cell phone rung.

"Ahhh... hello?" I answered, yawning.

"Hey baby." Stephan said.

"Hey. Where you at?"

"I should be there in about ten minutes."

I yawned again. "You might wanna speed cause I think I'm about to fall asleep."

"Girl don't fall asleep on me." he said.

I laughed. "Well you better hurry yo ass up!"

I turned the TV. back on and waited a couple more minutes until he got to my house. As soon as I let him in, I went straight to the bedroom to lay down.

"Aw, you not gone come get in the shower with me?" he yelled from the bathroom.

"Don't you see what time it is?" I yelled back. "No. I'm going to bed."

I was really only telling half the truth. I had too much on my mind. I wasn't in the mood for sex. Time was never a problem for me to get it in. I put my pajamas on and laid down. As I listened to the shower water run, I found myself soaking up my pillow with tears. A rush of emotion came over me. I wanted to just scream. I began to think of my parents. How could they just leave me all alone? My daddy was supposed to be here to hold me and my mom was supposed to make all my problems go away. I cursed them for leaving me. I cried because I knew Deli was lonely. I wanted to tell her that she wasn't alone. The way she looked at me when Kristian's name came out of her mouth had me feeling as I if I was staring right into a mirror. I was suck and had no idea as of what to do next.

I heard Stephan cut the water off and I immediately dried my eyes with my shirt. I didn't want him questioning me or trying to figure out what was wrong. I just wanted everything to go away. He came into the room and got in the bed. He smelled so damn good.

"Bae, you sleep?" he asked.

I just laid there with my eyes closed, pretending to be sleep. He leaned over and kissed my cheek, then cuddled up behind me. It was so sweet. Then he wrapped his arm around me and fell asleep. I needed his comfort. It made me feel a little bit better.

15

I went down to Exotic Rain to force Lando to give me my job back. For a while he was handling all my bills while I was getting myself together. Now Stephan was doing it. At first, I didn't mind, but it was starting to annoy me. Some days I didn't mind staying in and relaxing, but most days I'd rather be out doing something.

It had been about a month since I'd seen Deli or talked to her. I had written plenty of letters, but she never replied. I knew she didn't care to talk to me. She had no idea that I was hurting just as bad as she was. I wanted to tell her so bad in my letters but I just couldn't. I wanted to tell her face to face that Kristian was doing the same thing to me as he was doing to her.

Somehow, in the mist of both of our problems, Prii and I had become kind of distant. She was so busy trying to get Na'Priice back, that I barely got to see her. Things were getting worse because I felt as if I was getting lonelier and lonelier by the day. Stephan was working so much that I was only seeing him at night and on his days off. I had to do something before I went crazy and dancing seemed like my best bet. After a few no's, I had finally convinced Lando into letting me come back into work. There were a few new faces, but besides that, everything was pretty much the same. The same hoes that were there when I left, were there when I came back.

"So, what brings you back to the cat house?" Princess asked, as I walked into the strip room. "We thought you were gone for good."

"Now, why would yall go and think a thing like that?" I asked sarcastically.

"Maybe, because you haven't been here in months." she said.

I sensed the tension in her voice. I found it quite amusing. I knew they were going to be mad the moment I stepped back in that bitch. I didn't respond. I just kept walking, knowing it would piss her of even more. I sat down at my station and waited for the next bitch to say her piece. Sure enough, the next one to open up her mouth was the last bitch I wanted to hear from.

"Where's your sidekick?" Missy asked. "She plan on coming back too?"

My first thought was to slap her. I knew coming back to the E.R. was going to be a challenge because dealing with these bitches took a lot of patients. I knew that if was to slap one of them that Lando would send me right back home. I didn't respond to Missy because she was a kid to me. I didn't want to let her get to me.

She smacked her lips as I continued to ignore her.

"Helloooo…." she said. "I know you hear me talking to you."

"Oh, I'm sorry. Were you talking to me?" I asked.

She smacked her lips again. "Don't get smart."

I chuckled. "Sorry sweetie, but I been smart." I replied. "And if you got something to say to me you can talk to me after hours because that's around the time ill consider talking to kids."

I turned around to my mirror and watched her feel some type of way. I continued to prep myself before I had to hit the stage. I didn't have time to play with these bitches. I came to work!

16

About a week in and I was back on top of my shit. These silly bitches were watching my every move and probably my every dollar. I didn't care though. I just continued to smile and go about my business.

There was this new chick named Dasani that worked at the club. A little short dark skinned girl with a huge ass. Another young one that Lando probably called himself "saving." She wasted no time in becoming my new shadow. She followed me everywhere, gossiping and explaining to me about which bitches she did and didn't like. Only I could care less because I didn't give a fuck about none of these bitches in the club. I pretended as if I cared as she went on rambling about bullshit. Its clear that she was young minded and probably didn't have anybody, which reminded me of the way Nyprii had taken me under her wing when I first came to Exotic Rain. Maybe I felt a little obligated.

A couple weeks later, I was laid up with my boo watching The Wood, after some good morning love making. I sat in between his legs as we both chuckled and laughed at all the funny parts.

"Suck, never chew." I said to Stephan, quoting Roland.

Stephan grabbed me and began nibbling on my neck. As I playfully acted as if I didn't want him to do it, when what he didn't know was that we were about to go round four of sex in the AM. Just as I felt him beginning to stiffen back up, there goes the damn doorbell.

DING DONG!

I got up and went to go look out the peep hole. It was the delivery man. I hadn't ordered anything lately, so I wondered what it could be. Without anymore hesitation, I anxiously opened up the door.

"Yes?" I asked.

"Hi, I have a special order for a Ms. Secret McKay Adams."

He then looked at the package to make sure he was pronouncing my name right.

"That would be me." I replied.

"Alrighty, can I just get you to sign here, then its all yours." he smiled, handing me his clipboard and pen.

I quickly signed for it as we exchanged items and I let him on his way. There was no return address on the package so I had no clue as to who it was from. I tore open the box and to my surprise, there was a teddy bear, a rose, a diamond necklace, and a card. My first thought was that Stephan had pulled a fast one on me. I picked the card up and it read...

"Hello beautiful,

I've been missing your precious face. I'm in your town for a while on business and thought I'd send you a few gifts to make you smile. Hope you enjoy,

Quam,"

By the time I had finished reading the card, I found myself smiling from ear to ear. It was so sweet. After all this time I was still on his mind. Well, I guess my juices were a bit addictive. But I cant even front. As good as his sex was, I don't know how I ever let him slip my mind. With everything that had been going on, I had completely forgotten all about Mr. Jamaica. Just as the thought of me hooking back up with him crossed my mind, reality checked back in.

"Who was that bae?" Stephan asked, walking into the kitchen.

My heart damn near jumped out my chest.

"The delivery guy." I managed to get out.

"What you done bought now?" he asked sarcastically, walking over to me. He seen the teddy bear and made a face.

"Nothing. Somebody sent me something." I replied.

"An old boyfriend or something?" he asked, picking up each item one by one.

He picked up the necklace and held it to the light.

"No." I said, snatching the necklace out of his hand. "He's just this guy I met when the girls all went to Vegas. He was just being nice."

"Yeah, a lil too nice." he said.

"Hmmm… do I sense a little jealousy?" I laughed.

"Jealous my ass. You better tell that nigga you only got one supplier."

I got up and went to go sit on his lap. I knew he felt some type of way. His jealousy was turning me on.

"Awww, you so sexy when you're jealous boo." I said sarcastically, kissing him on his neck.

"You think I'm playing Secret. You better let that nigga know something."

He was going on and on and wouldn't shut up about it. I slid down between his legs and pulled his boxers down. I knew how to shut his ass up.

"Don't make me have to whoop his ass. I aint finna be… oh shit!"

And that was all it took. As soon as my tongue touched his dick he aint have shit else to say but "damn girl." After that, he picked me up and laid me on the kitchen table, tossing all of my gifts to the floor. I really didn't care though. I was just ready to finish what we started before the delivery guy came. Flashbacks of Mr. Jamaica popped into my head making me wetter and wetter. I felt so bad thinking about him while I made love to my man, but I couldn't control it. As long as Stephan didn't know what was going on, I figured I'd continue to imagine Quam fucking the shit out of me and get away with it… at least just this once.

We finished up and went to go get in the shower. We washed each other up and got out. It was almost time for Stephan to go to work. As he got dressed I went into the kitchen and made him something to eat. I was about ready to go back to sleep.

Later on that day, I called Prii to see if she was at home. It had been weeks since we had had some serious girl time. I missed her. And plus I wanted to see what was up with Na'Priice.

"Hello?" she answered, sounding all nonchalant.

"Well damn, is this really the greeting I get after I aint seen or talked to yo ass in forever?"

"Hey girl. What's up?" she replied with the same voice. I started to get annoyed.

"Shit, I was just calling to see what you was up to."

"Oh. Where Stephan at?" she asked.

"Girl, he at work. Aint no telling if he coming back over tonight or not." I replied. "What's your plans for tonight? You wanna go have some drinks or something?"

She sighed. "Probably not. Imma just go see Priicy and come home. I don't really feel like doing nothing else."

"Oh, okay." I said. Not knowing what else to say.

I didn't want to beg her to come hang with me. All I wanted to do was just go out and take our minds off things for a while. I guess she just wasn't feeling up to it. I was a little annoyed because I missed her, but I wasn't going to trip about it. She probably was on her period and just didn't want to be bothered. I don't know, but whatever the situation was, I wasn't feeling it. It was definitely time to pull the plug on this conversation because it was dead.

"So you sure don't want me to go see Na'Priice with you?" I asked, once more, giving her the benefit of the doubt.

"Naw, I'm okay." She replied, just as I expected.

"Aight, well let me get up off this phone then." I responded, hanging up without her response. I was a little salty.

For the rest of the day I just kind of laid around and watched some movies until it was time for me to leave. I didn't really feel like dealing with the bitches at the club, but I had to go into work and make this money. I had plenty of money saved up, but more money was better. I got my black ass up and took my ass to the club.

A couple days later, Prii called my phone with so much excitement in her voice. I almost didn't pick up after the way she blew me off the other day. She was lucky I loved her.

"Hello?" I answered dryly.

"Girl….. Guess what?" she yelled into the phone.

I really wasn't in the mood to play any guessing games with her.

"What Prii?" I asked.

"Come open up the door!" she yelled again.

I slowly got up and took my time to go open up the door.

"What do you want?" I asked sarcastically, as I swung open the door.

"TETE!" Na'Priice yelled, running up and hugging me.

"Oh my God!" I yelled, picking him up and squeezing him tightly. "When did you get home?"

"Today." he replied.

I looked up at Prii, noticing her smiling with tears rolling down her face, which caused me to tear up. I grabbed her and hugged them both. I was so happy for them.

"So how in the hell did this happen?" I asked, as we sat down at the kitchen table.

"Girl, I don't even know. One minute they telling me I cant bring him home because no evidence of that bitch being responsible was coming up anywhere. That was just two days ago."

Now I knew why she had blown me off. I figured she'd probably given up hope. Tired of fighting for something that was rightfully hers. I could understand why she didn't want to be bothered.

"I went home that night and prayed til I couldn't pray no more." she continued. "Then this morning, walking into that courtroom, I felt like God was on my side. I looked over at Shanell, who couldn't help but to roll her eyes."

"Ugh, that bitch." I said.

"I know right?" Prii said. "And girl, any other day I would have been trying to wring that bitch's neck, but today, I just smiled at her. I sat down next to my lawyer and waited to see what was going to happen. They called some man up on the stand who I guess was CJ's dad."

I automatically knew she was talking about the nigga who had pulled me off of Shanell.

"What did his punk ass have to say?" I asked.

"He sung like a canary." Prii said.

"What?!… He snitched?" I asked shocked.

"Girl yes." she said. "Something about her neglecting his son and giving him alcohol too. I knew as those words were coming out of his mouth that I was getting Na'Priice back."

"That shit is crazy." I said.

"I know. And my favorite part about it is that they both have to do a minimum of 2 ½ years."

"Are you fucking serious?!" I yelled, looking over at Napriice to see if he heard me swear. "You're lying! They gotta do time? Both of them?"

"Yeah, Shanell was doing time off tops, but he's doing time for knowing about it and not doing anything about it. "

"That's exactly what they get." I said. "I'm so happy for you Prii!"

I reached over and hugged her again.

"Me too." she said, hugging me back. "I know one things for sure."

"What's that?" I asked.

"My baby aint going to no more bootleg babysitters." she said as we both laughed.

Weeks later, I checked the mail and there were two letters in it. I had already known that one of them were from Quam. He had been sending me numerous letters since the first one. He was always saying how he needed to see me and how he couldn't stop thinking about me. I thought it was cute at first, but as they kept coming, it began to get a little creepy. I had only met him once and he was behaving like he was in love with me. I mean, we did have sex, but it was just a fuck. A really, really good fuck, but that was it. I was beginning to think that Mr. Jamaica was becoming a little obsessed with me. Questions began to form in my mind like how did he even know where I lived? Or why he never left a return address? Or why he was still even in my city? What business could he have possibly been doing for this long? I didn't even bother to open up and read his letter. I tossed it to the side. I opened up the second letter, which didn't say who it was from, and it read...

"Dear Secret,
It took me to swallow my pride and everything else in me to write you this letter. I know you could probably care less about anything I have to say right now after the way I treated you when you came to visit me. For that, I apologize. The way I acted was un-called for. There's just so much built up anger inside me that I don't know what to do with it. I had no idea how to just come out and say it. I didn't want to feel like I'd be wasting my time. I didn't think that you would care. Ever since the day you came to visit, I been eager to tell you what happened."

As I read each line, tears just began to fall. I was so happy. I couldn't believe Delilah had actually decided to reach out to me. I honestly didn't think that I would ever hear from her again. My heart pounded as I began to read on.

"In some way I felt like I owed it to you to know. I guess I kind of feel guilty for leading yall on to believe that I was dead. But anyways, I'm writing to let you know that Uncle Kristian was raping me in that house we called a home. Crazy thing is, I always knew it was happening to you too. I just wanted you to come out and say it first. I looked up to you, so I depended on you to give me the courage to have a voice, but you didn't. Instead, you just left me there alone. You escaped while I stayed to suffer. At the time, I didn't understand how you could just leave me there. I just knew you knew what was happening to me because I knew what was happening to you. But when I looked into your eyes that day you came to visit, I could tell that you had had no idea . I felt more sorry for you than for myself at that moment. I just wanted you to know that I do still love you Secret. You'll always be my big sister. It wasn't fair what happened to us, but life clearly goes on. Right? Life steered us in two different paths and one of us just so happened to turn out better than the other. I don't know if you'll ever see aunty Karen again, but if you do, please tell her that I am truly sorry for everything.

- sincerely, Delilah"

I sat there crying as I re-read the letter again and again. Kristian had really done a toll on us. Delilah was right. The shit that I was doing was no better than the shit she was doing. I was selling my body just as she was. I wanted things to be different. We needed a new start somewhere. I didn't care what it took. Even if that meant leaving Nyprii, Na'Priice, and Stephan here and moving to a different state so that me and Delilah could have our lives back, then so be it. I had enough money for the both of us to pack up and leave. There was nothing but heartache and pain here in Minnesota. IT hurt me to think about leaving Nyprii and I hated to think about leaving Stephan, but I had to do this for me and Deli. Even if Deli didn't want to leave, I was determined to make her leave with me. I had no idea as to where we would be going, but I knew we were getting the hell up out of here. First thing first, I had to get her out of jail. I grabbed a pen out of my purse and went to go sit down at the table so that I could write her back.

"Delilah,

First off, I just want to say thank you so much for writing me back. I never expected that you would, but thank you. I know I was wrong for leaving you alone. It was selfish of me to only think of myself. I never even suspected that he was doing anything to you. Especially since you were his blood niece. If it means anything, I promise you that if I did know about it, that I would have NEVER left you there with him. I guess since it was happening to me so much, I never stopped to think that the shit could be happening to you. My heart hurts so bad for being so careless. We weren't blood sisters but that shit couldn't have made us any closer. I am soooooo sorry Deli. I promise I'm going to make it up to you. None of this shit was our fault. We didn't ask for this shit so therefore you don't have anything to apologize to me about. I completely understand exactly how you're feeling. I came up with a plan for the both of us to get through this together. I got enough money saved up for us to get away and start our lives over. Remember how we always said we wanted to stick together like glue when we were younger? Work, live, grow into grannies together? I believe we can make it right Deli. Kristian does not have to control our lives forever. As long as we're in this together, we can do this. Ill be up to visit you so we can work on getting you out of there. I love you sis. See you sooner than later!

Secret,"

I quickly ran and mailed her letter off. I wanted it to get to her as soon as possible. I wanted her to have enough time to read it, think about it, and agree to it by the time I went to visit. I was just so ready to leave. I knew she just had to agree to it. It seemed as if it was just the perfect plan.

I waited about a week before I went to go visit Deli. I figured that that was just enough time for her to get my letter, read it, and take my plan into consideration. Nyprii decided to walk me in this time, just in case I decided to have another panic attack. When I got to the desk to sign in, I couldn't find Delilah's name.

"Excuse me sir?" I said, to the fat man sitting behind the desk.

"Yes?" he replied.

"Can you tell me why my sister's name isn't on here?" I asked.

"I sure can." he said. "And what might her name be?"

"Delilah Johnson."

I stood there patiently as I waited for him to look up her info in the computer. I could tell by the look on his face that he was getting ready to tell me some shit that I didn't want to hear.

"I'm sorry that you had to find out like this miss," he said turning a slight pinkish color. "but your sister passed a few days ago."

"Sh... She what?" I asked, not thinking I heard him correctly.

"She committed suicide. I'm so sorry miss." he said again.

My stomach began to turn. I was too late. A numbness came over me. I knew my tears were falling, but I couldn't feel them. I had fallen to my knees and it took a minute for me to realize that two guards had picked me up and was walking me back out to the waiting area. Prii was out there waiting and quickly rushed over when she saw me.

"She's dead." I said, before she could even ask.

"What? What happened?" she asked confused.

"She killed herself." I responded. I didn't have any emotion.

I didn't want to be in the facility anymore. I just wanted to go home.

The 45 minute ride home was completely quiet. I knew Nyprii had about a million and one questions for me, but she was silent. I couldn't believe that Delilah was gone. I began to wonder if she had even gotten a chance to read my letter. Tears began to fall uncontrollably as I thought about her not even getting a chance to read it. Nyprii reached over and held my hand as tears also rolled down her face.

"I'm so sorry about your sister Secret." She said as we pulled up in front of my apartment.

I didn't know what to say so I just nodded my head.

"Do you want me to come in?" she asked.

"I'm alright." I responded as I got out.

She sat there for a minute as I walked up to the door, probably debating on if she should pull off or not.

"Are you sure you don't want me to come in?" she yelled out the window.

I nodded again . I really didn't feel like talking about anything. I just wanted to wake up from this nightmare. How did things just go so wrong? When did they get this bad? My life was a complete disaster. I couldn't win for losing. I felt drained. Life had sucked everything out of me. I began to question God.

"I must have been a mistake huh?" I yelled out loud as I sat on my bed. "A fucking accident?!... Why is this happening to me?!"

I stared up at the ceiling waiting for an answer. He didn't respond.

"I HATE ME!" I yelled again. "What did I ever do to deserve this fucking life you gave me?!"

Still no response. I stood up, looked around my bedroom, and a fit of rage came over me. I just went crazy. I knocked everything off the dressers, knocked the television off the stand, cracked the mirror, tossed all of my clothes out of the drawers, and threw my stereo into the wall. I couldn't control myself. It didn't end there. I also trashed the kitchen and the living room. Pots, pans, dishes and silverware were everywhere. In the living room, I had pushed my 50 inch TV down, broke my glass table in the middle of the floor with a steel skillet, and threw couch pillows every which way. When there was nothing left for me to destroy, I sat down in the middle of the floor and balled my eyes out. I was barely 23 yet and I had lost my fucking mind. I realized that it sounded like a bunch of people knocking at my door. I knew it was probably my nosy ass neighbors, which I only seen every blue moon. I didn't care for them. I didn't care for anybody. Not even my damn self at the moment. I figured they'd heard all the commotion down in my apartment and wanted to come stick their noses somewhere that they didn't belong. Then I heard the police.

"Ma'am, this is the police! Open up!" Some lady cop yelled as I ignored her.

I stood up and went into the bathroom to find my aspirins. I wanted everything and everybody to just go away.

"Ma'am, open up!" the cop yelled again.

I ignored her once again and went into my bedroom. I opened up the bottle and began to pop multiple pills into my mouth. I didn't care anymore. Life was nothing more to me and I was tired. Delilah had gotten out, so why couldn't I? I had no idea as to how many pills I had taken, but as I laid there, I felt myself beginning to drift off. As things began to get dark f or me, I heard Nyprii's voice.

"Wake up Secret!" she shouted as she was shaking me. "Help!" she cried.

I laid there slowly dying as my best friend held me in her arms. How in the hell did she get in here? I thought. Then I heard the cop.

"Keep talking to her. It helps to keep her conscious." she said.

"Secret, please don't do this to me!" Prii cried. "I need you bitch!"

I wanted to tell her that I was sorry, but I couldn't move.

"Secret PLEASE!" she screamed. "All I have in this world is you and Na'Priice! You can not do this to me!"

I still couldn't move. My eyes began to close and I couldn't control them.

"Noooooooo!!!!" I heard Prii yell one last time.

As my eyes closed, I felt somebody tug on my shoulder.

"Hey ma-ma." a familiar voice said.

"Mom?" I asked, confused.

"Why are you doing this ma-ma?" she asked.

I couldn't say anything. I just grabbed her and didn't want to let her go. My tears poured out as I squeezed her tightly.

"You know this aint right." she said, hugging me back.

"But I've missed you so much mama."

"We've missed you too baby girl." said another voice.

I turned around and it was my daddy. I hugged him even tighter and didn't want to let go. In that moment I was feeling like that eight year old girl again.

"You have to go back baby girl." Daddy said.

"You have so much to live for ma-ma." Mama said.

"Like what?" I said, crying.

"There are two beautiful people depending on you to be strong ma-ma."

I wondered if she was referring to her and daddy or Prii and Stephan.

"Its too hard." I cried.

"Baby girl its not hard. Life's only hard if you make it hard. You're a fighter. You are MY daughter. I refuse to let you go out like this." Daddy said.

"But daddy…"

"But daddy nothing baby girl. You have to go back!"

"I aint got no more life left in me." I replied.

"Yes you do ma-ma. You cant give up. We been riding wit you this whole time. You've grown beautifully, and we're proud of you." Mama said.

"You can do this baby girl. I know you can." Daddy added.

They both hugged me tightly and didn't let go. I cried because I knew I couldn't stay. As bad as I wanted to, I knew I had to go back. Just then, I heard the sirens, and felt something in my throat as I was gagging. They were pumping my stomach and there was just so much pain.

"Here she is. She's coming back!" One of the paramedics yelled.

"Whew, that was a close one." One of the other paramedics responded.

They rushed me to the hospital where I was now stable. Nyprii, Lando, Stephan, and Na'Priice were at my bedside when I came to. As I opened up my eyes, Nyprii grabbed my hand. Nobody said anything right away.

"I'm... sorry yall." I said with a raspy voice.

"Prii began to tear up.

"Shhh... just rest bae." Stephan said.

I couldn't believe that after all the crazy shit that he done put up with me, he was still here by my side. I knew that this man had to truly love me.

"You okay tete?" Na'Priice asked.

"I'm okay baby." I said, with a tear rolling down my face.

"Don't cry." he said, wiping my tear away with his little hand.

I looked around at everybody and realized that I did have a family. I guess I created it along the way. I hadn't noticed that these same people had stuck by me through everything. Even though, neither one of them knew my whole story, they stuck around anyway.

"We love you Secret." Nyprii said, as she continued to hold my hand.

"I know." I replied, smiling.

17

Days later, I was doing better, but I couldn't leave the hospital just yet. They wanted me to talk to one of the hospital psychologist. I guess they wanted to make sure that I was in my right state of mind before they released me. When I got into the counselor's office, it was just like I had seen on movies. The little couch chair was there that people usually laid on to get comfortable and spill their guts out, while the counselor listened. To my surprise, my psychologist was a black woman. She shook my hand and introduced herself to me as Janet. We sat down and she immediately began to question me. She asked me all sorts of questions about my childhood and growing up. I was a little skeptical about telling this stranger my business, but something about her made me feel like I could trust her. I also remembered how Stephan had told me that it helped him out a lot when he was younger. It couldn't hurt to at least try. And besides, if I wanted to better myself, I guess I had to start somewhere. As soon as I opened up my mouth, it was like the words just started spilling out. I began to tell her everything. All the way from the beginning to the end. I was talking so much, that I hadn't noticed the hour with her had went right past. She suggested that I meet up with her every once in a while at least to check in and let her know how I was doing. I must admit that it did feel good to get a lot of stuff off my chest.

As I waited back in my hospital room for the nurse to bring me my release papers, one of my doctors walked in.

"Hello Secret." she said with a huge smile on her face. "How are you feeling?" she asked.

"I'm feeling a lot better." I replied.

"That's great!" she said. "I have some even greater news for you."

I sat there waiting for her to continue talking.

"You're expecting!" she said with an even bigger smile.

"Uh, expecting what?" I asked, not ready for to say what she was about to say.

"Congratulations! You're having a baby!" she shouted.

"I... I'm having a baby?" I replied in disbelief. "Are you serious?!"

I couldn't believe my ears. A baby? After the way I had cursed God? He was blessing me with a child? I was at a loss for words. Maybe this was exactly what I needed. Something to call my own. Something to feel like I needed to live for. Tears fell from my eyes. I was overwhelmed with happiness. I hugged the doctor as if she was the one who impregnated me. I had no idea how I was going to tell Stephan, but I knew I just couldn't wait to tell Prii. She was on her way to pick me up and I couldn't wait for her to get here. Ten minutes later she was walking through the door with the nurse who was bringing my discharge papers.

"Prii, oh my God! Guess what?" I said, not waiting a minute later.

"What?" she asked smiling, not even knowing why.

"I'm three weeks pregnant!" I shouted, grabbing my tummy.

"Oh my God!" she shouted, hugging me tight. "You just found out?"

"Yes! You're about to be an aunty." I shouted as we continued to hug and jump up and down.

"This is crazy! What did Stephan say?" She asked.

"He doesn't know yet." I replied. "I haven't called him yet."

"Why the hell not?" Prii snapped.

"Because I want it to be a surprise." I said. "He'll know when the time is right."

"And when is that?" she asked, rolling her eyes.

"Prii, I'll tell him okay. Just don't go opening up your big ass mouth."

"Okay, okay. Fine!" she said. "I guess ill keep quiet."

When we got to my apartment, I had completely forgot about my little fit of rage before my overdose. I almost didn't want to go in.

"Prii, I don't think I wanna go in there." I said.

"Its cool. Just come on." she said, getting out of the car.

I sighed and followed right behind her. I decided to check my mail before we went in. I knew there wasn't anything in there that I needed, I just wanted to stall.

"Ain't no need in checking that mail." Prii said. "I already did that."

"So where's my mail?" I asked.

"Its inside." she replied, smartly.

"Why you say it like that?" I laughed. I knew she must have seen one of Quam's letters or something in there.

"Because I just remembered that you forgot to tell me something." she said. "Mmhmm, you thought you was slick. I read the letters from Mr. Jamaica."

I laughed even harder. "Prii, don't you know you can go to jail for reading other people's mail?"

"Whatever!" She said, snatching the keys out of my hand and opening up the door.

When we got inside, the place was completely spotless. It was like I hadn't tore anything up. I had a lot of brand new shit. A new TV, glass table, couch, etc. I turned to look at Prii.

"You did all of this?" I asked.

"Of course!" she said, cheesing.

"Damn Prii, don't take all the credit." Stephan said, coming from out of the back room smiling.

"Okay, fine. He did do most of the work and paid for everything but, I did fluff a few pillows and pick up a few forks." Prii responded, laughing.

We laughed as I walked over to Stephan and kissed him. I couldn't believe they had went out their way.

"Yall did not have to do this." I said, tearing up.

"Well, I wish you would have said that sooner. I done broke a nail, got dirty, and sweated my edges out. You owe me." Prii said.

I laughed. "Shut up Prii."

"I'm just playin boo. You know we couldn't leave you hanging." she said.

I hugged the both of them. I knew at that moment that these just had to be the two beautiful people my mom was referring to. They were everything to me.

"Thanks you guys." I said.

A couple hours past and it was once again time for Stephan to go to work.

"Bae, I promised Nyprii that I would give yall some alone time." he said. "I gotta go to work, but I took off work tomorrow so we can spend the whole day together."

I got up and walked him to the door. I kissed him and hugged him tightly. I didn't want him to leave, but he had to go. I stood in the doorway pouting, as I watched him slowly pull off. When I could no longer see his taillights, I sighed and prepped myself for crazy Prii. I knew this night was going to be interesting.

"So…?" Prii said, as I sat down next to her on the couch.

"So…. What?" I asked.

"I'm ready for you to tell me everything." she said.

"What's everything?" I asked chuckling.

"No, I'm serious." she said with a straight face. "Tell me about your sister."

I took a deep breath because I knew tonight was the night that I had to tell Prii everything. There was no way that I was getting out of this one. I guess I was prepared to tell her. So for the next couple of hours, we sat and talked over a couple glasses of wine. Even though I had heard that wine wouldn't harm my baby, I vowed that this would be my last drink. I told her everything just like she wanted to know. I didn't leave out any details. She sat and paid close attention to every word that came out of my mouth. I could see the tears in her eyes, but she didn't let them fall. As I spoke, I realized that for the first time, I couldn't cry. I didn't see any reason to. Even when I talked to Janet about it, I cried like a baby. I guess I was all cried out. It was time for me to start being strong. It still hurt so bad, but I couldn't let it defeat me.

"That shits deep." Prii said sniffling with tears rolling down, as I came to a closure. "I'm so happy you finally told me."

"Yeah, I feel better about it to." I replied, as she hugged me.

"So, where do you go from here?" she asked.

"I guess I gotta move forward and get prepared to bring this baby into the world. I wanna be a great mom." I said.

"You will." Prii said. "I know you will."

I smiled and hugged her again.

"Okay! Enough of this mushy shit." Prii said, cheesing. "I have a little secret of my own to share with you."

"Oh Lord!" I said, trying to prepare myself. "Okay, tell me."

I was buzzing a little bit and she had drank way more than me, so I knew she was feeling herself. Wasn't no telling what was about to come out of her mouth.

"So… Lando and I are…"

"Fucking?!" I shouted.

She made a guilty face and nodded her head yeah, laughing.

"Bitch I knew it was gone happen." I said. "But how did this come about?"

"I don't know." she said. "He was just there for me. I mean, he's always been there, but when Na'Priice was gone, he really was by my side. He wouldn't let me give up." she smiled.

"Awww, Prii…" I said. "That is so cute."

"Shut up." she said chuckling.

"No really, it is." I said. "I always knew yall had a thing for each other."

The conversation brought me back to when I was nineteen and I had just met Lando. I remembered me wanting him to be mines because he was such a boss. I remembered him taking me to my first strip auditions before I even wanted to become a stripper. When I found out that he was just trying to recruit me, it turned me off. I didn't even think to want him after that. Life worked in so many crazy ways. I thought about how different I would probably be feeling right now if Lando and I would have ever dated, or even had sex for that matter. I chuckled thinking that the conversation could have went way different. I was glad that Lando was more of a big brother to me than anything. I was so happy for the both of them.

"Yeah, I know." She replied, sipping on her drink. "So, what's up with you and Mr. Jamaica?"

I told her how I thought he was obsessed with me and how he had been sending me numerous letters. I explained to her how I had to hide them from Stephan so he wouldn't trip out.

"Do you really think he's crazy?" she asked.

"You don't?" I asked, confused.

"I mean, yall did fuck Secret. Maybe he just really wants to see you." she said.

I looked her upside the head.

"What you looking at me like that for?" she said, laughing. "You the one that said you had a magic pussy. Not me."

"Shut up!" I said, tossing a pillow at her. "So what do you suggest I do?"

"Go see the man." she said.

"Go see him?!" I slurred. "And what about Stephan?"

"What about him?" She asked.

"Bitch, if he catches me, its over it!" I snapped.

"What he don't know, wont hurt'em." she replied. "I know you wanna yank on them Jamaican dreads again."

I cracked up. "You must be drunk."

"So!" she laughed.

"And anyways, if I did wanna go see him, there ain't no way to get in contact with him." I said.

"Maybe if you opened up and read your letters, you would know that he's been telling you to meet up with him at the same exact place in each of the letters. Some restaurant called Cashmere's downtown." she informed me.

I laughed because Prii had really been reading my letters with her nosy ass.

"Girl, he says he goes there every day from 5pm to 7pm." she continued.

"Prii, doesn't that sound a little weird?" I asked.

"No, not really." she replied.

"That's because you like that crazy shit." I laughed.

"So, are you gonna go?" she asked.

"What if I don't like the food?" I asked, trying to come up with an excuse not to go.

"Well you don't have to eat it Secret. Just go see the man!"

"Okay, okay…" I said, still not sure about the situation.

We got off the Mr. Jamaica subject and began to talk about a bunch of nothing. I missed having our girls nights like we used to. It had been a long time since we just stayed up all night sipping and talking shit. I was happy things didn't change between us after I the crazy shit I had just done. We didn't even bring up the fact that I tried to kill myself. We just acted as if it didn't even happen.

"Where's Na'Priice?" I asked after I realized hours later that he wasn't with us.

"Girl he's at Lando's." she said. "I guess they call themselves having a 'guy night'."

"A guy night?" I asked, thinking that it was so cute.

"Yeah girl. Talking bout they finna stay up all night watching cartoons, eating junk, and playing video games." she said.

I began to wonder what would Stephan be like with our child. I couldn't wait for the right time to tell him about the baby. I wanted him to be just as happy as I was. My hand rested upon my flat stomach as I began to wonder about the sex of my baby. It didn't matter to me if it was a boy or a girl.

I told the doctors that I didn't want to know until it got here. I just couldn't believe that I was going to be a mother.

In the mist of all my thinking, I turned to look at Prii's drunken ass, who had somehow fallen asleep on me. I got up and got her a cover. I let her stretch out on the couch while I went to go get in my bed. The wine had me ready to snuggle and snore. I curled up under the covers and dosed off.

Later on that night, I had had a dream about Delilah. We were young again and standing in front of our old home. I held her hand as we began to walk up towards the house. We reached the front steps as she let my hand go.

"I cant go with you." she said.

I begged for her to come with me.

"You have to be brave sister." she said, as tears began to fall.

I didn't want to go in alone, but I knew I had to do it for the both of us. I reached the top of the stairs, took a deep breath, and went in. As soon as I stepped over the threshold, I was awakened by the smell of pancakes....

18

"Damn Prii, you got it smelling good up in here." I said, wiping the sleep out of my eyes and walking into the kitchen.

To my surprise, it was actually Stephan in the kitchen. Prii was nowhere in sight. He was standing over the stove wearing nothing but socks, boxers, and a du-rag. Just how I liked him in the morning.

"You know that girl cant hook it up like I hook it up." He said confidently.

I chuckled. He was right. Prii ain't have nothing on him when it came to cooking. Hell, I ain't have nothing on him and I could cook my ass off. I walked up behind him and wrapped my arms around him as he continued to scramble some eggs.

"Good morning." I said, kissing his upper back.

"Good morning to you." he replied, turning his head halfway so that I could kiss his lips.

"What you wanna do today?" he asked, as I sat down.

"I don't care. I'm just glad I got you all to myself today." I said, as he smiled and prepared our plates.

We finished up eating and went to go get in the shower. As I stood there letting the hot water hit my body, Stephan stood behind me massaging my breast and kissing my neck. He slid one hand down between my thighs as I slowly began to wind my hips and grind up against his hard dick. Between me and the water, I couldn't tell which one was more wetter. Stephan loved to sex me in the shower. It was his favorite spot in the house. He slid inside me from the back as I held on to the front of the shower wall. After that, he turned me around, picked me up, and slid me down onto his dick. After a several good strokes, I was coming almost instantly.

By the time we got out of the shower, I was slightly weak in the knees. We went and cuddled up in the bed and just talked about things. I wanted so bad to tell him in that moment that I was pregnant, but I just couldn't do it. I laid on his chest and soon found myself in another deep sleep. I must have been exhausted because I had fallen asleep for hours. As I awoke, I looked over to see if Stephan was on the other side of the bed, but he was gone. I began to feel bad about falling asleep on him after he had taken the day off to spend it with me. I stretched and walked into the living room, where I found him fast asleep on the couch. I figured that must have went in there to watch TV because he didn't want to wake me by turning the tv on in the bedroom. I started to wake him up, but he looked so peaceful lying there. I decided to let him rest. I turned off the television and took it upon myself to do something for him tonight. He was always catering to me, making me feel special, and making it known that he loved me, so I wanted to do the same in return. I quickly and quietly gathered every candle that I owned, lit them, and placed them all over my apartment. I was nervous because I didn't want to wake him up during the process. Praying that he didn't wake up, I ran into my bedroom and threw on this sexy little lingerie outfit that I hadn't worn yet. I had ordered it a long time ago and been wanting to wear it ever since, but couldn't find the right time to wear it. Tonight was perfect. I had the perfect pumps to match. I wanted him to catch me in it when he awakened from the aroma of my lasagna specialty. I sprinkled on a little Love Spell, threw a few curls in my hair, and looked in the mirror. I was looking and smelling so good, that I almost wanted to touch my damn self.

I finished putting the last layer of noodles and cheese on my lasagna, preparing to throw it in the oven. I must have been in the zone because I didn't even hear Stephan walking up behind me.

"Damn girl! What's all of this?" he asked, smacking my butt.

"Just a lil' something." I replied, bending over to tease him and put the lasagna in the oven.

"Is that so?" he asked.

"Yup." I said, walking over to kiss him.

He immediately picked me up and sat me on the counter.

"Uh un.." I said, pushing him away as he tried to feel me up.

"What you mean no?" he asked.

"You have to wait." I said.

"Oh, it's like that?" he asked, backing up.

I smiled and nodded, proceeding to give directions to take off his shirt and get up on the table. All the while, I'm stuffing my face with strawberries and whip cream as he did what he was told. I hopped off the counter and went to go grab the baby oil.

"A nigga finna get a massage?" he asked, watching my every move.

I climbed on top of his back and began to oil him down. After he was oiled down, I began to stroke and massage his back and shoulders. I knew I was doing a hell of a job because he couldn't help but to moan and tell me how good it felt. One minute I was massaging him and caressing him and the next minute we were cracking up on the floor. Somehow, in the mist of me kicking off my pumps to get a little more comfortable, the table had collapsed. It happened so fast that all we could do was laugh. It was relaxing as we laid there with the candles all around us. I guess we must have worn the table out from sexing on it so much. Even though we were now laying on the floor on top of a tabletop piece, it was actually really romantic with all the candles around everywhere. I felt like I could lay there forever with him. I reached up and grabbed the strawberries and whip cream to spicin' up the mood.

"You want some?" I asked, dipping a strawberry into the whip cream and placing it in between my breast, which were sitting up quite nicely in my bra.

"Hell yeah!" he responded, crawling over to me and burying his head between my titties.

He finished eating the strawberry and began to tongue my nipples. It felt so good, but I stopped him and laid him down. I licked down his chest and undid his pants with my teeth. I covered the head of his dick with whip cream, which was standing so attentively. I licked around and around until all the whip cream was gone. Then I took him fully into my mouth without any hesitation as he moaned and groaned. He was loving every bit of it. After that, I rode him until the stove went off for the lasagna. I made our plates as we sat there naked, eating on the tabletop. I didn't want the moment to ever end.

A couple days later, Prii was constantly calling and bugging me about the whole Quam situation. She kept suggesting that I go see him and set things straight so that he could stop sending me the crazy letters. I suggested back that she go set the record straight for me because I really didn't want to go deal with the crazy Jamaican. She had finally talked me into going and I was convinced that it would be easy.

About a week later, Prii dropped me off a couple blocks down from the Cashmere's restaurant. For some reason, I was nervous. I didn't want to be dropped off right in front of the restaurant. Prii complained about having to wait in the car because she wanted to come in and be nosy. I decided against it and told her to go park somewhere close in case I had to make a run for it. She whined and did as she was told.

As I walked up to the doors of the restaurant, I found myself really nervous. This feeling was way different from the feeling I had when I had first met him in Vegas. I walked through the doors and looked around. I must admit that the place was nice and cozy. It wasn't too long before I spotted out the nicely built, dread headed Jamaican. He was sitting down at a far table next to the window, which he had happened to be staring out of. He hadn't noticed that I entered the restaurant. I took a deep breath and proceeded towards him. As I got closer, he must have felt me coming his way because he quickly turned and saw me. He stood up and greeted me as I sat down at the table. I couldn't help but to smile at him because he was smiling at me.

"Hello Secret." he said. "I cant believe you are here."

"I cant believe I'm here either." I replied.

"How have you been?" he asked.

Before I answered, I thought about all the crazy mess that I had been through since I last seen him and took a deep breath.

"I've been doing okay." I said.

"Just okay?" he asked, looking confused.

I nodded my head. "I've been doing alright." I said.

"Well, you look good." He responded, looking me up and down.

I started to regret the fact that maybe I shouldn't have let Prii help me get dressed. Maybe we over did it a little bit. She was all about the 'Three C's. 'Cleavage, Curves, and Cakes.' Something about leaving a man to thirst for me after I shut him down. Prii was always coming up with something. I couldn't keep up with her crazy ass.

"Thank you." I replied. "So, how have you been?"

"I'm doing a lot better now since I have the privileged of seeing your beautiful face." he said. "Did you enjoy the gifts?"

I thought this was the perfect time to ease in something about Stephan so that he would know how this little date was going to end up.

"I thought your gifts were sweet." I said, smiling. "Although, my boyfriend wasn't to keen on the fact that another man was sending me gifts."

"Oh, yo.. your boyfriend?" he stuttered.

"Yeah, we been together for a while now." I replied.

Just then, a waiter by the name of Milo walked over to us.

"Hi, I'm Milo. Ill be your server for the evening. Can I start you two off with something to drink?"

"Ill just have a shot of Hennessy and the lady can have whatever she wants." Quam responded.

"Ill just have a water. I'm not all that hungry." I added.

I didn't even plan on staying that long. Besides, I knew Prii was in the car probably pulling her damn hair out. I was trying to get this date over with as quickly as possible. The waiter walked away and we continued our conversation.

"You're even more beautiful than before." Quam said. "It's a shame that you are taken."

He slid his hand across the table to hold mine. As he touched me, something went through my body. A slight wetness formed between my thighs. I couldn't help it. He was still just as sexy as he was in Vegas.

"Yeah, I know." I said, sliding my hand away from his. "That's why I had to come here to tell you that I cant accept anymore of your letters."

He looked down at my hand and made a face as if he was confused.

"Don't tell me that you're about to break my heart." he said.

"Well, not intentionally." I replied. "To be honest, I didn't think that I would ever see you again."

He began to frown.

"What do you mean?" he asked. "I thought this was what you wanted?"

"What?" I asked confused.

"Here's your drinks." Milo said, placing our drinks in front of us and walking away.

"You don't remember?" He asked.

"Remember what?"

"When you said you wanted to see me again."

"What are you talking about?" I asked nervously.

He was starting to freak me out. He dug into his pocket and pulled out a small, slightly wrinkled up piece of paper, and handed it to me.

"Open it up." he said.

I began to open up the small piece of wrinkled paper. It read...

"Quam,

Thanks for the trip to Jamaica. I had a lot of fun. Maybe we'll see each other again someday.

Secret."

It was the note that I had left on the night stand in his hotel room from the last night that we had hooked up in Vegas. Now I was realizing that I wasn't being paranoid. This man was really crazy. I awkwardly looked up at him, wanting to know why he was carrying around this old ass note.

"You see?" he said. "This is what you wanted."

I sat up in my chair and looked down at his empty shot glass.

"Um, I think you done had one too many shots of that Hennessy." I said.

He chuckled as if I was joking.

"Secret, its only right that you come back to Jamaica with me." he said, trying to grab my hand as I pulled away again.

"You're trippin'." I replied. "I told you that I wasn't available. What part of that don't you understand?"

"Yes, I do understand. But he cant do for you like I will. Please just come with me." He begged. "I have to have you."

"The man I'm with now is all the man I need." I said. "I love him. He does a lot for me."

I could sense Quam's frustration as I went on rambling about how good Stephan was to me. He slammed his fist into the table when I told him that I would never leave Stephan for him. I was astounded.

"This isn't fair!" He shouted. "I'm the one that loves you."

I looked around embarrassed. I couldn't believe that he was behaving the way that he was.

"What is your problem?" I asked, slightly whispering.

"That man doesn't love you like I love you Secret." he said. "I want to marry you, have beautiful babies with you, take care of you. Why wont you let me?"

"Excuse me?" I replied.

He was really freaking me out. It was definitely time for me to get the hell up out of that restaurant.

"I think I should just go." I said, puling my purse strap up over my shoulder.

As I stood up from the table, he grabbed my arm.

"Don't walk away from me." he said.

My heart was racing. I didn't know what the hell to think. The man was completely delusional. He really believed that we had something together.

"You need help." I replied, snatching away from him.

As I walked towards the door, I could feel his eyes piercing my back watching me. I turned to look at him one last time before I walked out and shook my head in disbelief.

"This isn't over!" he yelled, as I stormed out of the restaurant.

When I got in the car, Prii could tell by the look on my face that things didn't go so well. Before she could even ask, I started going off. I cursed her for talking me into going as I explained everything that had just went down. The man was completely deranged. She began to laugh as if the shit was hysterical.

"Its not funny Prii." I snapped. "I really wasted my time coming here."

"Well, at least now he knows that you don't care to get anymore of his letters." she said.

I was furious, but I hoped she was right. He was definitely going to be wasting his time

sending them. Now that this little date was over, it was time to get back to my man.

19

Weeks had past without any letters or gifts from Quam. Prii was right. That crazy ass man was able to catch on. I was convinced that I wouldn't have to deal with him anymore.

I was about two and a half months into my pregnancy, and morning sickness was kicking my ass. I still hadn't told Stephan about the baby and was hoping that he hadn't noticed any changes. Although, he did witness one of my morning vomits, I was able to throw him off. Luckily, we had tried out some new Asian restaurant the night before, so I told him that the chicken didn't sit too well in my stomach. Valentines day was right around the corner, which meant my birthday was coming up sooner than I had expected. It seemed kind of wrong to be keeping the baby a secret, but I planned on telling him on one of those special days.

Meanwhile, back at Exotic Rain, I was trying to keep everything under control. I wasn't showing, but I didn't really want to be there. It was just a way to keep the baby secret on the low from Stephan. I had to make shit look normal.

Every time I turned around, Dasani was right there on my heels. Secret this and Secret that. She was becoming aggravating as hell. Always in everybody's business. The bitches at Exotic Rain always had my name in their mouths and here comes Dasani, ready and willing to tell me who, what, where, and when it was said. I had finally gotten tired of it and told her to keep it to herself because I wasn't concerned about anything that those bitches had to say. She was so busy worrying about what they were saying about me, when she didn't stop to notice that they couldn't stand her ass either. They couldn't stand the fact that she was always following up behind me like a little puppy. Hell, I could barely stand it. Another reason they couldn't stand her was because she was young and pretty. She wasn't all washed up like the rest of them. You could just tell that Dasani was fresh, while the rest of them were used and recycled. Even though Dasani was always being messy, she had potential. She was smarter than she led on to be. She was actually only stripping to pay for her school. I loved when she talked about doing something with herself instead of worrying about the rest of the girls in the club. Eighteen years old and had her mind set on wanting to be a business woman. I told her if she could just quit being so messy, that she had the potential to pull it off the day that I decided to invite her to my apartment, was the day I found out that I wasn't going to be able to get rid of her. Her and Prii had had a lot in common, so I was happy that we all were able to clique right off the back.

"Nooooooo....." I yelled in my sleep, as I laid there having another dream about Delilah.

We were both crying as we were being pulled apart from one another. It was weird that both faces of the persons pulling us away, just so happened to be Kristian's. Almost as if he had a twin. As I kicked and screamed for him to put me down, I watched Deli being carried away on Kristian's shoulder as the sight of her faded away. I could still hear her voice as she yelled out for me to go to Karen.

When I woke up the next morning, I knew exactly what I had to do. I had to make arrangements to meet up with Karen. I didn't exactly know how or when I was going to do it, but I knew I had to do it. The repetitive dreams were only signs of Deli crying out and begging me to get this over with. The thought of her not being able to physically be here with me killed me inside. It dawned on me that I no longer had Karen's number. It didn't take long for me to search for it in the phone book though. As I hesitantly picked up the phone to dial her number, my heart began to race. I was nervous because I hadn't spoken to her in a long time, but even more nervous because I didn't want the wrong voice to answer at the other end . It rung a few times before it was answered.

"Hello?" Karen said, answering like I had awakened her. It took me a second to speak.

"Hello…?" She said again.

"H… Hey." I managed to get out.

"May I ask who's calling?" she replied.

"Its me, Secret." I said.

"Secret?" She asked, as if she couldn't believe it.

"Yes, its me."

"Oh, my sweet baby." she said. "Hey!"

"Hey mom." I replied. It felt kind of good to hear her voice again.

"Its been so long. How have you been?" she asked.

"Its been kind of rough." I chuckled. "I've been managing though. How have you been?"

"Oh, I've been hanging in there." she replied. "I miss you so much. Why haven't you been to visit me?"

I couldn't believe the things she was saying after she had practically disowned me. She didn't want anything to do with me. I started to tell her that even if I wanted to come back to that house, which I would never, she was the one who didn't want anything to do with me because of the lifestyle I chose. I guess she must've forgot.

"Its just been a lot going on ma." I said, not wanting to go into detail about why I really hadn't spoken to her.

"Well, I have something for you." She said. "I've had it for a few weeks now."

"What?" I asked. "What is it?"

"I want to give it to you in person." she said.

"Good, because I was calling to tell you that I wanted to meet up with you. I have something very important to tell you." I replied.

We arranged for her to come visit me later. I invited her to my house because there was no way that I was stepping foot back into her house. The last thing I wanted to do was see the face of the devil himself. I just wanted to tell Karen what she deserved to know and get it over with. Now I was even more anxious to see her because she had something for me. I had no idea as to what it was, but I couldn't wait to find out.

Time was ticking and it was getting closer and closer to the time for her to be coming over. It felt as if I had a million butterflies in my stomach. I didn't know how I was going to tell her about Kristian, her only brother whom she admired so much. It was going to break her heart, but it needed to be said. Whether she believed it or not, I had to do this. At least for Deli's sake. I sat looking out the window, waiting for her to pull up. I picked up the phone and called Prii so that she could kind of calm my nerves a little bit. She told me to just be straight forward with Karen. She said I didn't need to hold back anymore because I had already done that enough. Prii was right. The best way to go about it was to be straight up. I sat on the phone with Prii for about fifteen extra minutes until I saw the car pull up. I went to greet her at the front door and took a deep breath before I let her in. I opened up the door and she immediately grabbed me and hugged me like she never wanted to let me go. It seemed as if we had been hugging forever. I knew that by the time I was ready to let go, she wasn't, but she did anyway. We sat down and she couldn't help but to smile and stare at me.

"I don't even know where to start." she said. "Its been so long."

I reminded myself to just be straight forward and stick to the main reason as to why I invited her over here. I knew that the longer I waited, the harder it would be for me to get it out.

"Okay, ill start." I said, taking another deep breath. She grabbed my hand and proceeded to give me her full undivided attention. I could tell by her eyes that she knew that I was getting ready to tell her some serious shit. I informed her that I just wanted her to listen to what I had to say before she said anything. I then opened up my mouth and began to speak. As my lips began to move, everything began to seem surreal. I couldn't believe that I was finally sitting here telling Karen the very secret that I had been keeping from her after all these years. She really just sat there and listening, nodding, and dropping tears. It hurt my little heart to see her cry, but she had to hear the truth. I told her everything from Kristian, to Delilah committing suicide. As I watched her take it all in, I couldn't wait to hear what she was going to say. I was now ready to let her talk. She then opened up her mouth and told me that she had already known about Delilah being alive. She then also told me that Delilah was not only in jail for prostitution, but she was also in jail for murder. She said Delilah had murdered numerous people. People who were still walking the earth whom she'd had exposed. I wasn't understanding what she was saying to me.

"The police called me a few months ago, when they first caught her and told me that Delilah was in jail for prostitution and seventeen counts of deadly exposure."

"Exposure?" I asked again. "I'm not following you. Who did she expose?"

"Delilah was going around purposely exposing men to aids!" She shouted.

I placed my hand on my chest and couldn't believe the words that I was hearing. Tears just began to fall from my eyes.

"And its all my fault." Karen said, crying. "I had no idea that my brother was doing this to you girls."

"Its not your fault." I said, trying to comfort her. "You didn't know."

"All the late nights I was working." she continued, shaking her head.. "I can only imagine how scared you must have been every time I walked out of that door. How could I have been so blind? How could I have let this happen to you girls?"

She threw her face into her hands and began to cry hysterically.

"I'm so sorry Secret!" she shouted."

"Its not your fault." I said again, hugging her, and wiping her wet face.

For a second she just sat there shaking her head in disbelief. Out of nowhere, she stood she said she had to go.

"No, you don't have to leave." I said, not wanting her to go.

"I'm sorry, but I don't think I can do this right now." She said. "I brought you girls into my home and didn't protect you. And now one of you is dead. Ill have to live with that for the rest of my life."

She reached into her into her purse and pulled out an envelope.

"This is for you." she said, handing it to me.

She hugged me again tightly and let me go. "I have to go."

As I watched her walk out the door, I sat back down on the couch and stared down at the envelope in my hand. It had my name written on it in Delilah's hand writing. I slowly tore it open. It was another letter from her. It read…

"Secret,

If you're are reading this right now, this is my last letter to you. I sent it to aunty Karen's so that you wouldn't get it right away. I read your last letter you sent to me and I only wish that I could participate in your future. I'm sorry to tell you like this, but I have Aids. A man whom I trusted gave it me. Yes, it was Boppa. When I first learned that I had it, something in me went black. I turned so cold. I hated men, and I hated everything about them. I wanted these men to feel low, dirty, and contagious just as I did. I know I was wrong, but I continued to go around having sex, taking money from men, and giving them something that they would have to live with for the rest of their lives. I called myself teaching them a lesson. Still, I knew it wasn't right, but I didn't care. I don't regret what I've done, and I'm pretty sure I'm not going to ever regret it. So you see, I just don't deserve the new life that you offered me. I'm not a good person, and I refuse to pretend to be. I just wanted you to know that I love you and I will always love you. I just ask that you tell Karen what happened to us. She deserves to know. But after that, I don't want you to hold on to it anymore. Let it go. You deserve to go on and live the new life that you planned for the both of us. Get married, have some kids, and start over. I don't want you to feel bad for me because ill be free soon. Ill be just fine. I love you sis. Stay beautiful...

Delilah..."

~~~~~~

"Hello?" I said, answering on the first ring. Nobody replied.

"Hello....?" I said again. I was beginning to get annoyed. Somebody had been calling and not saying anything for the past couple of days. It was frustrating the shit out of me. I was almost about ready to change my number.

"Happy Valentines Day baby!" Stephan said, walking into my room with a tray of breakfast.

"Awww, thank you boo." I replied, signaling for him to lean down and kiss me. "Happy Valentines Day."

He had cooked me a bacon, ham, and cheese omelet. It smelled so good. I was only hoping that this little baby was going to let me keep it down. Morning sickness was no joke. I was throwing almost everything back up. Next to my plate was a gift. I looked down at it and then back up at him.

"Open it." he said.

I quickly unraveled the little string that was wrapped around the little gift box.

"Bae, I hope this ain't another one of your 'IOU' tricks." I said, referring to the past gifts that I had received from him.

I opened up the small box and inside laid a single key.

"What in the world is this to?" I asked, taking it out the box.

Stephan just stood there with a big grin on his face. I really wanted to know, but he was acting like he wanted me to guess.

"Can you just tell me please?" I begged. I was so anxious to know.

"Go look out the front window." he said.

"Swear to God!" I yelled, automatically knowing what it was. I jumped up and headed for the front door, stopping in my tracks.

"Wait a minute." I said, turning around. "I hope I don't look out this window and see a damn bike."

Stephan burst into laughter.

"Just go look." he said.

"Mmmhmm…" I replied, as I continued to the window.

When I opened up the door I couldn't believe my eyes. There was a white Benz sitting in front of my apartment with a big purple ribbon sitting on top of it. I turned back to look at Stephan.

"What is this?" I asked

"That's yours." he replied, sounding the horn with the extra pair of keys he pulled out of his pocket.

"No its not!" I said, covering my mouth in disbelief.

He handed me the keys he had in his hand and kissed me. "Yes it is."

I slipped on my shoes and ran out to the car as he followed right behind me. The baby must have had me so emotional because I got in the driver seat and before I knew it, there were tears rolling down my face. Stephan hopped in the passenger seat and quickly wiped my tears away.

"So… what you think?" He asked.

"I think you're crazy." I said chuckling. "I cant believe you did this."

"You deserve it." he said. "I just wanted you to know that I appreciate you."

"I love you." I replied.

At that moment I already knew what I had to do. I took him back inside and sat him on the couch. I walked into the bedroom and got the pregnancy papers that I had hidden. I felt as if the moment couldn't have been any righter. I walked back in the living room with my hands behind my back.

"What you doing?" he asked smiling.

"Close your eyes." I said.

As he closed his eyes, I took a deep breath and placed the papers in his hand.

"What's this?" he asked, opening his eyes.

"Read it." I said, sitting down beside him.

I watched as his eyes kept tracing over the date of me finding out. I could tell that he didn't care to go on. He had finally took his eyes off the paper and focused them on me. He didn't look like he was happy.

"Is this some real shit?" he asked.

My heart was racing as I smiled and nodded my head yes.

"So, you're pregnant?" he asked again.

"Yes bae. I'm pregnant. We're having a baby." I responded, a little confused as to why he didn't sound so happy.

"And you've known about this since December right?" he asked.

I felt myself beginning to get a little agitated. I wasn't feeling the tone of his voice.

"Yeah, so?" I replied.

He stood up from the couch.

"So you've known all this time and you're just now telling me Secret?" he snapped.

I didn't know what to think. I couldn't believe he was trippin' on me. I never thought this would be his reaction. Especially after the way the morning was already going.

"Bae, I just wanted the moment to be right when I told you." I said, trying to keep calm so that the situation wouldn't turn ugly.

"You're damn near three months pregnant. Anytime before this would have been right Secret." he said. "What's so perfect about the timing now huh?"

"Why are you trippin'?" I said, now raising up off the couch. "I thought you would be happy!"

"Happy?" he shouted. "Why should I be happy about you keeping this baby a secret from me?"

"Why does it even matter when I decided to tell you?" I asked. "You know its yours!"

He did a little chuckle. "Excuse me?"

"You acting like I just told you that the baby ain't yours or something." I said.

He chuckled again and looked down at the floor.

"Well damn," he said, looking back up at me. "Is it?"

I looked him upside his head as if I didn't understand what had just came out of his mouth.

"Excuse me?!" I snapped. "Are you serious right now?"

I was so confused. Stephan was not acting at all like his normal self. It had to be something else wrong. I had never seen this side of him. It was taking everything in me to keep my hand from going across his face. I had no idea what was going through his head, but I wasn't having it.

"I'm just saying, there's a reason you waited this long to tell me right?" he said. "Just be real with me."

"I am being real with you!" I shouted.

"Naw, I don't think that's my baby." he said, shaking his head.

My feelings were so hurt as he had let those words leave his lips. I was so mad that I couldn't bring myself to tears in front of him. Who the hell was he to think that he could just disrespect me? I thought this man really loved me. In a matter of twenty minutes he had completely transformed into a total stranger. I didn't know who he was standing in front of me. I couldn't stand to look at him anymore. As far as I was concerned, my valentines day was over.

"Get the hell out!" I snapped.

"Now you want me to leave?" he asked. "Without telling me what's up?"

"I said get out!" I shouted.

I was beyond pissed and he just acted as if he didn't care. He was being so inconsiderate about my feelings. I didn't understand how he could really question if this baby was his. I wasn't fucking nobody but him.

"Its cool. Ill leave." he said, putting on his coat. "But while I'm gone, I advise you to go on down to your job and figure out who that baby's father is."

As those words came out of his mouth, I found myself throwing my fist into his face. He was treating me like a hoe. Wasn't I the same bitch that he had just bought a Benz for? The same bitch he had been riding for since the first day he met me? The same bitch who he claimed to love on a daily basis? What the hell was going on? I was so confused. After I popped him in the face a few times, he turned me around and grabbed my arms across my chest. I couldn't get out of his grasp and I frustratingly began to cry hysterically.

"Let me go!" I shouted. "I hate you!"

"Calm down!" he shouted back.

"I cant.. believe you!" I said, between sobs. "You just like all the rest of these niggas!"

In an instant, I head butted him and he let me go. As soon as my arms were free, I turned around and slapped the shit out of him and jumped back.

"You need to calm yo ass down!" he snapped, forcing himself not to slap my ass back.

"No, you need to leave my house!" I demanded, pointing at the door.

He shook his head and checked his bottom lip to see if he was bleeding.

"I'm out!" he shouted, walking out of the door.

I quickly ran and locked the door behind him. I slid to the floor and buried my face in my arms and cried for about five minutes. When I finally had the strength to get up, I grabbed my phone and called Prii. It rung a few times too many until it was answered. She usually answered on the second ring.

"Hello?" I said, as the person on the other end just sat there.

"Prii?" I said, damn year yelling into the phone.

By this time I was sure that she hadn't noticed that the phone was answered. At first, all I could hear were muffled voices, but I couldn't quite make out what was being said, or who was saying them. Then I heard a bunch of movement as if the phone was being scuffled around.

"Hello.....?"! I shouted.

They still couldn't hear me. As I was about to just give up and hang up, I began to hear loud moans in the background.

"What the hell?" I thought.

These motherfuckers were having sex in my ear. I instantly hung up. I didn't know whether to be jealous or disgusted. Prii was over there having a wonderful valentines day with Lando, while I was at home having the worst day ever. You damn right I was jealous! I picked up the phone and dialed Janet's number. It had been a couple weeks since I had last spoken to her. Selfishly, I hoped that she wasn't out enjoying her valentines day with anyone because I really needed to talk.

"Janet Banks." she said, answering.

"Hey Ms. Janet." I replied. "Its Secret."

"Oh, hey Secret. Is everything okay?" she asked.

"No, not exactly." I said. "But if you're busy I can just call back later."

"No sweetie. You're fine. What's going on?" she asked, sounding so concerned.

I immediately began to cry. I was definitely an emotional wreck.

"Stephan and I just got into it." I cried. "I told him about the baby and he tripped out."

She had been known about the baby because I had told her about it during one of our previous sessions.

"Don't cry." she said. "Tell me what happened."

I explained to her how he went from reading the papers, to his whole little demeanor just changing.

"It caught me so off guard." I said, wiping my tears. "Especially after the great morning we were having before everything went down."

"Has he ever behaved like this before?" she asked.

I told her that he had never even cursed at me out of anger before, let alone treat me like some random bitch. It was like he crumpled up my feelings and tossed them in the trash.

"I haven't given him any reason to think that I would ever cheat on him. How could he question if this baby was his?"

"What lead him to say that?" she asked.

"He's mad because I waited so long to tell him." I said. "He feels as if I should have told him sooner."

The more I replayed his voice in my head, the more upset I got.

"Well, most men have this same problem." She said.

"Problem?" I asked. "I'm not following you."

"Just listen." she replied. "Most men are usually over the top ecstatic about becoming a father. Especially, a new one. But, it also comes along with a fear."

"A fear?" I asked.

"Yes. A fear." she said. "In most situations it'll feel more like he doesn't trust you or try to find ways to get out of not facing it because they're afraid."

"But he's knows me though." I cried. "He really reacted as if I was somebody else."

"They behave in different ways." she said. "I don't think its ever intentional to hurt your feelings, or make you feel low, or degrade you. Men just refuse to be hurt, so they try to flip the script just to make sure that his feelings, pride, and emotions aren't fiddled with."

"Sounds like you're giving them a reason to be disrespectful." I replied.

I wasn't really feeling where she was coming from.

"No no no. That's not what I'm saying. Its never okay to let a man disrespect you." she said. "What I'm saying is, most men make this same mistake when it comes to these situations. Bringing a baby into this world is a big thing for them. Believe it or not, its sometimes bigger for them than it is for us. Men lash out because it's a bit much for them to handle at first."

"And that's okay?" I asked.

"In my opinion, yes." she said. "Especially if you know you have a good man. If your man lashes out at the beginning, then nine times out of ten he's going to come to his senses later. What you don't want is, a man that's going to lash out later on down the road."

"Why is that?" I asked.

"Because, now you can determine if you're ready for this, rather than it be too late later."

"Ready for what?" I asked.

"Ready to continue to have this baby with or without him." she said.

I swallowed hard. I didn't want to be without Stephan. I really loved this man. It was my destiny to be with him. I understood that there was a possibility that he could just play me to the left and leave me to be a single mother, and I took it upon myself to accept that. I just hoped that that wasn't the case though.

"Ms. Janet I'm going to have this baby with or without him." I informed her confidently. "I won't force him to play his role in our child's life, but if Stephan is the man that I know he is, he'll step up and do what's right."

This was my baby. A life that was growing inside of me. How could I take away a life that was going to give me so much life?

"I'm glad to hear that." She said. "And I can tell from the way you speak of him in our sessions that he really loves you. I'm sure he'll do the right thing."

At that moment I felt as if I was going to be okay. I knew everything would be just fine. I didn't need a man to complete me. This baby was going to fill any void that I had ever had. Even though Stephan did snap out, I knew that wasn't the real him. I knew he loved me and that he would be back. I just hoped that it wouldn't be too long before he got his act right, because I wasn't going to wait forever. I understood that he was afraid, and I was willing to deal with that. Hell, I was scared my damn self, which was probably why it took me so long to even tell him about the baby. The hour and a half that Janet spent putting everything into perspective made me realize that I was ready for whatever was coming my way. I was ready to work on me and Stephan and see where things would lead to, but first we had to get passed this little situation that we'd had earlier. I thanked Janet for all of her help as we came to the closure of this over the phone session, and told her that I would see her in a few weeks to let her know how everything was going.

I hung up with her and dialed Stephan's number. Just as I suspected, he didn't pick up for me. I called a few more times after that, but he still didn't pick up. I thought to go hop in the car and drive over to his place, but I decided to leave him alone so that he could gather his thoughts together. As I was getting up off the couch to go get in the shower, there was a knock at my door. I had no idea as to who it could be.

"Who is it?" I yelled, looking at my reflection through one of the picture frames hanging on the wall. I knew I looked like an emotional wreck.

"It's me!" the voice yelled back. I still couldn't make out the voice.

I went over to look out the peephole and saw Dasani standing there.

"Damn it!" I whispered aloud to myself. I didn't really feel like being bothered by her, but it was too late for me to just shut up and act like I wasn't home.

"Hey D." I said, opening up the door and letting her in. "What's up?"

"Girl, its cold as hell outside!" she said, shivering. "What you got to eat up in here?"

I completely ignored her question.

"What the hell is all of this?" I asked, noticing she had a bunch of valentines day gifts in her arms.

"Well, this one is from me to you." she said, handing me a big ass red teddy bear that held a heart that read 'will you be mine?' on it.

"Awww, thank you D." I replied, hugging her. "You didn't have to do this."

"Girl please!" she said, pushing me off of her. "I'm probably the only one in the world without a valentine today. The least I could do was give out gifts."

I laughed. "Girl, you so crazy."

Sometimes I would forget that she was only eighteen.

"And who's is all of this?" I asked, referring to the box of chocolates, the roses, and the teddy bear that she was still holding.

"Oh, I believe this is yours to." she said, sitting it down on the living room table. "But it ain't from me though."

"Then who is it from?" I asked, confused.

"I don't know." she said. "It was just sitting in front of your door when I got here."

The gift tag on the teddy bear read 'anonymous.'

"Girl, I think you got yourself a little secret admirer." Dasani said.

"More like a stalker." I replied, knowing that the gifts had to be from Quam.

Even though I hadn't heard from him in months, this shit had his name written all over it. How dare he drop these gifts off in front of my doorstep that quick? What if Stephan would have been here? He would have really been accusing me of some shit. And worse, why was Quam lurking around my apartment? Shit was starting to get out of hand.

"So where's my boo at anyway?" Dasani asked, jokingly referring to Stephan. "It's valentines day. Ain't yall supposed to be together?"

She often liked to joke around and say that she was going to take Stephan from me because he was too much man for me to handle. To be honest, I didn't trust the little bitch as far as I could throw her. Karen used to say that there was always a little truth behind every joke. I didn't understand too much when I was younger, but as I got older, it made so much sense. I often liked to 'joke' back with her and tell her that she wouldn't live to tell it. So I dared her to try me. There was so much truth behind that joke, that I couldn't even call it a joke.

"Girl he had to go run some errands." I lied. There was no reason for her to know that we had got into it.

"On valentines day?" she asked. "Hmph. Men!"

"So you know Prii gone be mad if she don't get no gift from you." I chuckled, switching the subject.

She cracked up. "Trust me. I already know." she said. "I dropped hers off first."

We both laughed knowing how much of a brat Prii could be.

For the next couple of hours we just sat there chit chatting. Dasani had found some Tequila in the cabinet that Prii had left over my place one night. She had already been wasted when she got here that night so I hid the tequila in the cabinet and forgot to give it back to her ever since.

"You want a shot?" Dasani asked, not knowing that I was pregnant.

"Naw, I been laying off the liquor for a while." I replied, refusing to tell her about the baby. I really wasn't in the mood to talk about it since Stephan had tripped out on me.

"Come on!" she begged. "Its valentines day, our dates are nowhere to be found, and we're just sitting here. Let's get fucked up!"

She poured a shot and reached it over to me. "Here, take this." she said.

"Girl, I'm not taking that." I said, shooing her away. "I'm not even in a drinking mood."

"Fine then!" she whined. "More for me."

As I laid back watching her take shot after shot after shot, I thought it was hilarious seeing her transform from sober to drunk. I could tell after about her sixth shot that she was lit.

"Don't you think you done had enough?" I asked, as I watched her stagger around everywhere.

"Girl naw. I got this." she replied, pouring herself another shot. "If I was you, I'd be wanting to feel like me."

All I could do was laugh at her. She was definitely fucked up. Her young ass was handling that Jose' Cuervo though.

"Here Secret." she said, walking over to me with another shot she poured. "Pleeeeaaaassseee drink this."

"I said I didn't want none." I replied, pushing her back away from me.

"Bitch just drink it!" she slurred.

As the scent of tequila on her breath transferred to my nose, I immediately felt nauseous. I covered my mouth and darted for the toilet. The whole time that I was vomiting, I could hear Dasani talking shit.

"You need to learn how to hold your liquor!" she slurred to me. "Light weight!"

When I finished throwing up, I grabbed a towel to cover my nose with. I was preparing to go in and steal the bottle from her. She clearly didn't need anymore if she had forgotten that I was still sober.

"Prii should've came over with us." she said, as I walked back into the living room.

I ignored her and walked over to screw the top on the bottle and hide it.

"Naw, you don't need no more!" she yelled from the couch, assuming that I was getting ready to pour me a shot.

She didn't even care that I was ignoring her. She just kept on running her mouth. For some reason, Prii had happened to be her topic of discussion. I wanted her to just shut up and pass out, but she just kept talking about Prii this and Prii that. She was sounding as if she was obsessed with her. I laid on the love seat across from her and let her talk me to sleep. I hadn't even realized that I'd fallen asleep, when I was awakened by Stephan gently pulling the cover back from over my head.

I looked over at Dasani who was now passed out slightly snoring. As I sat up on the couch trying to wake myself all the way up, I couldn't believe Stephan was standing over me. I was so happy to see him. He grabbed my hand and walked me to the bedroom. I let his hand go, hopped in the bed, and snuggled up under the covers without saying two words to him. Even though I was happy to see him, I was still pissed at how he treated me. He needed to know that. He stripped down and cuddled up behind me. At first, he didn't say anything. He just held me. And after about a minute, he spoke.

"I fucked up bae." he said, finally. "I don't know what I was thinking."

"I didn't respond. I decided to let him talk. I wanted to see what he had to say for himself.

"You know I love you Secret, and that I would never do anything to hurt you." he continued.

"But you did!" I snapped.

"I know baby, I know." he replied. "I didn't mean it though. Its just been so much going on, and I didn't know how to deal with it all."

"Like what Stephan?" I asked, frustrated because I didn't want to hear any bullshit come out of his mouth.

He sighed and turned over lying flat on his back. I turned to look at him. I can tell that he had a lot on his mind.

"Talk to me." I said.

He took a deep breath.

"Well, for the past month my step dad has been in a coma." He said, sounding as if he didn't want to continue. "I had no idea that he was even sick, let alone suffering from brain cancer."

My heart fell into my stomach. I felt so bad because Stephan admired his step dad. He had helped Stephan and his mom out with so much. He was like their super hero or something. Stephan took to him as if he was his real father. I knew Stephan loved him with his whole heart. Mainly because of the love and care that Michael had for his mother. I had never even seen Stephan cry before, but it wasn't a surprise to me when I heard him began to choke up.

"My mom never once told me that he was sick." he continued. "Then one day she up and calls me to spring this coma shit on me. I never even seen it coming."

As he was speaking, I began to wonder how the hell he managed to keep all of this in the whole time. He never once mentioned to me that his step dad was sick. I guess it really wasn't any of my business. He had done a hell of a good job pretending as if everything was fine. I didn't suspect anything at all. Not talking about it was probably his way of not wanting to deal with it.

"Why didn't you tell me?" I asked. "I could have been there for you."

"I couldn't bring myself to talk about it and I didn't want you to have to worry about anything." he said.

"What do you mean?" I said, sitting up on the bed. "That's what I'm here for bae."

As he stared up at the ceiling trying not to drop any tears, I grabbed his face and stared him in his eyes to let him know that I was serious. He reached over, grabbed my waist, and laid his head in my lap.

"They pulled the plug on him today." he said, beginning to cry. "My mom called me this morning and told me."

For a second, I didn't even know what to say. All I could do was hold and comfort him.

"I am so sorry bae." I said, hugging and kissing him.

It hurt me to see my baby hurting. I began to tear up as I thought about Michael not being able to see our child be born. I knew that that was something Stephan would have really wanted. Stephan's mother was the only grandparent that our child was probably going to have. I hadn't heard from Karen since the day she left and it wasn't no telling what was probably going through her head. What was even worse was that his mom stayed about two hours away, which meant that it was going to be hard for her to see the baby as often as she wanted. It was already hard just for him to go visit her as it is with him having to work all the time, but he made it work. But now, that Michael was gone, I knew it was going to be even harder for him to leave his mom alone and come back. This was going to be so difficult for Stephan. I held and rocked him as he wept in my arms until he fell asleep. He had stuck by my side through a whole bunch of shit, and I was ready to do the same for him in return.

20

The day before my birthday, Stephan had confessed something else to me. He told me that another reason why he spazzed out on me about the baby was because he had been in a previous relationship with a girl who had lied to him about his daughter for three years. He said that early on that him and his ex-girlfriend didn't work out, but he was always there for his daughter and whatever she needed. I guess when his alleged daughter had gotten hurt one day and had to go to the hospital, they needed his blood but he wasn't a match. Now I could really understand where his whole assumptions of me telling him a little bit too late could have came in to play. But had I'd known that, I would have told him sooner. I was just happy that he had finally got it off his chest.

Stephan had suggested that I ride up to Winona with him to meet and spend some time with his mother. At first I was a little skeptical about it because it didn't seem like the right time to be meeting her, but he said that she had been dying to meet me. Stephan and I had been talking for a while now and not once had I even spoken to his mom on the phone. I can admit that I was a bit nervous. He had explained to me that his mom was one of the most sweetest people that you could ever want to meet. I believed him, it was just that the thing that didn't sit too right with me were the circumstances that we were meeting under. The whole ride up to Winona I just kept reminding myself not to say or do anything wrong. I just wanted everything to be an easy going visit.

"Bae, we here." Stephan said, slightly nudging me.

Somehow in the mist of all my thinking, I had fallen asleep. I slowly opened up my eyes, yawned, and sat up. I took a look around at my surroundings and noticed that we had pulled up to a big ass brown and white house with a few people on the porch. It kind of took me by surprise because I didn't expect for it to be a family gathering. I got out the car hesitantly and tried to shake off my nervousness. I had so many butterflies in my stomach that I began to feel them in my esophagus. Stephan walked around to me and held my hand. I guess he could tell that I was a little nervous.

"Just be cool bae." he said, as we began to walk up towards the house.

"Look who done finally made it!" shouted some man with a huge belly. "We all been waiting on you. Get over here and give your uncle some love boy."

"What's up unc?" Stephan said, hugging him, as the few other people kind of formed a line to get their hug from him.

Awkwardly, I just kind of stood there trying to keep a smile on my face because I could feel their eyes on me, dying for him to introduce me.

"I ain't know all yall was going to be here." Stephan said.

"Chile' please!" said some country lady. "You know yo mama always throwing some last minute shit."

I could tell she was from like down south or something by the way her clothes, nails, and hair was done up. It didn't bother me though. I actually thought it was cute.

"Uncle Steph! Uncle Steph!" Chanted some little girl, running out the screen door into Stephan's arms.

"Hey Coco!" he said, picking her up. "You getting big girl. How old are you now?"

She was the cutest little thing. Long curly hair with hazel green eyes.

"Five." she replied, holding up her hand to show him.

Then she looked over at me and waved shyly. As I smiled and waved back at her, she whispered something into Stephan's ear. He just chuckled and shook his head yeah.

"Everybody, this is Secret. The love of my life." he announced, grabbing my waist.

As soon as these words came out of his mouth, they were on me like vulchers. They were asking me all type of questions, telling me how pretty I was, hugging me and welcoming me into the family. After all of the outside meeting and greeting, Stephan had finally decided to go in the house.

"Where's granny?" he asked Coco, while she was still in his arms.

"In the kitchen." she responded.

Stephan grabbed my hand and we walked inside the house. There weren't too many more people on the inside. Just a couple more kids and a few adults. I was guessing that he probably didn't know them too well because he just spoke and kept on moving.

"Hey ma!" he said, as we walked into the kitchen.

To my surprise, she was a little petite lady sitting at the edge of a long table picking greens.

"Hey baby." she replied, as she stood up to hug and kiss him.

I recall a time when Stephan told me that his mom was about fifty years old. I was confused because this lady didn't look a day over thirty. She looked good for her age. And as for her height, she couldn't have been no taller than four and a half feet. I couldn't even imagine her pushing Stephan's big ass out. It was like Ripley's Believe It Or Not.

"And you must be Secret." she said, smiling and walking over to me. "I've heard so much about you."

"Likewise." I responded, as she reached in and hugged me. "Sorry to hear about your husband."

"Baby you don't have to be sorry." she said, holding my hands into hers and looking me straight in the eyes. "It's a part of life. By keeping him on that bed, I was only making him suffer. I had to learn to let go and let God so that my baby could be free."

As those words came out, I remembered Stephan telling me that his mom was all into the church thing. I took a second to reminisce on the times I used to go to church with Karen and Delilah. At the time I didn't care for church because I was still unsure of how I felt about God.

"My baby ain't suffering no more." She said with a big ole' smile on her face. "He was the greatest man I ever met."

A jealous Stephan cleared his throat in the background as we both snickered.

"You know you my number one baby." she said, kissing him on the cheek.

"Granny can I be your number one too?" Coco asked, cheesing.

"You are sweetie." she replied.

"Coco come on. Your daddy's outside." said some drunk woman, staggering into the kitchen.

"Why yall leaving so soon?" Stephan's mom asked.

"Ms. Stacy, I'm sorry but, my feet are killing me, I gotta work tomorrow, and Coco gotta get ready for school in the morning." the drunk woman replied.

She didn't even acknowledge the fact that Stephan and I were in the room.

Coco began to cry.

"I don't wanna go home yet. I wanna stay with my granny!"

"Come on Coco. I'm trying to be nice. Let's go!" the girl said, in a calmly manor.

"Well, its only 4 o'clock Chelle. I'm pretty sure big Coco wouldn't mind picking her up later." Ms. Stacy said.

"No, we're leaving. She can have a fit if she want to. This belt around my waist ain't finna play with her behind."

Coco just stood there as if she didn't hear the threat.

"Cor'Rielle Unique I do not have time for this. Go get your coat and boots." she slurred.

"Just let her…" Ms. Stacy started, but Stephan cut her off.

"Mom just let her go. You know how she get when she drinks."

"Nigga, what you mean how I get?" The drunk girl snapped. "You see I ain't said not one word to yo ass since you been here, but you just couldn't take it could you?"

"Please don't start!" Ms. Stacy yelled.

Woah, did I miss something? I thought. Come to think of it, it was a little awkward that they didn't speak. Obviously they had to know each other, seeing as though Coco was calling his mom granny.

"Naw ma, she always getting drunk acting a fool." Stephan snapped. "Take that bs to yo own mama crib."

"Fuck you Stephan!" she yelled, walking over and grabbing Coco's hand. "You ain't shit!"

Ms. Stacy just sat back down in her chair and continued picking greens. Me, not knowing what else to do, I sat down next to her and offered her my assistance. As we sat there picking greens, we listened as Stephan had followed her out the door to the front yelling back and forth.

"You need to go take some parenting classes witcha dead beat ass!" Stephan yelled. "My brother do everything for Cor'Rielle!"

I got up and went to go see if I could calm him down.

"He do shit for CJ to, but we all know he ain't the daddy!" he yelled again.

When I got to the screen door, Chelle was standing in the street hollering while her nigga and two kids just sat in the car.

"Fuck you, you bitch ass nigga!" she yelled. "You just mad cause you ain't my baby daddy!"

Stephan's uncle and one of his cousins were down there trying to get her in the car.

"Shut up bitch! You'll never taste this dick again! EVER!" Stephan yelled back. "You a hoe!"

"Baby calm down!" I shouted, grabbing his arm and pulling him back inside.

We went back in the kitchen with Ms. Stacy, who was now washing her greens off.

"Ma, I'm sorry for being disrespectful." Stephan said, after he had calmed down. "I don't know why you continue to let that demon in here."

His mom thought that to be hilarious and cracked up.

"Son, you are a mess." she said. "Roechelle is not a demon. She's just a little off."

"Ma, I'm telling you she's the devil's advocate." he laughed. "She's more than a little off."

Ms. Stacy just smiled and shook her head.

"Courtney couldn't even come in and say hi because he's so embarrassed by her."

It took me a minute to catch on, but I began to put two and two together. Realizing that Ms. Stacy had referred to the drunk bitch as Roechelle and Stephan referring to his brother as Courtney, I could have choked on my spit. I began to feel sick to my stomach. I mean, I knew Courtney couldn't have been his real brother because Stephan had just so happened to be an only child, but the fact that they were this close was throwing me for a loop. How dare the world be this small? I thought. What were the odds of Courtney and Stephan knowing each other? It couldn't have just been a coincidence. My heart raced as the thought of him actually coming in the house and seeing me crossed my mind. How awkward would that have been? I hadn't seen Courtney in years, since I left him for getting Roechelle pregnant. I began to wonder what Stephan would think of me if he found out about this situation. The room was spinning.

"Is everything okay in here?" said the big belly uncle that first greeted us outside.

"Yeah unc, we all good." Stephan replied.

"Boy I cant believe yall still go at it like that after all these years." his uncle continued.

"She's crazy Unc. Something is really wrong with her."

His uncle cracked up. "Yall gone get it together one day."

As they sat there cracking jokes and laughing, I just couldn't stop thinking about the fact that Stephan and Courtney knew each other. Could this really have just been a coincidence? I couldn't help but to think that somebody was playing some kind of trick on me. It could have been any other two men, but it wasn't. It just had to be these two in particular. My first love and the love of my life. This shit was really fucking with me. All I knew was that I needed to get the hell out of Winona, and fast before shit got real.

"Look Secret." Stephan said, showing me a picture. "This is Michael."

I looked down at the frail man on the photo. He looked extremely ill, but was smiling like nothing was even wrong. For a second, he looked as if I knew him, but I figured it was just a thought.

"He looks so happy." I replied. "I wish I had gotten a chance to meet him."

As I was handing him the picture back, they were handing me another one of him. This one must have been before he'd gotten sick because he looked way more put together. In an instant, my heart dropped. The man in the picture was definitely familiar to me. As a matter of fact, I knew exactly who he was. His nose piercing is what gave it away. Now I just knew somebody had to be fucking with me. The man in the photo was Uncle Mike. My dads old right hand man. I hadn't seen him since my eighth birthday. I could feel myself beginning to get sick to my stomach.

"Excuse me," I said, sitting the picture down and getting up from the table. "Where's your bathroom?"

"Down the hall to the left." said the uncle, as I darted for the toilet.

What the fuck?! I thought, as I leaned over the toilet. This shit was too much for me. First Stephan and Courtney, now uncle Mike was the mysteriously dead step dad? The world couldn't have possibly been this small. This shit couldn't have gotten any crazier… or so I thought.

Knock Knock…

Somebody was at the bathroom door.

"Just a minute." I replied, getting up to splash some cold water on my face.

"Bae, its me. Open up." They said.

I opened up the door and to my surprise, it wasn't Stephan on the other side. It was Courtney. I was in total shock as I stood there giving him the deer in headlights look. He came in and closed the door behind him.

"What the hell?" I thought as he then clicked the clock.

"What you doing?" I asked, completely freaked out.

"I miss you girl." he said. "I just wanna talk to you."

I was so confused because I could have sworn he'd left already.

"Do I even know you?" I asked, trying to play dumb. I knew it wouldn't work, but it was worth a try. I just wanted to get out that bathroom with him before Stephan came looking for me and caught us in there together.

"Secret please, don't play stupid with me right now. I'm not in the mood."

"Oh, you're trippin'." I said, as I tried to walk past him and out the door.

"Hoe, sit the fuck down!" he snapped, pushing me down onto the toilet. "Quit playing with me."

"What the hell is wrong with you Courtney?" I shouted, startled.

"Courtney, Courtney, Courtney…" he said, chuckling and shaking his head.

I looked up at him as if he had lost his mind.

"I miss the way you used to say my name girl." he said.

I rolled my eyes and just kept quiet as he continued.

"So, I see you fucking my brother now right?" he said. "Don't you hear how nasty that sounds?"

"Court, I had no…" I started, as he slapped the spit out of my mouth.

"Shut the fuck up!" he snapped. "I didn't ask you to speak."

I was confused be cause he did ask me a question. I guess it was rhetorical. I just sat there crying, holding the side of my face. Courtney had never put his hands on me before. I couldn't believe this was happening to me. Why hadn't Stephan came to check on me yet? I'm guessing that they had gotten the party started because the music had been cranked up.

"Oh, so you must have thought this nigga was better than me or something." he said. "I mean, I wasn't good enough for you or something?"

This nigga had really lost his damn mind. I was too scared to say anything because I didn't want him to hit me again. All I could think about was him harming my baby.

"You were supposed to be mines forever." he said.

I wanted so badly to tell him that he was the one who had played me. He played me for the drunk ass bitch that he's with now.

"You know I never wanted to be with Roe." he said. "You were always my queen."

He stepped back and chuckled.

"Wait… don't tell me you love this man." he said, looking at me deranged like. "Do you love him Secret? And don't lie to me."

I was so scared to speak, but I knew either way I would piss him off.

I closed my eyes and shook my head yes. If he was going to hit me again I didn't want to see it coming. He didn't though. He just chuckled again.

"So you see what has to happen now right?" he asked, smiling.

He was scaring the shit out of me.

"Please don't do anything crazy." I cried.

"You're fucking MY brother, and you think you have the right to sit up in my face and cry about it?" he asked, as he pulled out a pistol and sat it on the sink. "You love him more than you loved me?"

I couldn't take my eyes off of the gun. I just knew that I was going to die at this point. There was no way that I was getting out of this one.

"ANSWER ME BITCH!" he demanded, as I damn near jumped out of my body.

"Steph, I mean Courtney I..." I had fucked up. I was so scared that I had accidentally called him the wrong damn name.

"Hold up." he said, cutting me off, picking up the gun, and scratching his head. "What did you just call me?"

I stood up off the toilet because I knew he was going to try some crazy shit. How the hell did I manage to let myself call his crazy ass Stephan? Even though I was on my feet, all I could do was back up against the wall. He walked up on me and traced the gun down the side of my face.

"Bitch, I would fucking shoot you where you stand." he informed me, whispering in my ear.

"I'm so sorry." I cried.

He put his other hand around my throat as I closed my eyes.

"Shut up." he said.

As my eyes were closed, I prayed that God would send Stephan to run to my rescue. I cried hysterically as I thought of how fucked up this situation was. I stood there feeling so helpless. I had no idea that Courtney was this crazy. Who would have thought that whenever we ran into each other again that it would be under these circumstances? It was always one thing after another.

"Courtney, please!" I begged. "You don't have to do this."

"You really thought you'd get away with this shit?" he chuckled. "You must think I'm stupid huh?"

I just kept my eyes closed because I couldn't bring myself to look at him. He was really trippin' hard. I began to wonder if Roechelle had driven him crazy over the years. He probably blamed me for all the bullshit that he'd been through since I left. This Courtney was definitely nothing like the old Courtney I knew. He was so washed up and bummy like, which indicated to me that he had fallen off, and bad.

"What are you doing?" I cried as he began to rub his hand around my belly.

"This my brothers baby right?" he asked, going down to kiss and rub my stomach.

I didn't even bother to answer him. How could he even tell that I was even pregnant? I wasn't even all that big. Stephan must have told them about the baby.

"I said is this my brothers baby?" he shouted.

Scared to death, I shook my head yes with tears still rolling down my face. All I could think about was why hadn't anybody came to check on me, or even had to use the bathroom for that matter. It felt as if we were in the bathroom forever.

"No." he said, standing up. "This cant be right."

He began to pace back and forth, whispering to himself. I began to feel as if I was dealing with a schizophrenic. I had no idea as to what the hell he was talking to himself about, but I sure as hell wasn't trying to stick around to find out. As he stopped and faced the wall, continuing to talk to the little friends in his head, I decided to risk my life and make a run for it. As I darted for the door, I just wasn't quick enough.

"Bitch where you think you going?" he asked, grabbing me by my hair and slamming my head into the door. "You thought you was gone get away from me bitch?"

He tossed me to the floor and began to kick and stomp on me. I cried and tried my hardest to fight him back. He was just so big. I balled up into a fetal position as his size 13 foot came landing down on my body over and over again. My whole body ached as my stomach filled with agonizing pain.

"Help!" I cried, but I knew no one could hear me.

Courtney had finally got done kicking and pounding on me and walked out of the bathroom. I laid there in the middle of the bathroom floor bleeding, weak, and feeling sorry for myself. Nobody had came to my rescue. I was almost sure that I was having a miscarriage, how bad my stomach was hurting. I couldn't move. All I could do was cry. I just knew I was going to die from all the blood that I was losing. I just laid there and never wanted to get up. Once again, I felt like my life was over. My voice was so quiet as I called out for Stephan to come. Even though I knew he couldn't hear me, for some reason I just wanted to keep saying it over and over and over. I could feel myself slipping away slowly but surly.

"Baby!" Stephan shouted, shaking me. "Baby get up!"

For what seemed like seconds later, I had awakened at home, in my bed. Only to realize that I had just had a nightmare.

21

"Damn, this bitch is nice!" Prii said, getting into my car. "What the hell did you do to earn one of these?"

I laughed cause Prii had all the jokes.

"Girl you know my head game ain't one to be fucked with." I replied sarcastically.

"Well imma need some lessons." she said as we both cracked up. "So where we going first birthday girl?" she asked.

"I don't know." I said. "I guess we can go do some simple shit."

Hell, I was pregnant. There wasn't too much shit I could do.

"Simple shit?" she snapped. "Simple shit like what?"

"Hair, nails, spa. You know... The works!" I replied.

"Oh, that's your idea of simple?" she laughed, looking up at my nappy ponytail. "Well, ill go with you but I don't know if ill get anything done."

Pulling off, I realized that I wouldn't be spending my birthday with Stephan. He went up to spend some time with his mom and help her out with the funeral arrangements. I still couldn't believe the nightmare that I had had two nights before. That shit was crazy. When Stephan had woken me up out of my sleep, he was so concerned because he heard me saying his name over and over. I told him about what I had dreamed about and he thought it sounded crazy. He just held me in his arms until I was able to fall back to sleep. I believe that this was the reason for him not inviting me up to Winona with him. Even though, I really didn't want to go, I still felt some type of way about not going with him. I guess it just wasn't the right time to be trying to get all acquainted with his mother. And who knows, she might not have been so friendly as he lady in my dream. I quickly put the trip out of my mind. I was just ready to enjoy my birthday. 23 years young and I wasn't trying to be stressing about nothing. I couldn't drink, smoke, or be under the influence of any kind, so relaxation was all I had on my agenda.

We ended up picking Dasani up because she was blowing the back off of Prii's phone. The first few times Prii just let it go to voicemail because she said she really didn't feel like being bothered by her. I had gotten a weird kind of vibe about it, but Dasani did have a tendency to get on your nerves. Then Dasani began to call my phone, in which I decided not to answer either. I felt kind of bad because Dasani was our girl. She was just too much at times. Maybe because she was younger.

"This girl finna be calling all day." Prii said, as Dasani was calling her cell again.

"Does she always do this to you?" I asked confused. Dasani had never blew my phone up like this before. I guess because it was my birthday, she just had to be with us.

"Girl yes!" Prii replied. "Until I answer the damn phone."

I laughed, thinking that Dasani was obsessed.

"Just answer it." I said.

"Girl you know the first thing she gone say is come get her." Prii said. "I'm just saying, you being the birthday girl and all, its up to you."

"I don't care if she comes." I said. "She's cool."

Prii shrugged her shoulders and answered the phone.

"Hello?" she said, pushing the speaker button.

"Damn, why you avoiding me?" Dasani yelled into the phone. "I been blowing you up."

"Yeah, I know. Me and Secret went to breakfast and left our phones in the car." Prii lied.

"Yeah right. Let me talk to her." Dasani said.

"She right here. You're on speaker." Prii said.

"Happy birthday bitch!!!" Dasani shouted. "What are yall doing? Come get me!"

Prii and I glanced at each other and slightly laughed.

"Where you at?" I asked.

We went over to pick her up and went over to Ms. Suga's Hair and Nail salon. Ms. Suga was always hooking me up. Her shop was the best on the north side. When we pulled up, I seen Princess's little pink convertible sitting in the parking lot. I knew it was hers because the license plate read '2PRETTY' on it.

"So much for a stress free day." Prii said, noticing the car to. "This should be interesting."

"That hoe ain't finna stress me out on my birthday." I replied, getting out of the car.

"I been waiting to smack her ass." Dasani said. "I cant stand that bitch."

"The bitch been having it out for me ever since I started fucking with Lando." Prii said. "I think she's jealous."

"You know that's Lando's little runner up." I said, as we laughed, walking into the shop.

"Hey Ms. Suga!" Prii yelled to the back of the salon.

"Hey yall!" Ms. Suga yelled back waving as she was in the middle of bumping some girls hair. "Ill be up there in a minute."

"Oh wow!" We heard a voice say as we sat down. I turned to see Missy and Princess sitting up under the dryers.

"Look what the cat dragged in." Missy continued, staring us down.

"Naw bitch, ain't no cat drag us up in here, but ill be happy to drag yo ass out." Prii snapped back.

"Try me bitch!" Missy said, jumping from up under her dryer.

"No bitch you try it!" Dasani said, jumping to Prii's defense.

"No yall not! Not up in here yall ain't!" said one of the other employees who was sewing in another girls tracks. "Ms. Suga ain't finna have that."

Missy rolled her eyes and sat back down, continuing to whisper the rest of her little smart remarks to Princess. Princess always had Missy fighting her battles. Especially since Michelle no longer worked at Exotic Rain. I guess Michelle just couldn't take anymore of Princess's shit and found out that Princess was fucking her husband so she quit instead of sticking up to her. All princess had now was Messy Missy. So dumb and blind to the fact that Princess was only using her.

"Ain't nobody worried about these hoes." Prii said.

"They always got some shit to say." I added. "Miserable ass bitches."

"Hoes?" Princess asked chuckling. "That's not what Lando was calling me."

"Uh oh…" said an older back lady who sat in between us being nosy, instigating with her eyes as she looked back and forth at us.

"Bitch please!" Prii snapped. "My man don't want you."

"Oh really?" Princess replied, looking over at Missy as if both of them knew something that we didn't.

Prii folded her arms and waited for Princess to continue.

"I think you better double check with him about that." Princess said.

"Girl, shut the fuck up." I said, annoyed. "You just mad."

We hadn't been in the shop for fifteen minutes and these hoes were already giving me a headache.

"Mad?" Princess asked. "No baby. I'm not mad. But your girl should be."

"Bitch ill spit on you." Prii snapped.

"I swear if we wasn't up in this shop right now." Missy said.

"You swear what bitch?" Dasani asked. "What you gone do?"

It began to get loud again and the lady who was sewing in the girls hair cleared her throat and cut her eyes at us.

"Don't start." she said warning us, as we all calmed down again.

I felt like we were some little ass kids. If I wasn't pregnant I would have been dragged a bitch up out of this hair salon. I had no idea as to what was taking Prii and Dasani so long. I wanted them to get the shit over with. Princess and Missy were getting away with doing too much talking. They had never been this tough before. It was quite surprising to me. Missy had jumped out of her body a few times, but she's young. I expected it from her. Prii got up and walked to the bathroom and I cringed as she walked passed Missy's dryer. I envisioned her knocking her ass out from up under her dryer. Surprisingly, she didn't. She just simply walked right past her to the bathroom. I looked over at Dasani who was mugging both of them like she was ready to jump over and tear both of their limbs off.

"Secret, come on baby girl!" Ms. Suga yelled over to me.

I got up and walked all the way to the back of the shop to her chair. I told her plenty of times that she needed to move her chair up to the front because it was hot as hell in the back. And plus, it was where all the drama took place. You couldn't hear shit back here. As nosy as Ms. Suga was, I'm surprised she didn't have front row seats. That's why her next words weren't at all a surprise to me, as I sat down in her chair.

"Girl, so what's going on with Prii and Princess?" she asked, starting on my hair.

"Girl, let me tell you…" I replied, getting ready to gossip.

Then I noticed Prii coming out of the bathroom and got side tracked. I could tell she was up to something. She had that slick little look on her face. I watched as she sat down and whispered something to Dasani.

"So is you gone tell me or what?" Ms. Suga asked, snapping.

"My bad girl." I said, continuing to tell her everything.

So for the next thirty minutes, I sat there burning the hell up, as she stood behind me doing my hair.

"Girl, you look like a brand new bitch." Ms. Suga said, handing me the mirror.

"Thank you Ms. Suga." I replied, admiring my hair in the mirror as I swayed it from side to side. "Girl this is perfect."

"You welcome boo." she said, snatching her mirror. "Now, gimmie my money."

"Thirty right?" I asked.

She laughed. "Girl, its yo birthday. You know you my baby. Gone and get outta here."

"You sure?" I asked.

"Yeah girl, gone head before I change my mind." she replied.

I hopped out the chair, hugged and thanked her.

"Yeah yeah," she said, hugging me back. "You better go see what's up with your homegirl. I think something's up."

I walked back up to the front and noticed Lando standing next to Prii.

"Why you up here on that bullshit Princess?" Lando asked.

"Bullshit?" Princess snapped. "Well was it bullshit when you was fucking me Lando?"

Everybody in the front of the shop turned to look at Lando as we awaited his response. Even ole' girl who was doing the sew-in. She wasn't even telling anybody to be quiet anymore. Unfortunately, he just chuckled at her and grabbed Prii's arm.

"Let's get the fuck up outta here man." he said, proceeding to walk out the door.

"Hell naw!" Prii snapped, snatching away from him. "You ain't gone answer this bitch?"

Lando snapped back. "You called me up here for this bullshit, embarrassing me in front of these old ass ladies. I ain't got time for this shit. I'm out!"

He threw his hands up and stormed out of the shop, leaving Prii looking dumbfounded. Even though I knew Prii was only trying to prove a point to Princess, she did go about it the wrong way. She knew Lando was private. He couldn't have been fucking that nasty bitch Princess. He wasn't for none of this kind of bullshit. He had a rep to maintain.

"Well, did that answer your question?" Princess asked, smirking. "Bitch I always get the last laugh."

Before I could even blink, Prii had ran up and knocked Princess to the ground. It happened so fast that I don't even think Princess seen it coming. She laid there curled up as Prii kicked and punched her, until Buck the big black security guard came and snatched Prii up.

"Move around with that shit!" Buck yelled, tossing Prii outside.

Prii stood outside yelling and screaming, daring Princess to come out. I started to go out there after her, but it was still a bunch of commotion going on in the shop. Dasani and Missy were toe to toe in each others faces going at it. Bitch this and bitch that, followed by a bunch of other bullshit that I wasn't trying to hear.

"Fuck that shit. Let's go D." I said, grabbing her.

As the two of them continued to argue, I managed to drag Dasani out of the shop. I looked around and Prii was nowhere in sight. I figured that she'd be in the car, but she wasn't.

"Where the hell could she have gone that fast?" I asked.

We sat there for about ten extra minutes just incase she popped back up, but she didn't. Dasani wouldn't stop running her mouth about Missy and it was beginning to annoy me. I couldn't wait to drop her ass off. She just wouldn't shut the hell up.

"Uh un! Why you bring me here?" Dasani asked, as I pulled up in front of her crib.

"Girl I'm finna go home and lay down." I lied.

I really planned on finding Prii, but she didn't need to know that because she was getting on my nerves. I just wanted her to get out of my car.

"You're such a party pooper." she said getting out.

I just chuckled and shook my head.

"Bye D. Ill call you later." I said, pulling off on her ass. Sometimes she was just entirely too much.

I grabbed my cell and dialed Prii's number, but it kept going straight to voicemail. I started to get a little worried, so I called Lando's phone to see if he had heard from her, but his shit was going straight to voicemail to. In a way I was comfortable with that because it made me feel like they were together. I decided not to worry about it and went home. I knew she'd probably call me later on and tell me everything.

When I got to my apartment, I could hear Stephan's voice on the other side of the door, but I couldn't make out who he was talking to. What the hell was he doing back from Winona so early? I thought. I didn't care though. I was just glad to know that he was in there. I figured that it might have been Prii inside telling him about what happened. Little did she know, that she was about to leave because I wanted some birthday sex. Hot, sweaty, and nasty birthday sex. I needed it after the crazy ass day that I had just had. I started to put my key in the door, but Stephan beat me to it.

"Hey baby." he said, kissing me. "Somebody's here to see you."

"Who?" I asked, walking in.

"Hey Secret." the voice said, even before I could turn to see him sitting on the couch.

"Quam?" I said, as my heart fell to my toes. All I could do was frown. "Wha.. What are you doing here?"

What the hell is going on? I thought. Could I have been dreaming again or what? I was totally stuck.

"I know you didn't think that I forgot about your birthday." he said, walking over to hug me. "Happy birthday girl."

As bad as I wanted it to be a nightmare, it was far from it.

I smiled forcefully. I was dealing with a complete psychopath. Why had Stephan even let this stranger into my place?

"Aren't you happy to see me?" Quam asked. "I haven't seen you since we were kids."

"Kids?" I asked confusedly.

"Yeah bae, he told me about all the crazy shit yall used to do when yall was shorties." Stephan said, laughing.

Obviously he had no idea as to who the hell Quam really was. How dare Stephan let this bitch into my apartment? He let him come in and fill his head up with a bunch of bullshit like we were some type of long lost best friends or something. I officially had regretted having sex with Quam. He was being too unpredictable. It was scary because I had no idea what was going on in his mind. If he wanted to play, then that was exactly what I was going to do. I couldn't tell Stephan just yet who the hell he was because I didn't want him to flip on me. Even though it happened a long time ago, in Vegas, before I even met Stephan, I knew he wasn't going to take it so lightly.

"Yeah, its been a while." I responded. "Seems like just months ago I seen you."

I was referring to the crazy incident we'd had at Cashmere's. He chuckled because he knew exactly what I was talking about.

"Its just so like you to pop up unannounced." I said sarcastically, hoping it would piss him off.

"I tried calling a few times before, but it wasn't working out, so I decided that I'd just surprise you." he replied winking at me.

I instantly knew that he had to be the one calling and breathing in my ear. I wanted him gone. He needed to leave. He was doing absolutely too much. Sending numerous letters, playing on my phone, showing up to my place? I couldn't help but to think that I was going to have to really get serious with this man.

I pulled my cell phone out, which was vibrating in my pocket. To my surprise it was Nyprii. I excused myself from the living room, informing them that I had to take the call.

"Bitch, before you say anything about them hoes at the shop, guess who's in my house right now." I whispered into the phone as I went into the bathroom closing the door behind me.

"Girl who?" she asked anxiously.

"Girl Mr. Jamaica is in my living room right now as we speak." I said.

"Get the fuck outta here!" she shouted. "Why is he over there?"

"I don't know. He was here when I got here!" I whispered into the phone loudly.

"Are you serious?" she replied.

I went into detail about how he had been sitting here telling Stephan all these different lies about our history together. Prii began to freak out because she just couldn't believe that he was really that crazy. Then I told her about the crazy phone calls I had been getting before this surprise visit.

"What the hell is his problem?" Prii snapped. "Do you need me to come over there?"

"Naw, I got this." I replied, silently laughing. Prii was so damn hot headed. "Ill call you whenever he leaves."

"Bitch is you sure?" she asked. "You know I got this trigger that I been itching to pull."

I cracked up. Prii had had some gun sitting up in her closet catching dust. I always forgot about her having that ole' dusty thing.

"Bye girl." I said, laughing as I hung up.

I walked back in the living room where I found Stephan and Quam sitting across from each other having a grand ole' conversation. What the hell? I thought. Why was Quam doing this to me? I couldn't help but to think that there were plenty of other girls for him to mess with. Girls were probably throwing the pussy at him left and right. After all, he was very attractive. What was so special about me that he just had to be with me? My first instinct was to figure out how to piss him off so that he would leave. I walked over and sat on Stephan's lap.

"Sorry, I had to take that call." I said.

"That's fine." Quam said, getting a little uncomfortable as he observed me on Stephan's lap.

"So, what was all the chit chat about?" I asked, wrapping my arm around Stephan's neck.

"We was talking about you bae." Stephan said, wrapping his arms around my waist.

I watched as Quam squirmed in his seat, steadily getting uncomfortable the more Stephan and I touched each other.

"Yeah, I told him about how all the boys wanted you when we were younger, but I wouldn't let them get too close." Quam said, giving Stephan some dap.

As bad as I wanted to slap his hand away, I just sat there and kept my composure. Quam wanted to see me crack, but I wouldn't dare give him the satisfaction. I'm pretty sure he was loving every minute of being in my house and sitting on my couch.

"You plan on staying for dinner? Me and my love would love to have you." I lied, just trying to figure out how long he planned on being here.

He took a minute to answer me. I guess he was just stuck on the fact that I was really all over Stephan in front of him.

"Well, actually…" he said, standing up and looking at his watch. "I have somewhere to be."

That was like music to my ears. I couldn't wait for him to leave.

"Aye man, it was nice meeting you." Quam said, shaking Stephan's hand.

"Yeah, same here." Stephan replied.

I dreaded getting up to walk him out. I knew me being all over Stephan would make him feel some type of way. He was pissed!

"So this how you do me?" Quam asked as we stepped out the door.

"Why are you even at my house?" I snapped, trying to keep my voice down so Stephan wouldn't hear us. "You're crazy. I told you that I didn't want you. Why are you doing this?"

"But you're supposed to be with me." he said, trying to grab my hand in his.

"Don't fuckin' touch me!" I said, slapping his hand away. "What is it going to take for you to understand the words that are coming out of my mouth?"

He reached in his pocket and pulled out the same little wrinkled up paper that he had pulled out at the restaurant. I started too smack it to the floor, but instead, I grabbed it and ripped it up. I was so annoyed. I could tell that I had struck a nerve as I looked up at him. He looked so sorry.

"I love you Secret." he said, like nothing I was saying meant anything to him. Like he wasn't comprehending.

"Quam, I don't love you though." I replied. "And this is the last time that I'm going to tell you. If you come back to my house, I'm going to call the police."

I stepped back inside and looked through the peephole until he walked away. Looking like a sad puppy, he walked away with his head down. I almost felt kind of sad for him. Relieved that he was gone, I took a deep breath and walked to my bedroom where Stephan was. I figured that his jealous ass was waiting for me to come in there so that he could question me about Quam. To my surprise, he was standing there butt ass naked.

"Took you long enough." he said, standing with his dick swinging. "You ready for daddy?"

I licked my lips, walking over to him and pushing him down on the bed.

"What you think?" I asked, seductively stepping out of my clothes.

He sat back, propping himself up on his elbows and watched me as I undressed. I got down to my bra and panties and decided to turn some music on. It had been awhile since I had given him a little strip tease.

"Oh, you gone dance for daddy huh?" he asked as I stood at the foot of the bed, beginning to wind my hips.

I bit down on my bottom lip and climbed on top of the bed, standing over him. As I continued to twirl and wind my hips, Stephan just stared up at me smiling. I took my bra off slowly and tossed it to the floor.

"Damn bae." he said, chuckling.

"What?" I asked, still dancing, coming out of my panties.

"You even sexy with a pudge on you." he said, laughing.

"Fuck you!" I said, laughing and balling up my panties to throw them at him in his face. "No more for you."

I hopped down off of the bed and went to go turn the radio off. He had thrown me way off. How dare he notice my little baby bump? I was only about 3 months. I was already a little self-conscious about this whole gaining weight thing. I wasn't ready for it to be noticed. I mean, I noticed it, but I figured that it was because it was my body. I guess I was wrong.

"Bae come here. I didn't say you were fat." he said, laughing and getting up to follow me to turn the music back on.

"Whatever!" I said, rolling my eyes at him.

"Awww, you're still cute." he said, kissing my neck from the back and rubbing my belly.

He turned me around and picked me up, leaning me against the wall.

"Oh, you mad now?" he said, continuing to kiss on my neck and breast, as I pretended to pout.

"Am I heavy enough for you?" I replied sarcastically.

"Oh shut up." he said, carrying me over to the bed and laying me down. He made up for calling me fat. Yes indeed he did…

The next day, I got up and went over to Prii's house to see what was up with her and Lando, and also to fill her in on Mr. Jamaica's crazy ass. When I got to her apartment building, I called her phone to let her know that I was outside, but it went straight to voicemail. It was so like her to not have her phone charged. I parked and went up to the door. After a few buzzers, she still didn't answer, so I rang her neighbors buzzer to let me in. I walked up the stairs to her door, and let myself in with the spare key. I now knew that she was home because I could hear the music coming from her bedroom in the back.

"Hello?" I said, pulling off my wet boots by the door. I couldn't help but to notice that Dasani's boots were right next to mine.

"Uh un… I know these bitches hear me." I said aloud to myself as I tip toed to the back room.

"Hello!" I screamed, bursting into the room, stopping in my tracks.

"Oh my God!" Prii yelled, as Dasani jumped up from having her face in between Prii's legs.

"Woah…" I said, not knowing what else to say.

I just stood there and watched them scramble to get their naked bodies underneath the sheets. The shit couldn't have been more awkward.

"Looks like I'm interrupting something so…. I'm just gonna go." I said, walking out the room.

"Secret, wait!" Prii yelled, quickly following up behind me with a robe on. "Its not what you think."

"Girl, I don't even know what to think right now." I replied, continuing to put on my boots.

"We wanted to tell you." Dasani said as we unnoticeably realized that she had followed us out the room.

"Oh, so this is serious?" I asked, chuckling and shaking my head.

"Look, just call me later okay." Prii said, ready for me to leave.

"No, you call me when you're done babysitting." I replied, and proceeded out the door.

"Yeah, my cousin was right about you." Dasani said as I stepped out the door.

I couldn't help but to rewind and step back inside.

"Excuse me?" I asked confusedly. "Who the hell is your cousin?"

I looked over at Prii and she looked just as confused as I did. Dasani just chuckled as if shit were a joke.

"You know what? I don't even care." I said before she could even answer. "I'm just finna go."

I sat in my car for a minute because I just knew Prii was going to kick her ass out after that little remark. I didn't want to be mad at the fact that they were fucking around, but I was. Not only was Dasani young as fuck, but Prii was cheating on Lando with this little bitch. He was like a brother to me and he did everything for Prii. I just didn't understand it. I just hoped Prii knew what she was doing with that little sneaky bitch. Realizing that she wasn't kicking her out, I pulled off and drove back home.

About forty-five minutes after I had been home, Prii came banging on my door. I would have thought she was the police the way she was banging, but she was yelling for me to open up. I sat there for a second just listening, contemplating on if I should get up and open the door or play like I was asleep. Chuckling at the thought of playing sleep on her, I got up and opened the door.

"Okay, before you say anything, just listen." she said.

"Listen?" I asked. "Listen to what? You're a grown ass woman Prii. You don't owe me any explanations."

"Well, fine then." she said. "You might not wanna hear about me and Dasani, but I do have some shit that you do want to hear about."

"And what might that be?" I asked, rolling my eyes and sitting down, wondering what the hell she was about to tell me.

"Okay," she said, sitting down next to me. "Remember crazy Keisha from the club?"

I shook my head yeah. "What about her?"

"Girl, that's Dasani's cousin. That's who she was talking about when she said the smart shit to you."

"And where is this going Prii? You know I don't care about bitches gossiping about me." I said.

"Bitch, Dasani told me that Keisha was the one who attacked you and put you in the hospital."

I couldn't help but to be misconstrued.

"Keisha?" I screeched. "How does she know?"

Prii shrugged her shoulders. "Something about you snitching and getting her fired."

"How the hell did I get that bitch fired?" I shouted. "I didn't snitch on her."

"Girl, I have no idea. That's why I rushed over here to figure out what was up."

I sat there gathering my thoughts, trying to think back to the day that Lando fired Keisha. What could have given Keisha the slightest reason for her to think that I was the one who snitched on her? I thought. Nothing was coming to mind. I was so mad that I just wanted to hop in the car and go fuck her up, but I couldn't. This baby was the only thing saving her at this moment.

"Call Dasani." I said. It was obvious that Prii didn't know the whole story, so I needed Dasani to get over here and tell me everything face to face.

"She's not answering." Prii replied, after calling several times.

I was so mad. After all this time, I had gotten over that whole situation. I no longer had cared what had happened to me that night. I could have just went to my grave not knowing a damn thing. But Karen used to say, 'what's done in the dark, will always come to the light.' Shit was about to get real bright.

"Oh, remember? The same night you went to the hospital is the same night you had got into it with Peanut, and she said something about you being a snitch?" Prii said, jumping up.

I instantly remembered. I also remembered not knowing what the hell Peanut was talking about that night at the club neither. They were all just a bunch of bitches running off what the next bitch had said. That must have been the word around the club that night.

"Damn, so what you wanna do?" Prii asked.

I looked down at my belly, then back up at Prii and shook my head.

"It ain't too much I can do at this point." I replied.

Prii was furious!

"So we just gone let this bitch walk?" she snapped. "I cant deal!"

No matter how much bullshit Prii and I went through, we were sisters . She was down to ride for me just as much as I was down to ride for her.

"Hell naw I ain't letting her walk." I said. "She just better be in hiding after I have my baby. I'm going after that bitch."

We started laughing and slapped fives.

"Okay I was finna say, do I really gotta go handle shit by myself? Cause you know I will." Prii said laughing. "And by the way, you getting a little big girl. You only 3 months. What you been eating?"

I tried not to laugh, but I couldn't help it. Prii was such an asshole.

22

"Keisha, she knows." Dasani said, sitting on the phone with her cousin on speaker.

"What are you talking about now Dasani?" Keisha asked, sounding fed up with her.

It had been about two months since I found out about Keisha's crazy ass being behind the reason that I was in the hospital. I was about five and a half months pregnant and big as ever. I couldn't believe how big I was for five months.

A few days ago Stephan and I had just gotten back from a doctors appointment and were in the middle of a playful disagreement. He was a little upset because I told the doctor that we didn't want to know the sex of our baby. I had said that from the day that I found out and I planned on sticking to it. While we were in the middle of our little dispute, we had gotten a knock at the door.

"Who is it?" I yelled, wobbling to the door.

It had just so happened to be Dasani, all beat up and bruised, looking for Prii. Prii was down at Na'Priice's new daycare, for family day. There was no way she was just going to up and leave from with her son. I told Dasani she could stay at my house til Prii got done doing what she was doing. Part of me wanted to throw the little bitch right back out my front door, but I was too nosy for that. I wobbled my big ass into the kitchen to get her some ice for her eye. Stephan excused himself out of the living room as I sat down with her on the couch. All I had to do was ask what happened and she immediately began crying and pouring her heart out. She started from the beginning and told me everything. She said that Keisha put her on to Exotic Rain so that she could make a few dollars to help with school, later on to find out that it was just to keep tabs on me and be all up in my business. Dasani said she only agreed to it because she knew how crazy her cousin was and what she could do to her.

"Nobody was ever supposed to get hurt." She said. "It was all supposed to be fun and games. All she would wanna know was what we did and what we talked about every day. It sounds crazy, but that's just what Keisha is. She's crazy. After a while I think she became obsessed with you, which I think only pissed her off even more. That's when she broke into your apartment. I promise I had no idea that she was going to do that."

"So, who told this crazy bitch that I snitched on her?" I asked, really wanting to know. I wanted to know who had sent Keisha off.

"Nobody." Dasani replied. "She said she saw you on the phone with Lando right after the fight with her and Princess."

I just shook my head and laughed. Keisha and I had been pretty cool in the club. We had never even bumped heads before, so I don't know why she would even think that I would snitch on her. She accused me of snitching on her because she saw me on the phone questioning Lando of his whereabouts. I wish she would have just approached me then… when I wasn't pregnant. I was so mad that I could have slapped the taste out of Dasani's mouth, but somebody had already beat me to it. I just couldn't believe this shit.

"I took yo ass in and you betrayed me D." I replied, looking at her in disgust.

"I know…" she sobbed, burying her face into her hands. "But if it means anything, I cut Keisha off after I got to know you and Prii."

"If it means anything?" I snapped. "Bitch, she almost killed me. I don't give a fuck about you cutting her off. Fuck both of yall!"

I can tell by the look on Dasani's face that she was hurt by my words. I didn't care. The young little sneaky bitch got what she deserved and I didn't feel the least bit sorry for her.

"Damn bae, is everything cool in here? What's going on?" Stephan asked, peeking into the living room. I guess I had gotten a little loud since he felt the need to come check on us.

"Yeah, we good bae." I replied, as he went back into the bedroom.

"So who did this to you?" I asked, turning my attention back to Dasani.

"Keisha did this to me." she replied, still crying.

I chuckled. "Keisha?" I couldn't help but to feel some type of way. "For what?"

I mean, I knew the bitch was crazy, but damn. She really had done a number on Dasani's face. How could she do this to her little cousin? Her blood?

"She got mad because I told her about me and Prii." Dasani said.

"Well damn, was you asking to get yo ass beat?" I snapped. "What made you tell her that?"

"Because I love Prii and Keisha doesn't want me to be around her." she said. "The bitch told me I crossed her, and before I knew it, I was getting up off the ground with a bloody face."

"So now you want Prii to comfort you and make you feel better right?"

I can admit that I was going a little hard on her, but I couldn't help it. I had lost all respect for her silly ass. There wasn't a fuck in me that I could give her about her tears.

"Prii is a grown ass woman, with a son. She don't need another child to be raising. And besides, she's already involved with someone. You know that."

"Secret, I ain't never felt this way about another bitch. I care about Prii a lot, and yeah, I know she's with Lando, but I also know she has feelings for me." she replied. "I just wanna talk to her."

I got on the phone and called Prii, telling her to come over as soon as she was done doing what she was doing. I didn't tell her why, I just told her as soon as she could.

"TETE!" Na'Priice shouted, coming through the door. I knew he missed me just as much as I missed him because I hadn't really gotten the chance to see him as much since he started his new daycare.

"I misseded you!" he said, hugging me.

"I misseded you too!" I replied, mocking him and adding an extra 'ed' on missed. "I heard you was a big boy in school now."

He shyly shook his head yes. "And I got a new toy." he said, holding up his little yellow truck.

"Cool!" I said. "Let's go show uncle Stephan your truck."

I walked him back to the bedroom where Stephan was watching some basketball game on TV.

"Uncle Stephan look what I got." Na'Priice blurted out, without wasting no time.

"Dang, where you get that from?" Stephan asked, acting as if it was just the coolest thing ever.

"Uncle Stephan can Priicy stay in here with you for a while so we can handle some business?" I asked.

He shook his head yeah as I walked back into the living room with Prii and Dasani. Prii was already going at it.

"Why you let that bitch do this to your face?" She snapped. "Imma fuck her up!"

Prii calm down!" Dasani said.

"Naw, I'm tired of this crazy bitch doing shit and getting away with it." she said. "Somebody needs to teach this hoe a lesson and I think its gone have to be me."

"Prii, I told her about us." Dasani said.

Prii looked up at me and then back at Dasani.

"What about us D.?" she asked.

"I told her that I love you Prii." Dasani said.

"Dasani, listen to yourself. Do you hear yourself right now?" Prii snapped. "Me and you were just fucking around. It was all fun and games D."

"So you mean to tell me you don't have feelings for me Prii?" Dasani asked. "You didn't feel nothing when we were together?"

"No D. I feel for you because you're my friend. I don't have feelings for you. I'm not gay." Prii replied.

Dasani looked like she could just throw up.

"So that's all it was then?" Dasani asked. "Just for fun?"

Prii shook her head yeah. Dasani looked up at me and I just shrugged my shoulders because I didn't know what else to say. I wanted to say I told you so, but I was sure she caught my drift. So that was it. Prii had laid it out for her. I don't know what their plans were for the future, but I know we had to most definitely deal with this bitch Keisha. So this is what lead us to the conversation with Keisha and Dasani on the phone. Prii was determined to get in Keisha's ass. We sat across from Dasani on her couch listening to the whole thing, preparing to set Keisha's crazy ass up.

"Secret knows about what you did to her." Dasani replied.

"You just had to open up your big ass mouth huh?" Keisha snapped. "I should've known I couldn't trust a rat."

I couldn't tell if Dasani was scared, or just trying her best not to say anything smart, but she was doing a hell of a job at keeping her composure.

"Keisha, she's not the one who snitched on you. You owe her an apology." Dasani said.

"A...An apology?!" Keisha was furious. "Bitch do you know who you're talking to?"

You could tell that Keisha wasn't used to Dasani talking to her like this.

"I'm just saying, you need to own up to what you did and be a woman."

Keisha began to chuckle and we could hear her clapping her hands in the background.

"Bravo little cousin. So you wanna play super save a hoe now? I guess that ass whoopin' the other day wasn't enough for you huh?" Keisha said.

Dasani looked at us across from her and by the way she was breathing, you could almost see her heart come through her chest. She was scared as hell. Prii shook her head in reassurance to let her know that she had her back.

"It ain't even like that cousin." Dasani said.

"Oh really?" Keisha asked. "Then what is it like then Dasani? Please, enlighten me."

"I just wanted you to know that Secret knows and that you should watch your back."

Keisha did a fake yawn, as if she had gotten bored with Dasani's conversation.

"Yeah, okay. Imma watch my back Dasani. Is there anything else you would like me to know before I hang up on you?" Keisha responded, nonchalantly.

"Actually, yeah." Dasani said. "I was wondering if you could come get all your shit from my house. I'm doing a little spring cleaning and I would hate to have to throw all your expensive belongings in the dumpster."

That last statement must have sent Keisha through the roof. I guess she didn't mess around when it came to her personal shit.

"Bitch, if you even think about touching my shit, imma kill yo ass. I see that bitch got you over there pussy whipped huh? Got you talking all out the side of yo neck and shit. But its cool though, I got something for yo ass. I'm on my way!"

CLICK!

Prii and I began to hoot and holler because our plan had worked. For a minute I was starting to doubt Dasani. I ain't think she had it in her. She knew just what to say to push her buttons. The whole thing was to get Dasani to say something to Keisha that would make her want to come over and beat her ass. To be honest, I didn't think it would work. I guess Keisha must have been hungry because she was eating right out the of the palms of our hands.

About an hour and a half had passed and we hadn't heard from Keisha. I began to think that she had really bluffed us. She wasn't coming. Prii had gotten impatient. She had Dasani calling and calling Keisha's phone. If the bitch didn't think anything was up at first, I'm pretty sure she did now. Another fifteen minutes had passed and Prii had gotten fed up.

"Damn, where is this bitch at?" She snapped. "You think she's coming or not? I ain't trying to waste no more time waiting for her ass not to come."

Dasani shrugged her shoulders. "I don't know."

"Well, its getting late. I don't think she's coming." I chimed in.

While Dasani sat there looking scared and lost, Prii and I got up and got ready to go.

"Wait a minute." Dasani said, getting up. "I can call her moms phone and see if she's heard from her."

"Her mom?" Prii asked.

Dasani shook her head yeah. Prii and I just looked at each other. Dasani was so young, dumb, and desperate. I can admit that what we were doing was childish as hell, I get that. But Dasani was really trying to set her cousin up to get her ass whooped. Even going to the length to getting her aunt involved. I guess Keisha had really did a number on her growing up. She treated her as if she was her puppet. I believe Dasani was just out for revenge.

"Hey aunty. Is Keisha around." Dasani asked, as we sat back down and listened to them on speaker.

"You haven't heard?" asked Keisha's mom, sounding as if she had just got done crying or was getting ready to cry.

We all looked at each other confused.

"No... heard what aunty?" Dasani asked.

Her aunt began to cry. "Keisha's been in a bad car accident."

Prii and I gasped at the same time.

"Wha... what?" Dasani stuttered.

"They said she was speeding, to only God knows where, and as she was running a red light she crashed into a semi truck." Her aunt cried.

"Oh my God! Is she okay?" Dasani shouted.

"No." the lady cried. "The doctors said she could be paralyzed from the waist down."

Dasani's eyes filled with water. She was at a lost for words. I found myself placing my hand across my chest in disbelief. The shit was sad as hell. Even though we were trying to lure her over to Dasani's to get her ass beat, I still felt bad about it.

"Paralyzed?" Dasani replied. "Like permanent?"

"Yes Dasani!" Keisha's mom snapped. "Your cousin will never walk again!"

She hung up on Dasani and left her sitting there looking dumbfounded. There was an awkward silence for about thirty seconds.

"I'm so sorry D." I finally managed to get out.

A part of me didn't want to be sorry for her because after all, Keisha was the one who had attacked me, but I couldn't help it. I had a heart. I felt for Dasani. She was young and confused. I had no idea as to what she was feeling at the moment.

"Man fuck that shit!" Prii snapped. "D. I know that's your cousin and all, but the crazy bitch had it coming to her. Karma's a bitch!"

Dasani looked up at Prii as if she couldn't believe the words that were coming out of her mouth.

"Prii stop." I said, feeling bad.

"Fuck her!" Prii replied. "Lets not forget that she almost killed you, and the fact that she was on her way over here to beat Dasani's ass again. God don't like ugly."

Prii was right, but it wasn't the time for all of that. She should have been comforting Dasani like I was doing. Hell, this was her bitch. Not mine.

It had been about three weeks since Keisha's accident. I hadn't heard from Dasani at all, but Prii told me that she had been right by Keisha's side, catering to her. It was funny to me that even though Keisha was paralyzed, Dasnai still felt the need to kiss her ass. Maybe she felt like it this was all her fault. The look on her face that day we dropped her off at the hospital had guilt written all over it.

"Wassup Prii?" I said, answering my phone.

She sighed. "Are you hungry? I'm coming over."

I could tell something was bothering her. I could sense it in her tone.

"No, Stephan cooked fish and spaghetti before he went to work." I replied.

"Well, is there any left?" she asked.

"Girl, there's plenty!" I said.

Prii got to my house in five minutes. She came in and plopped down on the couch.

"So... what's going on bitch?" I asked, sitting beside her.

"Lando dumped me." she replied.

My mouth dropped.

"What?... Why?" I asked.

She took a deep breath.

"He said he's closing down Exotic Rain and moving to Texas to start over with his daughter."

"Prii... that bastard had a baby on you?" I snapped. "Imma kill'em"

"Not necessarily." she replied, holding her head down.

"Then what are you telling me Prii. I'm confused."

She took another deep breath.

"The shit about him and Princess was true." she said. "He did fuck that nasty bitch."

"Are you serious?" I asked.

"Yeah, but he says he only fucked her once." she replied.

"Wait, so Lando's got a baby by Princess?" I asked.

Without looking up at me, she shook her head yes. I couldn't believe this shit.

"Oh my God Prii! Are you fucking kidding me?!" I snapped.

She told me about how the day after the fight with Princess in the shop, he came back to pick her up and he told her everything. He told her that they only had had sex once and he had gotten her pregnant. That was five years ago. He had a five year old daughter in Texas that he went to go visit every chance he got. La'Niyah was her name. He told Prii that she stayed down there with her grandma, Princess's mom. Mostly all of his important business trips down to Atlanta, were really down to Texas to see his baby girl. I didn't even know that he was taking all these trips like that. I guess since I was fat and pregnant and not working at Exotic Rain anymore, it was none of my business.

"Damn Prii," I said. "When was the last time he went down there?"

"Bitch, the day before Valentines Day." she snapped. "The nigga was gone for about a week. He lied and told me that we would celebrate when he came back, but we ain't do shit."

I thought back to when I had called her phone on valentines day and I heard moaning on the other end of her phone. Before I could even get my question out, she blurted out the answer.

"I spent majority of my valentines day with Dasani. That's when we first started fucking around." she said. "She came over and seduced me and I liked it. I needed it."

I didn't know how to feel knowing that it was her and Dasani instead of her and Lando on the other end of the phone that day. It kind of grossed me out, just a little.

"So why all of a sudden does he wanna make this big move now?" I asked.

"Because I told him about me and Dasani." she replied. "Girl, he spazzed out."

"Why would you even tell him about that?" I asked. "What happened to your 'what he don't know, wont hurt him' motto?"

She shrugged. "I felt like I needed to tell him before he heard it from somebody else." she said. "He cursed me out and told me that I had confirmed his decision. I guess he had been thinking about it for a while now. He packed all his shit up at my apartment and left me."

I shook my head in disappointment. I couldn't believe Lando. How dare he get mad at her for fucking with another bitch, when he was keeping his daughter on the low low in a whole different state? And on top of that, was sneaking out to go see her and lying about it. Niggas could be so backwards sometimes. I had lost respect for Lando. All this time I had thought that he was a real man. He was a fucking coward.

"Girl, I begged him not to leave me and you already know I ain't that type of bitch. I don't beg no nigga for shit!" Prii said, as I just shook my head agreeingly. "But I really loved that man Sii."

"I know." I replied.

"And even when I told him that I wouldn't even hang with Dasani anymore, he still said fuck me." She continued.

"That's fucked up Prii." I said, still in disbelief. "Well, its plenty of fish out here in the sea. You don't need him."

She shook her head and agreed. "You're right. I just cant believe that its over."

"So you really think his mind is made up? You think its really over?" I asked.

"Bitch, I know its over. Ain't nothing else to think about."

23

"I told you I would be back." Quam said, waking me up out of my sleep.

"Quam?" I replied, startled, trying to get myself together.

"Yes beautiful. Its me." he said.

I looked over to Stephan's side of the bed, which was empty.

"What are you doing in my house?" I asked, confused.

"I want to take you back home with me." he replied.

"Home?" I yelled. "What's wrong with you?"

I got up and ran to put my robe on. I had a habit of sleeping naked.

"You need to leave my house." I shouted.

"No." he replied. "Not until you come with me."

My heart was racing. I think he had finally just snapped.

"How did you get in here?" I asked, becoming more and more frightened.

I had no idea what he planned on doing to me. I just didn't want him to hurt my baby.

"No need to worry about how I got in. I just want you to leave with me." he replied.

He was persistent.

"I'm not going anywhere with you." I cried.

"I'm going to treat you like the queen you are." he said, as if he didn't hear what I had just said.

"Quam, you're not getting it!" I shouted, wiping my eyes. "I don't want you. You're fucking sick!"

He tilted his head and looked at me with this piteous look on his face.

"You don't really mean that." he replied, smiling and walking up to me.

"Please!" I cried and begged. "Please don't hurt me."

He grabbed my chin and gently kissed me on my forehead.

"Secret, don't you know by now that I could never harm you?" he said, using his thumb to wipe away my tears.

"Then why are you doing all of this?" I cried, wrapping my arms around my belly with my robe as tight as I could.

"Because I have to have you Secret." he replied. "I cant be without you any longer."

I held my head down and sobbed as he continued to speak, secretly cursing my vagina for getting us into this mess.

"I cant stop thinking about you." he said. "From the moment I wake up, to the moment I lay my head back down, you're on my mind. Secret, I dream you."

Why was he so serious? I thought. This was the type of shit that you would see in movies or something. It was scary, but it was all still so pathetic.

"Why me Quam?" I asked. "Out of all people, why'd you have to pick me?"

He shrugged his shoulders and looked down at my stomach.

"I just wanna help you raise our son." he said, trying to rub my stomach, but I smacked his hand away.

"This is not your baby!" I yelled getting fed up with his psycho bullshit.

Just then, I heard the front door close.

"Baby I'm home!" Stephan yelled. "They let me off early tonight!"

Quam and I locked eyes instantly. A look of rage filled his face, and I could practically see the steam coming from out of his ears. Little did he know, Stephan's voice was like music to my ears.

"So, are you going to tell him that you're leaving with me, or do you want me to tell him?" Quam asked, but before I could even get an answer out, Stephan had already walked in the room.

"Quam?" he asked, shocked to see him standing there in front of me. "What the fuck is going on in here?"

Quam just smiled at me.

"This what you doing when I'm at work?" Stephan snapped.

Quam backed away from me and turned to Stephan.

"Don't talk to her like that." He said calmly.

It took me a second to realize that it looked as if I was cheating. First of all, I was naked as hell underneath my robe, in my bedroom, with another nigga. And to make matters worse, Quam had told Stephan that we were long lost best friends from back in the day. There was no way that I could get out of this without explaining this shit to Stephan right here and now. I hated myself for not telling him about this crazy ass Jamaican the day he came to my house the first time. I honestly didn't think it would ever come to this. I thought Quam would eventually just give up, but obviously I was wrong.

"Bae, this ain't what it looks like." I said, running over to him. "This man is fucking crazy."

Stephan could do nothing but look back and forth at the both of us.

"Why is this nigga in your house Secret?" he demanded to know, gritting his teeth.

Quam just stood there listening as I cried and went into detail explaining everything to Stephan. I believe he was enjoying every bit of it. I told him everything. From the time we first had sex in Vegas, to the time he popped up at my house and filled Stephan's head with all those lies.

"Why you ain't been told me about this motherfucker?" Stephan snapped, mugging the shit out of Quam. "Nigga get the hell out of here!"

Quam shook his head no and sat down on my bed. "Ill leave when my queen is ready to come with me." he said.

"I'm not…" I started, but couldn't finish.

"Shut up Secret!" Stephan shouted. "Nigga, just cause your screws a little loose up there, don't mean I wont fuck you up. You best make moves."

In the mist of them going back and forth, I managed to grab my cell phone off of the table and dialed 911 and set my phone back down. I just wanted them to hear what was going on.

"Stephan, you just don't understand." Quam said. "I can't live without her."

"Please just leave!" I shouted dramatically so that the police would know something was up.

Before I knew it, Stephan had charged at Quam and they began fighting.

"Stop! Stop! Stop!" I yelled, holding my belly and trying to keep my distance as they rumbled and fucked my room up.

I then picked up the phone and begged for the police to hurry up and send someone. Fist were flying every which way. The dispatcher was talking to me, but I couldn't pay attention to her. I was too busy watching them fight. Then somehow, Stephan managed to hem Quam down on the bed.

"This ain't what you want nigga!" Stephan yelled, out of breath, staring down at Quam.

Quam chuckled and managed to reach in his pocket and pull a gun out.

"Oh my God!" I screamed. "Pease don't!"

Stephan raised up off of Quam and backed up.

"I didn't come here for all of this." Quam said, looking crazy. "I just came here for Secret."

Stephan just had his hands up the whole time and didn't say a word as Quam just stared and pointed the gun at him.

"Okay!" I cried. "Ill go with you."

I hoped that he would put the gun down, but he didn't. He turned his head towards me, but kept the gun on Stephan.

"You what?" he asked, sounding as if he couldn't believe what I had just told him.

"If that's what you really want." I sobbed. "Ill go with you. Just please put the gun down."

He smiled a little bit, but before he could put the gun down, Stephan charged at him again. The gun was still in Quam's hand, but while they were tussling he held it in the air as Stephan tried to take it out from him.

POW!

The gun went off in the air as my first instinct was to drop to the floor. I must have fallen to hard because I immediately felt pains in my stomach. They continued to fight as I cried out in agony. I began to have trouble breathing, as I crawled to my cell phone, which I had dropped when I fell.

"Please... help me." I cried to the dispatcher, who managed to stay on the phone after I had dropped it. "I'm... pregnant."

POW! POW!

Two more shots rang out, but I could no longer move. I felt myself beginning to pass out. The pain was unbearable.

"Ma'am, stay with me. Help is on the way." Was the last thing I heard the dispatcher say before I closed my eyes.

POW!

After awhile, I woke up in the delivery room, finding myself attached to a bunch of shit with my legs propped open.

"What's going on?" I asked, looking around, still kind of out of it.

"Sweetheart, we're going to need you to get ready to push." said one of the lady doctors. "You're in labor."

I looked around once more and didn't see Stephan, and for the life of me I tried to jump up off that table.

"Where's my boyfriend?" I shouted, beginning to panic.

All the doctors and nurses were struggling to keep me calm so that they could start the procedure, but I wasn't having it. I needed to know where the hell Stephan was and if he was okay.

"Ma'am, I need you to calm down. This isn't good for the baby." the same lady doctor said.

"No, you don't understand. I'm afraid that he might have gotten hurt." I cried, on the verge of hyperventilating.

"Okay, first, I need you to relax." she said. "Now, what is your boyfriend's name?"

"Stephan Williams!" I blurted out. "His name is Stephan Williams!"

The lady doctor looked over at one of her assistants and ordered her to go find any info on Stephan. Then she called the another assistant over.

"Okay ma'am, I need you to cooperate so we can get these babies out of you the safest way possible." she said.

"Babies?" I responded, looking down at her between my legs. "As in more than one?"

"Yes," she replied without bringing her head up. "You're having twins and the first one is coming now so I need you to push."

I tilted my head back and took a deep breath and pushed with all my might. It hurt so bad. Her assistant held my hand as I squeezed and pushed.

"Here he is!" the doctor shouted after about my fourth push. "He's handsome."

As bad as I wanted to smile, I couldn't. I was in so much pain, and I could feel the second baby trying to follow up right behind its brother. She handed my son off to one of the other nurses and got back to business.

"Okay, one down, one to go. You're almost done Ms. Secret." she said, trying to motivate me. "Get ready to push again."

I took another deep breath and pushed with all I had left in me. I was so tired.

"Come on Secret! You can do this!" the doctor yelled again.

I knew the nurses fingers who's hand that I was squeezing had to be broken by now. Although, it didn't seem to bother her too much.

"Okay, give me one more big push. You're doing good." she said.

I was hot and out of breath, but I had to get this over with. I took one last deep breath and pushed as hard as I could. I was determined to get that damn baby out of me with that push.

I had to because I don't think I was going to be able to push anymore after that one.

"Yay!!! You did it!" the doctor shouted. "Awww a beautiful baby girl."

I fell back on the bed , relieved that it was over with.

"Are my babies okay?" I asked with my eyes closed.

I had no strength. I was so exhausted.

"They are completely healthy." said the doctor. "Open your eyes and look at your beautiful babies."

She stood on my left side holding my baby girl, while the nurse stood on my right, holding my son. All I could do was cry. I felt bad because I really didn't have the strength to hold them in my own arms. I was so weak. As they began to wash my babies up, I had drifted off into a deep sleep.

"I knew you could do it baby girl." said a familiar voice. "We're so proud of you."

It was my daddy. I turned to see him and my mom standing hand in hand.

"I told you that you had two beautiful people to live for." my mom smiled, winking at me.

"You knew about these twins the whole time?" I asked.

She didn't respond. She just kept smiling at me. I couldn't believe all this time she had me thinking she was referring to Prii and Stephan.

"You fought a good fight baby girl." daddy said. "Now its time for you to go on and live a better life with my grand babies."

"Yes, its time for you to let us go and be happy." my mom added. "Be better than us."

I looked up at both of my parents, who looked so happy and proud of their only child.

"So this is the last time ill be seeing you?" I asked, tearing up.

My mommy smiled, but I could see the hurt in her eyes.

"No matter what, we'll always be right here baby girl." daddy said, placing his hand over my heart. It hurt me to see the tears fall down my daddy's face. I don't think I had ever seen my daddy cry before.

"We love you Secret." they both said, kissing me on each cheek.

"I love you too." I replied, as I was awakened by a familiar face.

"Hey baby."

It was Stephan, who was standing there with a cast on one arm and our baby girl in the other.

I raised up so fast and grabbed him and hugged him and didn't want to let him go. My tears began to fall uncontrollably.

"I'm okay." he whispered. "I love you."

When I finally let him go to take another good look at him, it took me a minute to realize that Prii was over in the cut playing with our son. I could almost cry again.

"Girl, I wish you would've told me that you was having two of these thangs." Prii said. "I had no idea that I was going to have to be a double god mom. I need another job."

Stephan and I burst into laughter.

"Prii you so crazy." I replied, as she handed me the baby.

"I'm just happy you okay girl." she said. "After this, I ain't trying to see you up in no more hospitals. This is like your second home."

"I know that's right." I said laughing. "So what happened to Quam? Did he got to jail?"

I looked up at Prii, who shot her eyes over to Stephan, who just looked down at me.

"He's gone." Stephan replied.

"What?" I said. "He's dead?"

Stephan hesitantly shook his head yes. I grabbed his shirt and brought his lips down to mine.

"Thank you." I said, kissing him. "For everything."

About two weeks later, we were chilling in our brand new home that Stephan had bought somewhere down the lines behind my back. He said we needed a brand new start. New house, new surroundings, new life. I was in the mist of changing our daughter Caleah, when I saw something shining in her diaper. It was a diamond ring. I quickly finished changing her and ran into the living room where he was playing with Caleb.

"Stephan, what is this?" I asked, as I felt my heart beat speed up. "I know this ain't what I think it is!"

I laid Caleah down in her crib because I was too excited and didn't want to drop her.

Stephan just smiled.

"Well, it is so… will you?"

He held up our son, who's shirt read 'Mommy will you marry daddy?'

My eyes filled with water as I ran over and kissed him at least a million times.

"Yes, of course I will!" I shouted.

He went to go put baby Caleb in the crib next to his sister and came back over to the couch. He grabbed me and started kissing me all over, getting my juices flowing, knowing that we couldn't have sex no time soon.

"Wait," I said, stopping him. "Before we make it official, there's some things about my past that I need to share with you that you don't know about."

He looked at me confused.

"Secret, whatever it is, let it stay in the past. I'm pretty sure there's a reason for it being in the past."

He was right, but I didn't feel right without him knowing the real me, my whole story.

"I know bae, but I have to share this with you. Its important to me. I want you to know everything."

He knew I was serious. He sat up and gave me his full undivided attention. I inhaled and exhaled and began to walk him through my whole journey of life. I told him detail for detail. Even though he knew some things already, I still wanted to refresh his memory. Just so he would know who he was really dealing with. By the time I was done, it felt like a weight had lifted off of my shoulders. It felt good knowing that he knew everything. The real me. Stephan just held me in his arms.

"Are you satisfied now?" he asked.

"Yes." I replied, looking up at him.

"Are you sure? We can gone and get married now?" he asked, sarcastically.

"Shut up and kiss me." I said, as I playfully stuck out my tongue and licked his bottom lip.

"You so nasty." he said, laughing as my phone rang in the kitchen. "Better get that. It might be the doctor."

Our doctor had been calling and checking up on us ever since we left the hospital. I got up to go answer and it wasn't nobody but Prii.

"Hey girl." I said.

"Girl, are you watching the news right now?" she asked, all in an emphasized tone.

"Uh, no." I responded. "Should I be?"

"Yes girl. Tune into channel 4. Shit done hit the fan. Imma call you back."

I walked back into the living room and cut on the TV.

"Who was that bae?" Stephan asked.

"It was Prii. She told me to turn it to the news." I replied.

I hit channel 4 on the remote and there it was. Prii was right. Shit had definitely hit the fan… and hard!

"A woman by the name of Karen Johnson is now in custody for the murder of her beloved younger brother, Kristian Johnson. There has not yet been any motives as to why she went into her brothers room at 2am while he was asleep and stabbed him multiple times, but we will surly get back to this story when we find out more…" said the news reporter woman, standing outside of my old home.

I quickly cut the TV off as my heart skipped a beat. I had about a million thoughts running through my mind all of a sudden. Oh my God. Karen had killed Kristian. I sat back on the couch and took all of it in. Kristian was dead and Karen was going to jail for murder? It had all seemed so surreal. I'm pretty sure Stephan didn't know what to think, being that I had just told him about everything not even ten minutes before.

"Bae, you good?" he asked, probably not knowing what else to say.

The situation was so bad, but it felt so good. I think that I was finally at peace knowing that Kristian was no more. He was no longer a factor. Over all, I knew I could rest knowing that Delilah could finally rest in peace. Kristian couldn't hurt me, her, or anybody else's daughter for that matter. He was gone forever!

"Yeah, I'm good." I replied, as I kissed my fiancé's lips once more.

That night, Delilah came to me in my dreams and thanked me. She told me how proud of me she was and that she knew I could do it. I sat and watched her sit on a cloud, floating away into the sky smiling. It was such a rush of relief knowing that she was happy… I was happy.